A *Thousand* SEAS

LATASHA BALL

To my mom Ginger and my dad Tommy.

Thank you for always believing in me and encouraging me to follow my dreams.
This book is for you. I love you both.

BOOK SUMMARY

All marriages have struggles. All duty has a price. All love has its limits...

Lillian White thought she understood sacrifice as a military spouse, but nothing prepared her for the harsh realities that lay ahead. When she takes a job in public affairs at the local Army post, she's thrust into a world where appearances matter more than truth, and where her marriage to a soldier is both revered and tested daily.

Enter Colonel Jackson Cooper – charismatic, handsome, and forbidden. In his presence, Lillian feels an unexpected jolt for the first time in her life, forcing her to confront the cracks in her marriage and the unfulfilled longings of her heart that leave her drowning in a sea of uncharted emotions. But in a world where infidelity is an open secret and emotional casualties are par for the course, pursuing her feelings could cost Lillian everything.

As tensions rise in her marriage and new role, Lillian must navigate the minefield of military life, confronting the ugly truths behind the polished facade. When a series of adversities strike, she's forced to question everything – her marriage, her loyalty, and her own identity.

If ever there is tomorrow when we're not together, there is something you must always remember. You are braver than you believe, stronger than you seem, and smarter than you think. But the most important thing is, even if we're apart... I'll always be with you.

-A.A. Milne

1

D*ear God, what in the world did I get myself into?* The heaviness in my chest lay thick as uncertainty filled my mind, trying to grasp the job interview that had just taken place. Like a robot under someone else's control, I obediently answered questions like I was reading off a script. At times, they grilled me like I was joining the military, instead of applying for a position working *for* the military. They wanted to see how well I operated under pressure.

"What would you do if a high-ranking military officer didn't listen to you while working on a project? How would you respond?" One of the interviewers, a short man with balding dark hair and chocolate brown eyes, recently retired from the military, yelled at me in a drill sergeant voice. His eyes narrowed, brazenly staring me down like we were about to have a standoff. I took it in stride and kept my composure. After the interview, I drove down the open road back to post, wanting to go anywhere except where I was expected to go. I was a military spouse. Trying my best to navigate and find my place in this often-foreign military world. Things were expected of me. It was a life I never imagined for myself growing up, but here I was once again wondering how my life turned out this way.

I drove up to post, patiently waiting for my turn to flash the security guard my military-dependent identification card to get back home. I thought about how being married to someone in the military was a future I never imagined for myself. There's no manual, no how-to guide for how to be the perfect military spouse. You simply hold your breath, jump into the deep end of the pool, and learn to swim as you go. What I didn't know was the minute you recite your marriage vows, you also unknowingly accept unspoken vows of putting your spouse and his military career first, understanding that your country may call him away at a moment's notice. It's assumed that you will smile, nod, and not ask questions that he may not be able to answer. Yet, you learn early on to wear this like a badge of honor, putting duty and the military's needs above all else.

This also means placing your needs last, and any ambitions you have will come second to your husband's military career. Before I got married, I was someone who was career-driven and excited about the bright path that lay ahead. Before I knew it, my days became filled with deployment care packages, deployment meetings with other spouses, dinners prepared daily with no dishes in the sink, laundry washed and folded, and doing my best to preserve a pristine home. All the while maintaining a full-time career. Nonetheless, it never seemed good enough for my husband. In the midst of all this juggling and people-pleasing, I had lost myself.

While I was trying to balance the responsibilities of being a military spouse and figuring out my career path, I was in-between jobs and temporarily working in marketing for a military housing company on my post. In the back of my mind, I knew the position was a steppingstone and could lead me to the job I was meant to have. One day, I received a phone call from a local government contracting company. They had a job opening in the public affairs department at the same post where we were currently stationed. The position was with an Army brigade and was a hybrid role due to the Covid-19 pandemic. I had interviewed for a technical writer position with them about six months prior. Even though the position didn't appeal to me at all, I still attended the interview, figuring it'd make for a good experience to have under my belt. They didn't wind up being awarded the contract for that role, and so I didn't get the job. Luckily, they remembered me and said I stood out during my interview and thought *this* role was perfect for me.

After hearing about the position, they expressed their excitement about bringing me onboard and offering me the job. I thanked them for their time and said I needed to think about it. I had my doubts. Working for the military never crossed my mind. Even being married to someone in the military had its moments where I wondered if I was also enlisted. Feeling stuck and needing some advice, I called my best friend Abbey, who happened to work in public affairs for the military. Abbey was in her mid-twenties with bright brown eyes and short jet-black chin-length hair brushed to perfection. She had moved up quickly in the ranks while working for the Army with her passion for structure and a strong work ethic. We previously worked together for a public relations firm, and I always valued her career advice. Her desk sat behind mine, and she quickly became my battle buddy, swapping war stories of working for a cutthroat public relations firm. I emailed her the job position to get her thoughts on the role.

"I don't know, Abbey," I told her on the phone hesitantly as I sat in my car on my lunch break one Thursday afternoon, mindlessly poking a bland tuna salad sprinkled with a few cherry tomatoes. "This doesn't really sound appealing to me, and it's outside of my wheelhouse."

She was not fazed by my hesitation and excitedly responded. "Lily, this is a great opportunity for you. That role is a perfect fit and you're going to enjoy it. You should go for it!"

That was Abbey. Always optimistic and not afraid to try something new. I was never as brave as her. I felt a light quiver in my stomach. "Really? You think so?"

Without hesitating, she said, "Yes! I know you, and I can see you really excelling in this role." I could feel the excitement in her voice as a small, hopeful smile formed across my face. I looked around as I sat in front of a house on post that was being used as our military housing office. My heart told me I was meant for more in life. Riding on the advice of my friend, I decided to take a leap of faith and accept the job with the military. Little did I know that one decision would change the course of my life forever.

It was September when I accepted the public affairs role and started work. Even though I was a wife to an active-duty soldier in the Army, I never thought in my wildest dreams I'd be working for the military—but here I was, getting ready for my first day as a contractor for the Army. My new job consisted of writing about various events happening on post for the Army's internal newsletter, along with writing speeches for the senior leaders at my new brigade. My first work assignment involved covering an awards ceremony happening on post. I had no clue about the details of this event and felt like I was flying blind, especially since I had no background whatsoever working for the military.

It was seven a.m., with the event starting at eight o'clock sharp. I was under strict instructions by my contract company not to be late. To me, being late in the military seemed like a cardinal sin. My husband had no issue reminding me of this as I often ran at least a few minutes behind, which always drove his type-A military personality up the wall. I anxiously paced my bedroom in my pink flannel pajamas and colorful unicorn bed slippers, wondering what I should wear to the presentation. Being a military spouse, attending events was one thing but attending as an employee working *for* the military was something altogether different. After trying on several outfits standing in front of my bedroom mirror, I decided on my definition of a safe ensemble—black dress pants and a fitted gray button-up dress shirt. As I looked at my reflection in the mirror, I carefully evaluated my outfit. I heard my husband's sergeant voice in my head saying, "No shoulders showing!" like he did when I fretted about what to wear when we first met the President of the United States while stationed on the East Coast. With a background in fashion working in marketing for a fashion college for more than seven years and a footwear company for two years, I took pride in looking my very best and knew the perfect outfit to wear for every occasion. But for some reason, this time, I was nervous.

I stood anxiously in front of my bathroom mirror, carefully applying my light pink eyeshadow that matched my pink cheeks. I carefully combed my long golden blonde hair back into a conservative ponytail. After finishing my hair and makeup, I took a deep breath as I gazed at my reflection in the mirror and gave myself a little pep talk: *Here we go. You got this!*

As I drove up to the brigade to attend my first on-site work event, my initial observation was how worn the buildings were. They were all the same bland, tan color and looked to be just as old as the post they were sitting on. I guess this shouldn't have come as a surprise since the majority of buildings on post were outdated and from the 1940s. Since this was my first post to be stationed on, I had nothing to compare it to. It was also my first official duty station in Arizona as the wife of an active duty servicemember.

When my husband and I accepted orders here more than ten years ago, I didn't want to go anywhere else and certainly not back to the East Coast. Arizona offered more than I expected when we first moved here. It was like no place I'd ever lived before, with breathtaking sunsets reflecting shades of bold orange, iridescent pink, and purplish hues painted across the sky. I also always felt most at home hiking or connecting with nature, exploring red rock buttes, trails reflecting vibrant wildflowers of all colors, and cacti of different shapes off in the distance. While most military couples move every two to three years, by the grace of God, we kept getting orders on this post. It was close to some of my family who lived in the area, which is all I cared about at the time. It also allowed me to have a career, a luxury many military spouses in my position can't afford to have.

I pulled up to the tan and brown auditorium and saw my new supervisor standing outside waiting for me. Ethan was a tall and slender fifty-something-year-old man with a strong journalism background who ruled with an iron fist and treated our internal newsletter like *The New York Times*. Little did I know that every article I wrote for the Army would be dissected by him while he took pleasure in grilling me. In my first observation of him, I concluded that he didn't have much fashion sense. I wondered how he selected his antiquated outfit. He wore khaki pants and a black button up shirt with gray penny loafers that I'm pretty sure I'd seen my grandpa wear. I wanted to give him some advice as a woman who once worked in the fashion industry, but I decided it was best to keep my fashion critiques to myself.

I parked in front of the two-story auditorium, which sat toward the back of the post. An empty feeling formed in the pit of my stomach, having no idea what lay ahead. I gathered my purse with my pink notebook and pen in tow and my voice recorder as my lifeline for getting through my time with the Army. Getting out of my car, I put on my face mask since the Covid-19 virus was still at the forefront of everyone's minds. I stood up—straight, like a soldier at attention—and confidently walked up to the auditorium where Ethan was waiting. He had to escort me into the building since I didn't have my government ID yet. We stood outside as the morning sun was shining high above us, with only a few clouds sprinkled in the sky. As I looked up at him, his red hair was slicked back perfectly without a single strand out of place and was also reflecting the bright sun beating down on us. I could see the seriousness in his chestnut eyes as he explained what to expect at the day's event. I listened attentively, trying to remember every word.

"This is an All-Hands event," he explained. "This is where awards are given out *only* to federal employees and not contractors. It's something that happens several times a year with the Army."

"That sounds nice," I replied. A blank look flashed across my face as I felt my body heat rising. *Why don't contractors receive awards?* I thought to myself, confused.

As we walked inside the building, a cold breeze hit me, and I realized the air conditioner must be on. I noticed the building was newer than the others and did look rather nice, with portraits hanging on the wall and a statue outside of some military person standing tall and proud, wearing a formal uniform with various ribbons and a serious look on his face. I had no clue who he was, but he must have been somebody important. *Wow, I feel like a fish out of water,* I thought to myself. *This is definitely not the fashion industry.*

I FOLLOWED Ethan as we walked into the large polished auditorium with two huge TV screens in the front of the room and several digital clocks displaying times from all over the world just above the screens. I looked across the auditorium and saw more than fifty military and civilian employees sitting in gray theater-style seats in the audience. Ethan pointed to several people in the room, explaining who they were. "This is Major Smith; he works in the front office. That man sitting down in the front row is Brett Jones, he is an engineer and works in the D Department."

He pointed to a man in a camouflage uniform, sitting with his back facing us at a long executive table in the front of the room. "The man sitting in the front of the room is our Colonel.

His name is Colonel Jackson Cooper." I glanced over at the Army officer, and out of nowhere, a rush of feelings and emotions hit me all at once. This sea of emotions was so intense, it took my breath away. I stood there completely bewildered, trying to gather my thoughts. The first thought that popped into my head was, *Oh my goodness, he is incredibly good-looking!* Shaking my head, I scolded myself, *What is wrong with you?*

Trying to shake off the emotional earthquake that just shook my life over those few seconds, I followed Ethan and sat in the middle of the auditorium, waiting for the event to start. Suddenly, the attractive colonel shot his head up, quickly looking behind him, and stared straight at me. He just as quickly turned his head back to the front of the room, but then turned around and looked back at me again. I sat there paralyzed, not able to move a muscle but entirely confused at the same time. *Why in the world is he looking at me?* I thought to myself. I looked down at my purse and realized the tape recorder was still in my bag. I needed to take it out and have it by the handsome colonel leading the All-Hands address to record his speech for my article.

I stood up from my seat and turned to my new boss. "Ethan, I need to put my tape recorder in the front of the room. Is that okay?"

"Of course, that's okay," he said with a smile on his face. With my heart racing, I walked nervously down the aisle to the front of the auditorium, where the handsome colonel was sitting in a large black leather executive chair.

"Excuse me, sir, can I please leave my tape recorder with you to record the event?" He looked up at me, and the first thing I noticed was his beautiful, piercing blue eyes. They were captivating in a way that caught your attention in a sea of people. I felt him grinning at me under his face mask.

"Well, I guess I'll have to be careful what I say then."

Completely stunned, I nervously replied, "Oh no, it's not like that." He laughed and smiled as he introduced himself.

"I'm Jack," he said in a charming voice, and he added, "I'm sorry. I didn't mean to keep staring at you. It's just that we don't normally see new people in here."

"Oh, that's okay," I replied, with my heart racing a mile a minute. "My name is Lillian… Thank you for letting me have my recorder by you." I quickly turned around and returned to my seat.

I sat in the gray chair next to my new boss, my eyes rapidly blinking with a stunned expression on my face. I was speechless. The colonel confidently walked up to the podium with his talking points in a white binder and began to address the audience as a PowerPoint presentation started playing on the large screen behind him. There was something about him. A confidence in the way he carried himself. The expression on his face told me he had experienced things that I couldn't even imagine and visited places I'd only seen in my dreams. It was obvious that he was a cut above the rest.

Trying to take in the event, knowing I was writing an entire article about it, I tried to concentrate, but the encounter kept replaying in my mind. Who was this man, and why did he keep looking at me? Was it *really* just that I was someone new? Something told me that wasn't it.

After the hour-long event, I nervously walked up to the front of the room and quickly grabbed my tape recorder from the long executive table. I was way out of my element. I knew I had to adapt very quickly going from being a military spouse to now an employee working for the military, having to learn the world in this new light. I had no clue how I was going to fit in. Feeling flustered, I tried my best to avoid eye contact with the handsome colonel. I pushed the entire experience out of my mind and raced home to write the article.

As I sat in front of a blank computer screen, armed with a tape recorder full of notes, a feeling of helplessness washed over me. "Somehow, I have to write an article about this event," I half-heartedly said to myself. After sitting for what felt like hours, I managed to write something. I sat at my desk in the corner of my living room, surrounded by pictures of my family and an inspirational quote framed on my desk. I took a deep breath and let out a defeated exhale. The article wasn't my best work. Ethan marked it up with his politically correct journalism remarks that I learned over time not to take personally. Part of me felt relieved to have the article completed, but I also couldn't help but wonder if it was setting the tone for how the rest of my career was unfolding with the Army.

Coming from a journalism background and having written professionally since the age of sixteen, seeing my papers *bleeding in red* after a round of edits was normal for me. It never dampened my passion for writing. My journalism degree sent me down endless changing paths of trying to figure out what I wanted to do with my higher education and ultimately with the rest of my life. Did I want to get into marketing? Did I want to be a journalist full-time? Did I want to get into public relations?

I so badly wanted God to just come down in a bolt of lightning and say in a booming voice, *Lilian, this is what you should do with your life.* But there I was, trying to figure it out on my own and feeling like I was messing up along the way or not doing something right, but it wasn't always that way, was it?

Growing up, I knew I wanted to be a writer. It was a calling deep down in my heart that I felt compelled to answer. Even though I grew up in the mountains outside of Yosemite and didn't have many resources, writing opportunities always found their way to me. I later caught the attention of my hometown newspaper editor, who offered me my first writing job while I was still in high school. I chose to follow that path. My parents also instilled in me the importance of a college education early on in life since I was the first generation in my family to graduate from college—a luxury they never had. "You need to go to college and get an education, so you don't have to depend on a man. It's important for you to be independent," my mom often told me growing up, her voice soft and yet curt. Going to college was a pathway that I was destined to go down, and I was determined not to let them down.

Because of keeping my nose firmly planted in my textbooks and staying focused on my growing journalism career, love never crossed my mind. Until the day I met Aaron, a thirty-eight-year-old, third-generation Army first-class sergeant, the day after I graduated from college. Aaron was a little taller than me, with green eyes and blonde hair sprinkled with flakes of auburn when it caught the sunlight. He was raised by his sergeant-major mom, who served in the Marine Corps. This strict upbringing had an impact on Aaron's personality as he always valued structure and following rules. As his mom got older, she developed a softer side that Aaron never seemed to have. When I started dating Aaron, getting married wasn't really in my plans, let alone marrying someone who was in the military. Besides, my career and college studies were my top priorities. Aaron relentlessly pursued me for two years even though I was adamant that dating men in the military was a bad idea. "You guys leave, and I'll get attached," I later told him.

"I may leave, but I will always come home," he said with a smile on his face that eventually won me over.

After dating a string of frogs in college that I knew weren't worth my time, I decided to give Aaron a chance and sent him a message on MySpace. Like a typical military person, he wasted no time jumping to the point. He bluntly stated that I broke his heart and led him on, which made me feel guilty. Having nothing to lose, I figured I'd give him a chance. We dated for a year as he showered me with handwritten letters and poems, and we did our best to maintain our long-distance relationship despite him being stationed in another town. When he proposed, it just felt like the right thing to do. At the time, however, I wanted to wait to get married, but of course, he didn't want to wait. "I waited two years for you," he said apathetically. "I don't want to wait any longer."

On the night of my graduation and the night before I was to get married, my grandpa had two strokes and did not tell a single soul for fear of ruining my big day. It didn't occur to me that maybe that was a sign from God that I needed to stop and think about if this was the right choice for me. Neverthe-less, I made a commitment, so I was going to follow through —even though during the first year of my marriage, when issues emerged, I found myself hiding out in my car with my mom on the phone. Maryland was in the middle of a snow blizzard, and I was two thousand miles away from home with tears running down my face. It was bright white outside, with only our mailbox barely peeking out from the mountains of snow surrounding my house. Even my mailbox was fighting to stay above the blizzard.

Taking shallow breaths, I let out a hard sigh and closed my eyes. "I want a divorce, Mom. I made a mistake, and I shouldn't have gotten married." With her conservative upbringing, my mom told me bluntly, "You made a commitment, and you need to stick with it." Her words stung like I had unexpectedly been bitten by a bee. Since she had recently divorced my dad, it occurred to me that maybe she didn't want me to follow in her footsteps. However, for me, things were about to change.

As I sat at my desk studying my marked-up article, I did my best not to feel overwhelmed in this new role. I slowly reviewed Ethan's requested edits, and wondered if this was what God wanted me to do for the rest of my life or just for now. The questions seemed never-ending. Regardless, I kept moving forward, not knowing what really lied ahead in this new world I was now a part of.

2

———

JACK

Jack stood at his white desk surrounded by mounting piles of paper, trying to collect his thoughts after his All-Hands address to the brigade. Even though he was reading from the prepared talking points in front of him during the event, he was distracted by the new woman sitting in the audience. He had never seen anyone quite like her before. She seemed out of place while nervously trying to talk to him, but he was unexpectedly taken aback by her beauty. Something about her kept drawing him in like a butterfly attracted to a fragrant, beautiful flower. Also, there was some-thing about her name…Lillian. That was a name he could never forget. Lillies were beautiful flowers. Jack forced himself to snap out of his trance. *What the heck is wrong with me? You know better than this,* he lectured to himself. She was just another contract employee. However, there was something about her…something different. He couldn't quite put his finger on it. She had captured his attention whether he liked it or not.

This is not good, he thought hastily to himself. At the

moment, he didn't need any distractions. With his responsibilities pulling him in a hundred different directions and his inbox that seemed to never sleep, he tried his best to push the new woman out of his mind. He opened his inbox on his laptop and tried to focus, going through emails he had received. His eyes drifted away from his computer as heat radiated throughout his chest. His blue eyes sparkled, and a weightless gaze formed across his face. Jack was feeling something in his heart he hadn't felt in quite a while…happiness.

3

———

There was no way of getting around it. I stood out whether I liked it or not. I was the new kid on the block. I found myself standing in my decrepit office building with my co-workers, waiting for our colonel to show up and give Ethan an award for a high-profile event he had spearheaded during the pandemic. I nervously straightened out my black collared shirt covered in red hearts. I was very girly and loved anything with pink, red, and hearts, but I didn't realize I was a walking billboard for love. I scanned the brightly lit office surrounded by rusted filing cabinets and wood laminate desks that looked regurgitated from the 1970s. Half-opened cardboard boxes from people who probably didn't want to move into the office, to begin with, were stacked four deep against the walls. I heard the door open from behind me, and the handsome colonel walked in like a breath of fresh air, holding a file folder with my boss's award. We were all wearing face masks because of the pandemic, but that didn't stop the handsome colonel from looking at me.

As we stood in a group of people, something drew me to

him, and I kept gazing over at him. His blue eyes caught my attention from across the room, striking and mesmerizing from afar. He was also sneaking glances at me, and for some reason, we were completely enthralled by each other's presence. Out of nowhere, my heartbeat quickened, and my face grew hot. I had no idea what was going on and wondered what it was about this man that had captured me in a way that I never experienced before. It's not like I was new to living on a military post.

Everywhere I went, men in service uniforms were going about their business—in and out of the gas station, commissary, and driving to and from work. I never gave it a second thought. But something about this particular man was *different*.

Ethan walked into the room and tried to act surprised, like he didn't know about his award. "Oh wow," he exclaimed. The colonel walked over to him, handed him the formal certificate displayed in a professional green folder, and smiled as the brigade photographer, Daniel, snapped their photo.

Wow, these people really like their awards, I thought to myself.

Jack gently laid his hand on Ethan's shoulder and smiled as he addressed the group. "While it certainly wasn't easy having to navigate through a pandemic, Ethan's strong work ethic and willingness to always put the mission first is what got us to where we are today." Jack then turned to Ethan and smiled. "Thank you, Ethan for always stepping up to the plate." As everyone erupted in applause, my focus was on this handsome man standing only a few feet away in front of me. After finishing his remarks, the colonel walked out of the building and back to his fancy office building situated in the middle of post. In my mind, his office seemed like someplace where the *Great and Powerful Oz* resided, but nobody had actually seen beyond his office door.

Meanwhile, Jack's military portrait was hanging everywhere. No matter what building I was in, his presence was felt throughout the post. Every corner I turned, there was his photo, proudly smiling with the American and Army flags displayed in the background. Along with his photo were hung signed memorandums about policies or the brigade's mission. I found it odd that his photo was plastered on what seemed like every other wall in the buildings throughout the brigade like he was the President of the United States. I started to realize, after seeing how people interacted with him, that everyone treated this man like he *was* the President. They carefully tip-toed around him, watching what they said when he walked into the room or had conversations with him.

After the hiring process had begun, but prior to meeting Jack on my first day, I had been faced with an important life-changing decision. A fork in the road of my life. My husband's orders were up here in Arizona, which meant having to move if nothing opened up at the current post we were living on. "I want to leave," he said, very declamatory. "I've been here almost my entire Army career, and I want to go somewhere else."

Now, most spouses say, "Yes, of course. We can look for orders elsewhere," in support of their husband's military career. I had done that in the past when we first took orders to the East Coast shortly after getting married, but something told me I needed to stay at my job. I reluctantly went to my bosses and explained my situation.

———

WALKING INTO THEIR MUSTY OFFICE, which reminded me of the Department of Motor Vehicles, I nervously sat down in the cold tan plastic chair in front of my bosses, Ryne and Ethan. I could feel Ethan harshly judging me with his glaring eyes as he sat next to Ryne, probably wondering why in the world I wanted to talk with them. Ethan had a reputation for micromanaging our team and overstepping when it came to anything published about the Army. Ryne, on the other hand, was the department manager, an insecure and overly stressed-out short man with dirty blond hair and coke-bottle eyeglasses. He obsessed over Jack's every move and latched onto him like a leech. As I did my best to slow my breathing, a wave of nausea hit me. I cleared my throat and took a quick breath.

"I know I've only been in my job for a couple of weeks, but my husband and I may have to move if there are no orders here," I hesitantly stated. "I love my job so far, and I love that I can serve my country with the skills and talents that God has given me. With that said, I want to ask if I can keep my job at the brigade and work remotely."

They both looked at me with blank stares. "Well, we've never been in a situation like this before," Ryne admitted. "As much as we'd like to let you work remotely, the truth is that if the colonel needs anything, we need you here. So, unfortunately, working remotely for the brigade is not in our best interest," Ryne explained to me.

My eyes widened as my mouth slowly dropped open, trying to let their words sink in. "Okay, I understand," I said rather defeatedly, like a robot following orders with no feeling whatsoever.

When the topic was first brought up about my husband's orders and possibly moving when I first started the job, their automatic response was, "Oh, no problem! We fully support military spouses." I quickly realized, after my many years of being married to an active-duty soldier, that the military's needs will always come first. This was something I didn't realize when I first got married. However, my new Army job was no exception to that rule.

Zoned out and wrapping my mind around what I'd just been told, I realized I had a choice. I could obey my husband's wishes to take orders elsewhere in the United States and quit my job, or I could find a way to stay here so that I didn't lose my job. I didn't know why, but this voice, deep down in my heart, told me that I needed to fight for my job. I needed to stay. There was a reason why, but it wasn't quite clear, other than I was beginning to like my job and found it very rewarding.

Arriving home later in the day, I pulled up to my basic tan-and-white townhome with terracotta shingles on the roof. Red woodchips were sprinkled throughout the front yard, with just a few plants that could withstand the extreme Arizona heat. The no-thrills home was a carbon copy of just about every home on the post. Out of the corner of my eye, I spotted that a few empty energy cans littered my neighbor's front yard. Aaron also never started his day without coffee and an energy drink to get him through the workday. I never understood why soldiers loved energy drinks and protein bars so much, but it seemed to be the two things that kept them going. Walking up my steps,

I took a deep breath as I slowly opened the dark brown front door, prepared to defy my husband's wishes. This would be the first time that I had spoken up against my husband.

I walked into the house to see Aaron standing in the middle of the living room wearing his camouflage Army uniform and tan combat boots. He was on his lunch break from work and routinely stopped by to eat and visit with our two rescue chihuahuas, Max and Charlie. They came running around the corner, greeting me as they heard me walk into the house. Aaron wasted no time jumping to the point.

"Well, what did they say?" he gratingly asked. I felt an empty feeling in the pit of my stomach as I fought off the sudden urge to flee. I carefully took a deep breath.

"They said I can't work remotely, and because of that, I decided that if you take orders elsewhere, I am just going to stay here." Aaron's eyes grew large. He stared at me with a blank expression on his face.

"What in the hell do you mean?" he spat out.

I continued, "Well, I've worked so hard to get this job, and I really love what I do. I don't want to leave. So, if you want to leave, that's fine, but I'm going to stay here."

I held my breath, waiting for a mini explosion to go off. This was something that I'd never done before, and it terrified me. Part of me wanted to be a supportive wife and just go wherever the wind took us. However, I wasn't about to give up my job just because he was tired of where we were stationed and wanted a change of scenery. Before, when orders were available on our post, he didn't even want to consider it. "Yeah, there's a couple of openings on this post but I still wouldn't take them," he bluntly stated. But now, with me working on post, our situation had changed.

"Okay," he said in a defeated voice. "I'll look for orders here and try to stay. If I don't find anything, I'll consider retiring so we can stay." I was flabbergasted. I stood there rapidly blinking, wondering if maybe I had misheard him. I wasn't expecting that, but I was also fully prepared to get an apartment and try to make it work here if he had to leave. A small part of me was also getting tired of the volatility that came with being married to someone in the military and longed for some stability. I simply wanted a break from always wondering about being forced to move every two or three years to a different post and having to start all over again.

The next couple of weeks were a total rollercoaster ride of emotions trying to find orders while he tried endlessly to convince me to move to different states, I had no interest in living in, like Mississippi.

"You wouldn't even need to work!" was the worn-out tune he replayed over and over again. "The cost of living is so cheap in Mississippi that you could just stay home, and we could even have a property with animals." He knew this was my dream and tried to use it to sway me to his side.

I shot back, "I don't have twenty years of work experience and an MBA to just stay home and do nothing! I like my job, and I want to stay." I held my stance like a strong post firmly planted in the ground, not allowing even the strongest of winds to sway me. My gut told me to fight for my job, and so I fought.

Right before my husband's orders were about to expire, a set of orders popped up on the post where we were currently living. It was with the Army reservists, something my husband wasn't too thrilled about. "They're weekend warriors who have no respect for authority," he said in his sergeant voice. "But I'll take them if you want to stay."

A sense of relief washed over me. I could stay and keep my job without having to hunt for my own apartment and try to make it work, living away from my husband and two dogs that I loved like they were my own children.

After I learned the news that we were staying in the area, I opened my work computer to send Ethan and Ryne an email. "My husband was able to find orders here so we are able to stay, and I can continue working for the brigade." I was still astonished at their lack of flexibility and non-existent support for someone who's a military spouse. Yet their everyday jobs revolved around "supporting the warfighter," as they often said. I decided to let it go. I was able to stay and keep working. I won the battle with Aaron, but was it worth fighting for?

4
———

I felt like I was living someone else's life. Doubt haunted me like a bad dream. Second-guessing my decision to challenge Aaron so I could keep my job working for the military—it was the shadow that wouldn't go away. The brigade held another event in the same auditorium a couple of weeks after my second encounter with Jack. To no surprise, Ethan tasked me to write about it. So again, armed with my handy tape recorder, I obediently drove to the auditorium, but this time felt different.

Sitting in the middle of the auditorium about ten minutes before the event was to start, I carefully got out my recorder and pulled out my pink notebook and two pens. As a former journalist, I always had two pens in case one ran out of ink. I sat straight as a board, waiting for the event to start. Then Jack walked in. I caught his eye, and with one sleek move, he gave me a subtle head nod. He continued walking to the front of the room where he was about to give a presentation on the latest technological developments for the Army.

I sat stunned, with my heart racing a million miles a

minute. Every single nerve in my body came alive. *Was he looking at me? No way,* I thought. *There's no way this gorgeous, successful, and brilliant man is looking* at me. My next thought was, why *me?* I wasn't anybody special for someone like him to look at me like *that.* What did he see in me? I had so many questions that I didn't know the answers to. He looked at me in a way that nobody had ever looked at me before—that I *was* a beautiful goddess that he might look at…but was otherwise entirely out of reach.

Meanwhile, I did my best to stay focused on the job at hand. Since Covid-19 was in full swing, I was still working from home, which I thoroughly enjoyed because it meant more time spent with my dogs. It also allowed me the luxury of managing my schedule teaching cycle at my local gym. While I was never sure what path to take for my career, teaching cycling was something I knew I was born to do. I loved the energy, making people smile while having fun and burning calories all at the same time. It was also my outlet for letting out stress from my day job, which was plagued by tight deadlines and my work being examined under a microscope by Ethan. I also felt like I was jumping through hoops as I was learning to navigate the military world I was now fully a part of as my personal and professional lives were colliding right before my very eyes. Despite all this, I was enjoying my job because it aligned with my passion for helping other people. I also discovered this newfound path of mission-driven work, which was very rewarding.

———

THE WORDS POPPED out of my computer screen like I was sitting in a 3-D movie theater. It had only been a few weeks since starting my new job and Ethan had asked me to come into the office to discuss edits to one of my latest articles. I held my breath, not knowing what to expect from him. He was extremely volatile, being hot one day and cold the next. My writing wasn't up to his high standards as the military had exceptionally high expectations—even if it was for an internal workforce newsletter hardly anyone ever read. I slowly walked into Ethan's office and found him sitting at the conference table waiting for me. In front of him was my latest article, completely unrecognizable with his multitude of edits.

Here we go, I thought bravely. I glanced up at him and saw the look of dissatisfaction written all over his face. I nervously bit my lower lip as my eyes darted toward the exit and back at Ethan. "Hi Ethan, I got your email about wanting to talk to me about one of my articles. What's going on?"

His nostrils flared, and his cold eyes glared at me from across the conference room table. He combed his fingers through his greasy red hair and adjusted his eyeglasses. "I'm going to give you the benefit of the doubt because you're new and have never worked for the military, but you've got some serious issues to work through with your writing."

I felt like the ax aimed at my job was about to come down at any moment. My head started to pound like a hammer. I took quick breaths as my mind went blank. I looked around the room and realized that we were the only ones in the building since everyone worked remotely part-time due to the pandemic. I was trapped and didn't see any way out. My nose caught the whiff of something unpleasant from the break room, and I realized Ethan must have just eaten his lunch.

"Okay, can you please explain what the issues are, and maybe I can do my best to work on them?"

Ethan let out a big huff in frustration. "For one thing, you need to start learning the acronyms. With you being married to a soldier, I expected you to know them inside and out, but I guess I was wrong. Also, you need to follow protocol. You can't just email anyone at this brigade asking for an interview. You have to go through *me* first, and I have to approve it."

Just when I thought he was done, he continued with his rant. "Lastly, under no circumstances are you allowed to talk to, nor even email, any of the senior leaders with the brigade. That goes for Colonel Cooper. The Army has a chain of command that we follow to a T, with the colonel being at the top."

I was shocked to hear him point out Jack specifically, but also, I wasn't surprised. I responded slowly. "Okay...I understand, but what if I'm writing a story and need to interview Colonel Cooper?"

Ethan looked at me and rolled his eyes. "Well, I highly doubt *that* will ever happen, but if it does happen, you will go through Ryne. He handles all the Colonel's military affairs."

Oh yes, Ryne, his gatekeeper. How could I forget? I thought sarcastically.

Ethan handed me my article. I looked down at my poor paper, hemorrhaging in red ink like it just fought a battle against Ethan's mighty red pen and lost. "I want you to look over my edits. Memorize them, and the next article you write, I want you to keep all these edits in mind, so we don't have this conversation again."

I somehow managed to smile. "Sounds good. Thank you again for taking the time to review your edits with me and I will remember them the next time I write. Did you need anything else from me?"

He responded matter-of-factly. "That is all for now. You can go."

I quickly replied, "Thank you. I hope you have a good day." I got up from the table and quickly walked out of the room. Part of me wanted to run out of that office and never look back.

Sitting in my car getting ready to leave, I felt like I was suddenly drowning in a job that I perhaps wasn't a good fit for. I shook my head while looking down at the floor. I slowly looked up at the parking spot across from me and saw Jack's name on his designated parking spot with his fancy navy blue sports car parked in it. He happened to work in the building across from mine. Slowly, I felt my adrenaline start to come down from being in fight-or-flight mode with Ethan.

The handsome colonel was becoming my silver lining for the trials I was going through with my job. At the same time, Aaron was on my mind. I felt conflicted about the feelings growing deep in my heart for Jack since I was married to Aaron. Even though my interactions with Jack were sparse, he was nothing like Aaron. Jack didn't wear his rank on his sleeve like other high-ranking military officers in his position— acting high and mighty like he was better than everyone else. Jack had a soft side to him, a stark contrast to his serious military side, the brief moments we talked at brigade events. He was not only easy to talk to, but he had a calming presence about him that told me I could trust him. I could tell him anything, and he wouldn't judge me. He was like no other man I had ever met. As if my adoration for Jack wasn't bad enough, Aaron was a first-class sergeant, and Jack clearly outranked him. This had trouble written all over it. I knew that if I wanted to keep my job—and my marriage—I needed to stay focused on doing my job and ignore my feelings for Jack.

After my verbal tongue-lashing from Ethan, I was on my way home, venting on the phone with my friend Amelie. We both worked together in the fashion industry after college—with her in product development and me in marketing. We became fast friends as we bonded over crazy requests from fashion stylists and worked for bosses who expected us to turn water into wine. With her soft-spoken voice and a smile that would light up any room, she had a way of always seeing the bright side of any situation. She sensed that I was having quite a day when she suggested we meet up for a drink to let off some steam. We decided on a quaint French bistro downtown, which happened to be one of my favorite spots since I adored anything remotely related to Paris.

I drove up to the restaurant and walked inside to find Amelie sitting at the bar, waiting for me, wearing tan sandals and black leggings. Her long caramel brunette hair hung loosely around her face, which happened to match her comfy caramel sweater perfectly. Her amber eyes sparkled as she caught sight of me walking through the front door. I excitedly walked over to her as she gave me a big hug.

"Hi!" she exclaimed. "It feels like it's been forever since I've seen you. I'm so glad you were able to find time in your busy schedule for us to have a quick drink."

"Oh my gosh, me too! It seems like I haven't had a minute to take a breath since I took this job with the Army. I'm wondering if it's going to slow down anytime soon, but I highly doubt it. How are you doing?"

Amelie replied as she took a quick sip of her wine. "Everything is going well. It seems like I haven't had a minute to slow down either, and the requests from the brides are never-ending…" Amelie was now a successful wedding planner, and I enjoyed looking at the beautiful, editorial-quality photos of her exquisite weddings, along with everything else that went with her job.

"I'm so proud of you and this amazing business you've built from the ground up. You're following your heart, and I'm so happy to see that doors are opening for you."

A big smile came across her face. "Thank you so much for saying that—what about you? Tell me what's going on at work. I'm sorry to hear that your boss won't seem to let you catch a break…"

I rolled my eyes and let out a huff. "It's just difficult to see the light at the end of the tunnel. I feel like I'm trying so hard, and I'm just not getting anywhere with Ethan. No matter what I do, he's not satisfied."

Amelie gave me a sympathetic smile. "Oh, I remember those days back when we worked for that clothing company in LA with our hard-to-please bosses."

I shot back. "Please don't remind me! The last thing I want is a repeat of my career in the fashion industry."

Amelie laughed. "Oh no, we don't want that, but it sounds like this job is different than working in the apparel business—starting with that handsome colonel you're working for…"

I let out a laugh. "I know, Amelie. He is so good-looking and charming, too. A small part of me wishes I had met him before marrying Aaron, but everything happens for a reason, I guess."

She replied hopefully. "I do believe everything happens for

a reason, and God wanted you to take this specific path for a reason. But it's important to recognize what you feel for Jack and why you feel this way."

I felt a sting of guilt in my heart. I knew she was right. This was the first time that I had developed feelings for another man that wasn't my husband. It was obvious those feelings weren't going away. "Yeah, I suppose I am feeling this way for a reason, and it's hard to know why at this exact moment. I think I need to sit down with myself, ask the hard questions, and not be afraid of what answers come up."

Amelie reached over and put her hand on mine. "I think that's a great start. I'm sure it won't be easy to do, but there's a reason why you're having feelings for Jack," she quickly added. "But I wonder…what if you ran into your colonel while on post with Aaron? Doesn't he outrank Aaron? Does Aaron have to salute him?"

I was stumped. Leave it to Amelie to think of something wild like that. Part of me hoped I would never be put in that situation. "Wow. I never thought of that, honestly. Thinking about Aaron having to salute Jack is a crazy thought, but what are the odds of us running into him? I don't think that will ever happen."

A questionable look came across Amelie's face. "Oh, I don't know for sure, but never say never. That's what I say. God seems to have a way of surprising us when we least expect it," she added. "And with your job, you have a lot more to give than what you realize. You have an advantage over your bosses because you've been in the Army world for a lot longer than they've been working for the military. Even though you're a military spouse, you still have something to offer that they don't have. That's tribal knowledge." I had never thought about it that way, but I had a feeling that maybe Amelie was onto something.

———

IT WAS like Amelie was staring into a crystal ball. Of course, she was right. Over time, I became a trusted resource when it came to understanding how the military thought on certain issues, all thanks to my active-duty husband and leaning on my experience as a wife to a soldier for almost fourteen years. I often found myself explaining things to people they didn't understand—like the importance of mustering. I found this baffling. How can someone work for the military for as long as they did and not understand these things? It blew my mind. After I explained to my new co-worker why the colonel felt mustering was so important, he got it.

"Checking in is a way of making sure you're okay," I explained to him. I then told the story of how my husband saved a soldier's life who was about to commit suicide, all because he didn't muster, aka check-in. "It's very, very important," I explained to my new co-worker. "This is why the colonel gets upset when people complain about mustering. Something as simple as clicking a freaking button, as he says, is not that hard, and it's for our own good."

Being able to give glimpses into the military way of thinking made me feel good because it meant I was showing my value, and I was glad to help where needed. A small part of me also wondered if this willingness to help others and go outside of my lane was a good idea in the long run. As I learned from being a military spouse and from my active-duty husband, going outside your lane is something that isn't welcomed. Everyone has a designated role to play, and that's just the way it is, but I was never one to follow the rules. Even when I first moved to post as a bright-eyed and excited spouse, my first experience living there was one I'd never forget—breaking a rule without even realizing it:

After driving onto post and showing the security guards on base my newly minted dependent identification card, I was on the phone with my mother-in-law, excitedly chatting away about my brand-new military life. As I pulled into the commissary, a man driving past me yelled out his car window, "Get off your phone!" I jumped out of my seat, completely terrified. My pulse started to race as I could hear my heartbeat thrashing in my ears. I quickly hung up the phone with my mother-in-law and pulled my car over to call my husband, telling him what happened.

"What were you thinking? You can't drive and have your phone in your hand!" He lectured me. "It's against post rules and if you get pulled over, I will be the one getting into trouble because I'm responsible for you."

I started to second-guess myself. I felt like a Pollyanna with so much yet to learn about military life and living on post. I squeezed my eyes shut as my legs felt weak. "I am so sorry! I had no idea," I told my husband apologetically. I was shocked by my first taste of military life. I realized that I had a lot of studying to do, which also included the new role of being married to a soldier.

That night, Aaron got home from work late—something that is a norm for people in the military. I often found myself trying to make dinner and have all the laundry washed and properly folded before he got home from work. This was a chore while juggling a full-time job. However, Aaron was particular about how his laundry was folded—specifically his brown undershirts. They had to be folded a certain way along with his socks, something they taught him during basic training.

Aaron walked in the door and dropped his work bag by the front door. Immediately, the smell of food cooking from the kitchen hit him. "Dinner smells great! What are you making?"

I responded in a bubbly tone. "I made spaghetti tonight!" Since I'm not much of a cook in the kitchen, my menu is rather limited, but I was working on building up my culinary skills and was proud of the dishes that I could make.

"Sounds good to me," he said enthusiastically. He sat down in the living room and switched the TV on as his favorite video game loaded onto the screen. A smile came across my face as I served him a plate of spaghetti. After he was done eating, I sat down on the couch next to him and reached over to give him a hug.

"I really missed you today," I said in a loving tone.

Unexpectedly, he pushed me away. "Ugh, I don't want you hugging me!"

I shook my head and started rubbing my forehead as tears welled up in my eyes. I longed for some sort of connection with him, but it was often met with rejection. "I just wanted a hug, and we hardly ever cuddle. I feel like I'm constantly asking *you* to hug me or be affectionate."

He looked at me and rolled his eyes. "You're being too clingy. My back and shoulder are hurting me, and you're making it worse." Feeling defeated, I got up from the couch and made my way to the laundry room to keep folding his laundry, so he'd have clean clothes to wear for the week.

—————

TAN and green duffel bags littered our living room like landmines. Deployment time was upon us again as Aaron was preparing for his six-month deployment to Belgium. The night before he was scheduled to fly out with his brigade, we went to dinner at a fancy Italian restaurant downtown. I wore a light pink tulle skirt with my gold glittery designer high-heeled shoes and a white button-up collared shirt tied at the waist. As I finished applying my make-up and putting last-minute touches on curling my hair, Aaron walked into the bathroom wearing a casual graphic t-shirt and blue jeans with his Converse sneakers. I looked over at him, and he was clearly annoyed.

"You don't need to dress up every time we go out. It's just dinner, not the Army ball," he said starkly.

Shock and disbelief hit me like a tidal wave, practically knocking me out. My head hung low as I felt my body crumpling in on itself. The comment impaled my self-confidence. I'd expect most significant others to say, "Wow, honey, you look beautiful," but nope, not my husband.

I responded angrily. "You know I like dressing up, so this shouldn't come as a surprise to you."

He hastily said, "Wear whatever you want. I don't really care."

That's right, I will wear whatever I want, and it's not like I'm dressing for you anyway, I annoyingly thought.

We arrived at the restaurant, and as we walked through the beautiful oak front doors, I looked up and spotted a beautiful crystal chandelier hanging above us. Black wallpaper with gorgeous paintings lined the walls. The smell of Italian food cooking in the kitchen filled the air. We were led to the booth closest to the front door. I sat down and set my pink clutch on the seat beside me as I adjusted my elegant skirt. Deep down, I didn't want to be at dinner with Aaron, especially after his snide comment about my outfit. However, I decided to make the best of it. The waitress, a woman in her early thirties, came up to our booth.

"Hello and welcome! Can I get you started with something to drink?" I ordered my usual lemon drop martini, and Aaron ordered a Coke. She looked over at me and exclaimed, "Wow, you look beautiful. I love your dress!"

I looked up at her and politely smiled. "Thank you. That's very kind of you to say." She handed us the menus and walked away. *Well, it looks like I'm not the one who's looking out of place,* I sarcastically thought as I looked around and saw other people dressed up, reflecting on Aaron's rude comment earlier in the evening about my dress.

The waitress came back ten minutes later to take our order. I decided on an eggplant lasagna while Aaron ordered the steak. "Perfect choice!" The bubbly waitress replied.

After she walked away, Aaron proceeded to vent about work. He had a new captain that he was working for, and he wasn't too happy with the overbearing officer who seemed to be stepping on Aaron's toes, taking over his responsibilities. "Just another typical officer who thinks he can do my job! He needs to stay in his lane and worry about his job and not be trying to do mine," Aaron huffed. He continued venting. "I just don't understand why I should take orders from this guy. It's not like he went through the same training I did. He has things handed to him on a silver platter. They don't have to work nearly as hard as the enlisted people do."

Anger started building up deep inside me as I thought of Jack. He's an officer, and he worked very hard. He wasn't like Aaron's captain. Jack had a dedicated work ethic, taking pride in serving in the military, whereas Aaron despised being in the Army. He always had something negative to say about the work he was doing and the people he worked with.

Surprisingly, I practically shouted, "That's not true!" I have no idea where this lion of a voice came from, and it startled me. Aaron's eyes grew large as he threw his head back.

"Where in the world did that come from? Why are *you* so defensive of all people?" he quickly snapped. "You've been working with officers at that stupid brigade of yours for way too long."

I felt the color draining from my face as tears started to build up in my eyes. *Don't cry! Don't cry!* I scolded myself. In the back of my mind, I knew he was wrong.

Right as I was going to respond to Aaron's rude comment, my heart started to dance. A little voice inside me said Jack was coming. I looked over at the front of the restaurant and saw Jack walk through the double doors with his wife. He looked across the restaurant and spotted me. We automatically locked eyes on one another. I froze in my seat as my eyes widened, and my breath started to shake. *Oh, my goodness, how did I know he was going to walk in the door?* I thought, shocked.

The hostess led Jack and his wife to a booth in the middle of the restaurant. His intense roaming gaze locked on me as he walked next to his wife. They sat down at the booth when I saw Jack whisper something to his wife. He got up and walked toward mine and Aaron's booth. I noticed this was the first time I had not seen him in a military uniform. Jack looked sharp wearing a well-fitted white button-up collared shirt, which seemed to perfectly complement his freshly pressed black dress slacks and black lace-up oxford shoes. He pulled the look together with a nice black leather belt. My heart started to dance even faster, and my breathing increased. Jack stopped in front of our table. His blue eyes twinkled as he looked down at me. A small grin formed on his face.

"Hello, Lillian, what a nice coincidence seeing you here tonight."

I tried to slow my breathing once again. "Hello, Colonel Cooper. It's nice to see you again."

Unexpectedly, Aaron shot up from his seat and accidentally bumped our table. He hastily turned to Jack and saluted him. "It's nice to meet you, sir. I'm Lillian's husband, Sergeant First Class Aaron White."

Jack turned to Aaron and returned the salute. Aaron quickly sat back down. Meanwhile, I secretly enjoyed seeing Aaron having to salute Jack. *Ha! I bet he's eating his words right about now!* I happily thought to myself.

Jack said to Aaron. "Lillian has been doing great things for the Army. We're very lucky to have her." He looked down at me with an endearing smile.

I replied, "Thank you, sir, that's very nice of you to say."

Aaron quickly chimed in. "That's great to hear, sir. I'm happy you're satisfied with the work she's been doing for your brigade. I've heard nothing but great things about you since she first started working there."

I snapped my head in his direction, trying my best not to glare at him for totally kissing up to Jack. *That's not what you were saying a minute ago!* I wanted to say, but I kept my thoughts to myself.

Jack responded. "That's very kind, but we're the lucky ones to have someone as talented as Lillian working for us. She is one of the best writers at our brigade."

A wave of shyness hit me. This was the first time I'd heard Jack pay me such a wonderful comment. "That really means a lot, sir. Thank you," I responded wholeheartedly.

Jack smiled broadly at me. "I will let you both get back to your meal, but it was nice seeing you again, Lillian, and it was nice meeting you, Sergeant White."

"It was nice meeting you too, sir," Aaron replied enthusiastically.

As I watched Jack confidently walk back to his booth, my eyes blinked slowly as a feeling of dizziness hit me. *I can't believe that just happened!*

Aaron turned to me as his eyes glistened from the unexpected encounter with Jack like we had just seen a celebrity. "Wow! Do you have any idea what it means to have the seal of approval from a colonel? That's a big deal."

Not paying attention to Aaron, I felt my mind floating away like I was struck by cupid's arrow. My eyes gazed off into the distance. I could hear Jack's voice in my head. *We're very lucky to have her.* I inhaled and took in the lightness growing in my heart. Aaron then leaned across the table, staring me down. His angry voice ripped through my daydream. "Hello? Lily. Are you listening to me?"

I quickly snapped out of my trance. "Sorry! Yes, I am listening to you."

Aaron then repeated in a condescending tone, "I said to have someone like a colonel on your side is not something that happens every day. Like I said, it's a big deal."

Oh, trust me, I know what a big deal it is because Jack is a very big deal, I thought to myself. "Colonel Cooper is a very nice man. From what I've been told by my other co-workers, he's not like other colonels at other brigades. He constantly shows his appreciation for the work we do."

Aaron responded, utterly shocked. "Wow, that's surprising. He sounds like a rare breed." *Oh, he sure is,* I thought to myself fondly.

I looked over and saw the waitress approaching with our dishes and another waiter following closely behind with our drinks. "Here you go," she said enthusiastically. "I hope you both enjoy and let me know if you need anything else."

I sat there quietly eating my meal as I was floating away in pure bliss with my heart still racing from the unexpected encounter with Jack. I looked over at Jack as he was talking to his wife. He kept glancing in my direction. I gave him a small smile as I saw his face slowly light up.

This was a wonderful surprise, and he sure did make my night, I thought to myself.

After we finished our meals, Aaron got up and walked to the hostess stand to take care of our tab. I slowly looked over at Jack, who was eating his dinner now with his wife—a petite woman with light brunette hair pulled back in a ponytail. Her black and gray floral dress came together with a black belt around her waist. I could sense the distance between them as she stared at her phone—ignoring Jack and their meal. I caught him discreetly glancing at me out of the corner of his eye. I felt the butterfly's taking flight inside my heart. I couldn't help but wonder if Jack yearned to have dinner with me instead of his wife.

Aaron walked up to the table. "Are you ready to go?"

Not really, but I guess so, I thought to myself. I stood up and saw Jack's eyes follow me as I walked out of the restaurant next to Aaron.

That night, I found it hard to sleep as I kept replaying the evening in my mind. *Well, Amelie was right!* I thought to myself as I remembered her asking about what if we ran into Jack. *I guess never say never!* I chuckled under my breath as I fell into a peaceful sleep.

5

———

JACK

A typical night out to dinner took an unexpected turn. Jack was quiet on the drive home from the restaurant. Rapidly blinking, he rolled down his car window with the cool night wind blowing all around him. He looked up at the night sky and noticed how bright the stars looked—so beautiful and peaceful with no clouds in sight. As he merged onto the freeway, he felt himself unexpectedly speed up as his mind started swirling with a hundred different thoughts after bumping into Lillian at the restaurant.

Seeing her outside of work took him by surprise, almost like seeing a wild animal for the first time in its natural habitat. He saw her in a new light—dressed up in that beautiful pink skirt, the soft light highlighting her rosy, pink cheeks and that subtle glow in her green eyes when she looked at him. He had never seen a more beautiful woman in his life. But there was something about the *way* she looked at him. Nobody had ever looked at him that way before. He also realized that nobody had ever made him feel more uneasy and nervous in his entire life. Here he was—an accomplished and powerful

Army colonel, and this petite, soft-spoken woman was making him shake in his combat boots. Jack closed his eyes and vigorously shook his head, almost as if he were trying to shake the thoughts out of his mind. *Even if I were single, there's no way I could be with a woman like that,* he thought critically to himself. She was way out of his league.

Sensing his distance, Jack's wife finally spoke up. "What is wrong with you? Why aren't you talking?"

Jack snapped out of his trance. "Nothing. I'm fine," he shot back.

Jack's wife took a deep breath and let out a small huff in frustration under her breath. "You haven't said more than two words since we left the restaurant. Does it have something to do with seeing your employee at dinner tonight?"

Jack's eyes darted from right to left. "No, she's just another contract employee working on post. She's nobody."

Jack's wife raised her right eyebrow and glared at him from across the car. "Okay, if you say so," she said with suspicion in her voice.

But was Lillian just nobody? Jack had his doubts.

6

———

Saying goodbye is never easy, no matter how many times you do it. For some odd reason, this time didn't hurt as much. I stood outside the parking lot on post as the old white school bus pulled up. Grabbing his duffel bags out of the trunk of our car, Aaron gave me a quick peck on the lips. Not the kind of kiss that you give the love of your life. The kind of kiss that was more routine. It had no feeling behind it whatsoever. "We've been through so many deployments they're all bleeding together now, but you'll be fine. Hold things down while I'm gone, and I'll be home before you know it." He sounded like he was running a quick errand instead of going on a six-month deployment.

I managed to smile. "I guess you're right. Have a safe trip and let me know when you land." Aaron looked over at Max and Charlie sitting in the passenger seat of our car. Tears started to fill his eyes. Not tears for leaving me. Tears for leaving our dogs. He walked over and patted their heads.

"Take care of our boys."

I lovingly replied. "Yes, they will be fine." The truth was

we were used to Aaron taking off and leaving for six or nine months at a time. They didn't know anything different. If it wasn't deployments, it was business trips and field training exercises. Aaron was always gone.

Aaron dutifully grabbed his duffel bags and boarded the bus. The boys and I watched as the bus drove away, leaving us in a thick black cloud of exhaust. Another deployment quickly came. How many deployments had I gone through? Six? Seven? At this point, I had lost count. Aaron was right. They were all bleeding together. As the realization of Aaron being gone started to set in, it was just me and my two pups at home keeping things going while he was away overseas.

By this time, I had had several interactions with the handsome colonel from Georgia. Flirty looks, smiles under our face masks, watching each other with quick glances when we were in the same room. All the while, I wondered to myself what this would lead to, if anything. I didn't quite understand it, but something about him made me feel a love growing in my heart that I had never felt before—not even for my own husband. At the same time, I felt guilty for having these feelings for another man that was not my husband. I didn't understand why it was so easy for me to picture myself married to Jack and having a little family of our own, and yet that was something I never pictured with Aaron. I knew this was all happening for a bigger purpose than I saw with my limited view of the situation. Something also told me that he thought about me all the time, too. I was on his mind probably more often than he'd ever care to admit. Meanwhile, I did my best to push the feelings down and ignore them, not telling anyone at work about what was happening between me and Jack.

———

Hi Lily! We've officially hit our one-month mark, as we're sure you're counting down the days until your soldier is home from Belgium! We would love to see you at our first Family Readiness Group meeting, where we'll be sharing the projects your service member has been working on since he left for deployment. Feel free to bring your favorite dish for the potluck!

I raised one eyebrow and gave the overly bubbly email a glassy stare. I sighed heavily. I dreaded attending military family events because I always felt like a rose in a field of thorns. I had very little in common with this group of women who always seemed to be gossiping left and right. I even remember hearing a story about a wife whose husband held a certain high rank, and she expected the security guards on post to salute *her!* Plus, here I was with no kids and working full-time, whereas the other spouses either had kids or were stay-at-home wives or husbands and didn't work. Regardless, I dutifully drove to the Army recreation center, where the meeting was being held, to get an update on how my husband was doing.

I walked into the recreation room, and right away, I was hit with the smell of cooked chicken and hamburgers. I saw a buffet of homemade food with delicious potato salad, corn on the cob, and appetizers. Kids happily played in the room with their friends while snacking on finger food. Spouses were huddled together in their cliques, excitedly talking amongst each other about their service members. All at once, a feeling of déjà vu hit me like I was in high school all over again, looking for my group of friends to hang out with. But this time, I didn't have any. Looking around the room, I spotted an open seat in the back. I took a deep breath and dreadfully sat down in the plastic chair, waiting for the event to start—all the while looking at the clock on my phone and trying not to run out the door. *I'm just going to find out the latest, and then I can leave.* I thought to myself.

As the adults in the room took their seats and the kids ran outside to play without a care in the world, the president of the Family Readiness Group from my brigade walked up to the podium and started to give introductory remarks.

A woman in her late thirties sitting next to me leaned over to another woman next to her and whispered, "Don't forget to stay for the meeting *after* the meeting."

My ears perked up. *What on earth is she talking about?* I curiously thought to myself. I opened my phone and found the email about the meeting. *That's interesting. There's nothing mentioned about a second meeting,* I thought to myself.

The woman sitting next to me whispered again to the other woman sitting next to her, "So, how are things going with your boyfriend since your husband left for deployment?"

My eyes widened. I tried to process what I just heard. *Did she say what I think she said?* I put two and two together—the meeting after the meeting was for the spouses who were cheating on their husbands.

Without warning, I felt immensely uncomfortable about what I overheard—like I had learned of someone's big secret that nobody was supposed to know. Except this time, it was common knowledge. I shifted in my chair, leaning away from the women sitting next to me. When a break came in the presentation, I immediately drove home, all the while feeling dazed and trying to soak in what I learned.

The second I got home, I called my husband to report back about the meeting, giving him a full rundown of what took place.

"I'm not at all surprised," he said frankly.

I sat there frozen. "What are you talking about? Did you not hear what I said?"

He responded. "Oh, I heard you, but what I'm saying is this isn't a surprise to me. Do you know how many troops I've talked out of cheating on their spouses? Some even have open marriages. Now granted, they're not all this way, but unfortunately, this is completely normal in the military."

I sat there in the middle of my living room, staring at Max and Charlie as they fought over their dog toy with the TV playing in the background. Everything became blurry. Time seemed to slow down. I was in total shock. Part of me couldn't help but wonder how the spouses could be so open about having other relationships. I heard stories in passing about military spouses cheating but for some odd reason, it seemed more common and accepted in the military.

Back when my husband and I got engaged, we visited my grandma in Missouri. At the mall, I went looking for self-help books on what it was like to be married to someone in the military. There, in the middle of this bookstore, I found a book for newly married military couples. I opened the book to a random chapter where the author bluntly stated that she looked forward to deployments and viewed it as a vacation away from her husband. At the time, it didn't make any sense. I loved my husband and didn't want to imagine being away from him for any length of time, let alone a six-month or eight-month deployment.

I realized that people had different ways of coping with that void or even filling it in altogether with someone else, but in my eyes, it didn't make it right. Now, here I was fourteen years later, developing feelings and lusting after another man for the first time since I got married. It was something that had never happened to me before, and I felt completely torn and guilt-ridden about it. I also wondered how different I really was from the women I met in my deployment meeting who openly talked about their boyfriends without a care in the world. I didn't want to follow in their footsteps.

———

ARTICLES ALWAYS CAME second nature to me. Writing speeches, on the other hand, sparked my interest because it was something new and challenging. They allowed for more creativity which I always appreciated. I often got tasked with writing the talking points for the senior leaders attending our brigade events. The events ranged from national monthly observances to leadership events. This time, I was tasked with writing Jack's talking points for our upcoming Veterans Day ceremony. *Jack's* talking points.

My mom and stepdad happened to be visiting that weekend and were excited to watch the event on social media, especially because they knew I wrote the colonel's remarks. It wasn't very often they had the opportunity to hear anything I'd written since I started working for the Army.

Picking out my outfit to attend the event, I wore a black knee-length dress with gold buttons, a small black belt, and my black-and-gold close-toed high heels. I paired the outfit with my fancy Army-inspired black long jacket with details on the sleeve that looked similar to an Army officer dress uniform. It was my favorite vintage coat. It was also cold that day since it was early in the morning. Still, I obediently stood outside the main building, waiting for the event to start.

From behind me, the double doors opened, and out walked Jack. He said "hello" to everyone and glanced at me as he walked by to stand in front, along with the other military people waiting for the event to start. As everyone watched the American flag being raised, I tried to concentrate, but my eyes were fixated on Jack. I wondered if he knew how good-looking he was. Standing confidently at six feet tall, he had a regalness about him and carried himself like a prince who stepped out of my childhood fairytales and into real life. He also had a charm and ease about him that brought people together when he was talking in front of a room, whether that was with ten people or fifty people. Everyone watched and listened to his every word. Yet he had a humbleness and a kind spirit that brought a smile to my face.

After the American flag was raised, a military officer kicked off the event with introductory remarks and shared his memories of Veterans Day, talking about his dad, who served and thanking all the veterans who continue to serve at the brigade today. After he was done, Jack stepped up to the podium. I was particularly excited because I wrote those talking points and poured my heart into them. It was the best speech I'd written for the Army thus far.

Jack started to speak in a soft and respectful tone when I noticed he stopped very briefly and corrected something that I wrote in his speech. When I submitted my talking points for editing to Ethan, he changed *Their Oath*, a military oath people repeat when joining the service, to *Their Oath of Enlistment*. Something told me that Jack wouldn't say it like that, and I was right. Not that it mattered much to Ethan, but to me, it did. I made sure everything I wrote was the very best, especially if it was something for Jack. As he paused and said what he was comfortable with, it made me smile because I knew in my heart that I was right. Deep down, a small part of me hoped for more opportunities to write Jack's talking points for future events.

After the speeches concluded, I made small talk with my co-workers as the rest of the brigade quickly made a beeline for the food trucks lined up in the quad area. The smell of freshly cooked tacos and hamburgers filled the air, which seemed to attract people from all over the post. Since I was a notoriously picky eater and a strict pescatarian, I decided to skip out on the food trucks.

As I turned to leave, I saw out of the corner of my eye that Jack, in mid-conversation with someone, stopped talking to watch me walk by. And not even hiding it but unintentionally making it blatantly obvious he was looking at me. Hot flashes automatically ran through my body as I forgot about how cold I was from being outside. I anxiously looked around and wondered if anyone else caught sight of Jack absently gazing at me.

Totally awestruck, I thought to myself, *Wow, he really likes me!* I felt like a silly schoolgirl unexpectedly catching the attention of my high school crush and not knowing how to behave.

———

THE NEXT WEEK, I attended the grand opening of an environmental testing facility situated on my post. Along with writing an article about the event, I was also asked to write a press release and pitch it to local and defense-focused media outlets, which I was really excited about.

The early morning of the grand opening ceremony felt cool and crisp. The weather oddly reminded me of growing up in California—chilly but not frigid, which I was thankful for. The ceremony was taking place outside, which meant I had to dress warm and look professional at the same time. I paired my black dress slacks with my long black peacoat. I accessorized the outfit with a knitted hairband that had a beautiful beaded feather on top. Along with looking fashionable, it also covered my ears and kept them warm. Since I had to wear my face mask, I felt covered from head to toe, bundled up like an Eskimo.

I drove up to the event, walked across the parking lot, and saw local city and state dignitaries starting to arrive for the ceremony, in addition to military personnel who also worked on the project. Sitting in the audience, I stared at the multi-story brick building in front of me. I quickly looked behind and saw Jack making small talk with Ethan. Like magic, I felt the strongest urge pulling me toward him like an invisible gravitational force. The feeling pulsated throughout my body like electricity.

I obediently ordered myself not to move. *Do not get up from your seat. Stay seated.* The feeling was something I had never felt before, let alone having to parent myself to not get up from my seat simply because I wanted to be close to him.

As I looked back at him, he quickly glanced at me sitting

in the audience. I snapped my head back around and felt my heart rapidly beating like rolling thunder in my chest.

Nervously fidgeting in the cold plastic chair, I felt the pressure of the event on me like a weighted vest combined with Jack's looming presence. I found myself tapping my pencil against my notepad, anxiously waiting for the event to start. I did my best to push Jack out of my mind.

Just focus on the event Lily, pretend like Jack isn't even here. Trying to change my focus from Jack to the event, I kept my eyes laser-focused on the podium as the post's brigadier general walked up to the microphone to give welcoming remarks. Brigadier General Stephanie Adams was a tall, slim woman with piercing chocolate brown eyes and jet-black hair pulled up in a tight bun. She had a reputation for commanding the attention of an army with her sharp voice and towering presence. When she spoke, people listened. A small condescending smile formed across her face as the audience was busy chatting away, unaware of her presence.

"Hello, everyone. Please find your seats. We are ready to begin," she said in a booming voice. Like watching ants scatter on the ground, the audience swiftly sat down in their seats. I watched as Jack made his way to the stage and sat down in the chair behind Stephanie.

"Hello, distinguished guests, coworkers, and our community. Thank you so much for being here today as we unveil this special facility. This is the first of many opportunities to leverage investments previously made by people just like you and the Army. It's these small service commitments that make a difference in strengthening our obligation to the Army and to our nation."

As I was rapidly jotting down notes from Stephanie's

speech in my notebook, I looked up and saw Jack's fixed glaze on me as a soft expression formed across his face. Aware of Jack's spotlight on me, I felt my inner temperature start to rise and the heat increasing in my face.

My eyes darted from left to right as I turned my focus back to my notes. *Just keep writing Lily, don't stop.* I instructed myself.

Stephanie continued to share her thoughts about the importance of this huge milestone, including planned Army projects and breakthrough advancements because of the laboratory. After finishing her speech, the audience erupted in applause. Stephanie politely smiled as she sat down in the chair next to Jack. I watched as Jack confidently walked up to the podium with his talking points in hand.

"Wow, that's a tough act to follow," Jack said jokingly to lighten the mood as the audience chuckled under their breath. "I'm going to go a little off script. Thank you so much for being here today. This is a project that is very important to me, as a lot of teamwork went into making this lab a reality. We rallied together when we faced challenges and overcame them while staying on schedule. We never compromised the mission, and I couldn't be prouder of what we all accomplished today." Once again, Jack always had a way with words when he went off script as the audience sat in a trance, listening to his every word. A small smile formed across my face as I did my best to hide my admiration for Jack.

Jack finished his speech as the crowd stood to their feet, applauding the smooth-talking colonel. Jack smiled brightly as he walked away from the podium and stood next to Stephanie. Two Army soldiers approached the stage with a bright red ribbon and a pair of large gold scissors. The scissors always made me laugh because they were simply gardening shears spraypainted in gold. One of the Army women, a short blonde-haired woman with sky-blue eyes and a dimpled smile, handed Jack the scissors as he proudly cut the ribbon in front of the newly minted building with a beaming smile on his face.

After the event concluded, I went on one of several scheduled tours of the environmental testing facility. As I listened to the tour guide talk about the construction of the building, including the projects lined up, I couldn't concentrate. I kept thinking about Jack and that powerful and compelling pull toward him. I also couldn't help but notice that daydreamy look in his eyes as he stared at me throughout the event. I was experiencing thoughts and feelings that I never felt before for anyone. Currently, I had more questions plaguing my mind than answers.

7

JACK

The alarm clock went off at four a.m. while the rest of the world slept soundly, not even thinking about the day. Waking up early was a habit Jack started when he first went to West Point, but today was the day of the brigade's highly anticipated environmental testing facility event. The grand opening was fresh in his mind. He wanted to get into the office earlier than normal to prep for the ceremony. He was the first one to arrive on post and almost always the last one to leave. His strong work ethic was instilled in him by his parents at a young age, something the military always appreciated. Jack started off the day with his usual five a.m. workout before getting to the office at seven a.m. He slowly walked over to his dresser and started quietly putting on his workout clothes with a dim light above him, so he didn't wake up his wife and their two cats.

He smelled the freshly brewed coffee in the kitchen. The timer on the coffee pot was always set for four a.m., so coffee was ready before heading out the door. After getting dressed, he grabbed his Army travel mug and filled it with black coffee, no sugar, no milk. Strong, just the way he liked it. While the enlisted troops preferred to down countless energy drinks to get through their day, Jack knew better. Always keeping a pulse on his health, he believed nothing good could come from energy drinks in the long run. With his coffee mug filled to the top, Jack was ready to take on the day.

Jack arrived at the gym fifteen minutes before his workout class started. Like clockwork, Jack put his wallet and keys in the locker room. He stood in the lobby of the brightly lit gym as electronic dance music filled the air, waiting for his workout class to start. It was a strength training class mixed in with cardio—a little bit of everything. It was important for him to get in a well-rounded workout before starting his day.

Working out was his way of sharpening his sword as he prepared for battle, not knowing what lay ahead but always being ready for whatever the day may bring. An athletic guy in his early twenties with short, wavy black hair and brown eyes walked into the room with a beaming smile on his face. "Good morning, everyone! Let's have you all get started on the treadmills for a warmup before we move onto the strength portion of our class." The people filed into the large workout room as the cheerful guy gave everyone a high five. He was clearly a morning person like Jack.

Walking up to the treadmill, Jack started off with a brisk walk. Before he knew it, his mind began to think about his tasks for the day as a mental checklist began to form. *I have a brief with Ryne at seven a.m. to discuss the ceremony, a meeting with the heads of each department at two p.m. to get ready for our yearly inspections…* Without warning, Lillian popped into his head. His face unexpectedly lit up as his heart felt a little lighter. Part of him wondered if he would bump into her today. He took a deep breath as he increased the pace on the treadmill, breaking out into a jog. He felt an unexpected jolt of energy under his feet.

———

AN HOUR LATER, Jack wrapped up his workout and made his way back home to get ready for work. Rolling down the windows, he allowed the crisp morning air to fill his car and lungs. Another busy day at the office was ahead for him. He gladly welcomed the challenge. Walking into the house, Jack's wife was still asleep as she lay on her back, snoring away without a care in the world. *I could never just stay home*, Jack thought hastily to himself. He knew working was part of his DNA.

As Jack hopped out of the shower, he pulled his crisp military uniform out of the closet and got dressed. He sat on the corner of his bed as he tightened his combat boots. He wore the same uniform for more than twenty years, and it never got old. Something about it reminded him of the purpose he served. A purpose bigger than him.

With no time for breakfast, Jack refilled his coffee mug as he ran out the door with his laptop bag in hand. Driving onto post, the security guards greeted Jack as he handed one of the guards his military ID.

Recognizing his name and rank, the security guard quickly saluted Jack. "Good morning, Colonel Cooper! We hope you have a good morning, sir," the guard said with a serious look on his face. Jack returned the salute as he gave the guard a small smile and a head nod. He grabbed his ID and drove onto post. Walking into his office, Jack set his laptop on his white desk as he started getting ready for the day. A quote from President Harry S. Truman in an oak frame hung above his desk: *Not Every Reader Is A Leader, But Every Leader Must Be A Reader.* Jack was a firm believer in reading books. On his desk lay several leadership books, including *The Art of War* and *The Seven Laws of Spiritual Success.* Always learning and studying. He believed there was always room for improvement to grow and thus be a better leader for his troops.

Jack sat at his desk. He opened his laptop and turned it on. He inhaled deeply as he gazed out his office window. With it still being early and nobody on post yet, Jack allowed his eyes to take in the empty parking lot with just his car parked close by. He suddenly wondered if Lillian would be working on-site today because of the ceremony. She had a habit of parking her car across from his, so he always knew if she was there. He allowed his heart to take in the warmth of her presence. Even if she wasn't in the room at that moment, her spirit was always there with him. He took her with him to each meeting he went to, each post engagement he attended, and in hall conversations with other senior leaders. She was simply always there.

8

Morning sunrises always held a special place in my heart. Being awake and spending alone time with God before the rest of the world came alive. I sat outside on my back porch, sipping my warm green tea out of my bright pink mug and taking in the moment. Beautiful laces of morning light spilled over the Arizona horizon as gorgeous strokes of orange painted across the sky. The serene moment was short-lived as I heard Max and Charlie barking away in the kitchen, summoning me for their morning breakfast. I took a deep breath as I walked into the kitchen and found them impatiently waiting for their food.

"I know you're so hungry! Let's eat breakfast, and then we can go for a hike while the weather is still nice," I happily told them. The little dogs started to bark in unison, almost as if they were more than happy to comply with my plan.

After breakfast, I packed a water bottle for the boys along with some bison dog treats to reward them for good behavior into my small hiking backpack and a few protein bars for myself. I also grabbed my tweezers in case they had an unexpected run-in with a cactus, something I learned the hard way with Charlie a few years back, so now I never go hiking without them. After hearing the jingle of my hiking backpack, the excited pups came running into my bedroom. It was time to adventure out for the day.

As we drove off post, I was more than happy to escape the daily demands of life, even if it was for a little while. Hiking was also my outlet for clearing my head with everything happening with Jack. I was secretly hoping for a moment of clarity being out in nature. Driving with the windows down, we breathed in the fresh morning breeze with the bright morning sun peeking through the clouds above us. Charlie hopped onto my lap like a little rabbit and plopped his head out the driver's side window—his favorite spot in my car. His big smile caught the attention of a couple sitting at the traffic light next to us. They looked over and smiled as they saw Charlie hanging his head out the window. It always made me smile seeing the happiness Charlie and Max brought to other people's lives, even if they were strangers on the street. They always got stopped for strokes and attention by admirers wanting to ask questions about them.

We finally made it to Wave Cave Trail, one of my favorite dog-friendly hiking spots. The trail was perfect for my senior pups, who were always excitedly ambitious at the start of a hike but, halfway through, looked to mom to carry them toward the end. I was often left wondering who got more of a workout on our hikes—me or them.

We got out of the car, and Charlie eagerly jumped out the second the door flew open. He ran down the rocky dirt road, barking with excitement about what lay ahead. I grabbed Max as I put on my light pink hiking backpack and yelled out to Charlie, who couldn't wait to take on the rugged desert mountain terrain. "Charlie! Wait for us before you go running down the trail like a crazy dog!" I chucked to myself as Charlie obediently came running back.

I looked across the desert landscape as I heard the open trail calling my name. The rock-strewn dirt path was accompanied by Saguaro cacti and green and tan desert shrubs scattered throughout the hillside. A warning sign about having your dog on leash was nestled on the trail as Charlie ran through the desert, clearly unleashed. We were never one to follow the rules, which was ironic considering that we were a military family. Following rules was a way of life living on a military post. Max, on the other hand, had no problem abiding by the rules. He was on his leash, happily trotting by my side as he explored some nearby shrubs and rocks.

We started our walk down the wide path, and we came to a wire fence that looked at least a hundred years old. I picked up Max and Charlie as we carefully weaved past the fence line and made our hike up the hill. Even though I was in great shape, thanks to my cycling classes, I started to feel myself gasping for air as our elevation increased. I glanced down at the boys as they gave me *the look.* It was time to pick them up.

"Okay, guys, I can carry you." I carefully scooped them up in my arms as I dug my feet into the ground and continued our ascent up the mountain side.

Once we reached the top of the mountain, I stopped and took in the beautiful Arizona desert landscape. With its awe-inspiring mountain rocky ranges and wildlife sneaking about throughout the desert, there was no place like it on earth. I spotted white arrows painted on rocks nearby telling us the direction to go in. "Perfect guys! Let's go this way. We are almost to the cave," I told the boys with a little relief in my voice.

I sat the boys down on the ground as Charlie ran in the direction of the cave, almost as if he could read the signs painted on the rocks. Max, on the other hand, decided he had enough hiking. He firmly planted his little paws into the dirt, standing his ground. A small grin formed across my face, sympathizing with my little dog. "Okay, Max, you win. I will carry you." I carefully picked him up as he made himself comfortable in my arms.

As I started to catch my breath, I caught sight of the cave nestled on the side of a mountain. I leaped into motion as I hyper-focused with the end goal in sight. "We are almost to the cave, guys! Let's go!" I told them enthusiastically. Hearing the excitement in my voice, Charlie charged up the mountain and ran into the cave. I followed closely behind him with a little bounce in my step.

I walked inside the cave and was surprised to see it mostly covered with sand. The boys and I made our way to the back of the cave. The inside was shaped like a wave and framed the Arizona desert landscape perfectly. I climbed on top of the wave as I felt my chest expand and let out a huge breath of relief. I closed my eyes and took in the moment. We made it. I looked down at Charlie, who was standing next to me, looking up with a big smile on his face. Max was happy enough to be in my arms and not walking. He could care less about the big accomplishment.

"We made it, guys! Let's sit down and enjoy some snacks."

I carefully made my way to the ground, setting Max on my lap.

Charlie made a beeline for my backpack, knowing he was about to get some yummy dog treats. My little boy had the nose of a bloodhound, and I thought he must have been a police dog in his past life. He managed to open the side of my backpack with his snout and stuck his head inside my backpack.

"Wait, Charlie! I can get the treats for you." I pulled out the treat bag as Charlie automatically sat, knowing the command was key to getting a dog treat. I laughed as his glossy eyes fixated on the dog treats in my hand. Not wanting to be left out, Max looked up at me and kept glancing at the dog treats. I handed each of them a treat. "You guys earned it! That wasn't an easy hike, but you both did a great job."

I pulled the cookie dough protein bar out of my backpack along with our water. I poured the cool water into the dogs' water bowl and took a sip of the refreshing water from my pink water bottle. I felt all tension release from my body and a comfortable wave of warmth on my face. My heart was full of gratitude with so much to be thankful for. Thanking God for this special moment, I allowed my eyes to absorb all that *He* created in front of me and in my life.

Even though I couldn't make sense of my personal life, I had to trust that it was all working out. *Just pray, let go, and trust. That's all you can do, Lily,* I thought to myself. Things looked so clear from up here as I sat on the massive rock wave surrounded by vast mountain ranges, beautiful desert plants, and rocks of different sizes scattered throughout the valley. I just hoped that I could keep this clarity when I returned to reality from my well-deserved time spent in nature. Out of the corner of my eye, I saw bright lightning strikes flashing out of the clouds. Even though it wasn't raining, random lighting was a normal occurrence and came with life in the desert.

After about fifteen minutes of rewarding ourselves for our hard work, it was time to go back home. Not being one to sit still, Charlie read my mind, and he started darting for the exit of the cave. He was more than ready to call it a day.

"Wait up for us, Charlie!" I called out to him as he stopped halfway and whipped his head back around in my direction. Blatantly disregarding my command, my defiant little dog continued to run out of the cave and down the dirt path. "Oh my gosh, Max, what are we going to do with him?" Max gave me a sympathetic look knowing all too well Charlie's mischievous ways. I grabbed Max and my hiking backpack and hurried out of the cave and down the road, trying to catch up with Charlie.

The three of us made it back to the car in one piece. I looked down at my boys, who were covered in dirt from running through the desert. The rough terrain also got the best of me as my hiking shoes were covered in dirt, along with my legs and shorts. I couldn't help but laugh to myself. "Wow, guys, we are a hot mess!" Charlie started barking as I opened the car door. With one graceful jump, Charlie jumped into the passenger side of my car and into the plush dog car seat. I sat Max down in the car seat as both boys began to eye my backpack with the dog treats. "Let's get home first, and then you can get your treats," I lovingly told them.

Driving back to post, I felt the endorphins from my adventurous hike leave my body. Reality was starting to set back in. I pulled up to the post gate where the security guards were waiting. One of the guards, a tall guy in his late thirties with a muscular build and black hair, signaled for me to pull forward. I quickly reached over and took my dependent identification card from my purse. This caught the attention of Charlie and Max. They both jumped on my lap, ready to bark at the guards. I slowly pulled up to the gate as the guard reached out to grab my identification card with a big smile on his face.

"Should I ask for their IDs as well?" he asked jokingly.

I started to giggle. "Well, you can try, but I'm not sure if you'll get it from them!"

He scanned my identification card and handed it back to me. "I've seen your dogs for years now, and they still bark at me…"

I glanced over at Max and Charlie, who were barking like a pack of hyenas. "I am so sorry! They bark at anyone who comes up to my car."

The friendly guard laughed. "It's okay! They're just doing their job, and I'm used to it at this point. I hope you have a good day."

I smiled at the forgiving guard as we drove away. I looked down at Max and Charlie, who settled back down in their car seat, exhausted from their barking spectacle. As much as I wanted to be upset at them for causing a stir every time we came on post, I just didn't have the heart to be mad at my adorable little dogs.

We carefully drove through post as I set my cruise control to twenty-five miles per hour in hopes of not catching the attention of any military police wanting to pull people over. I parked in front of my townhome as I felt the sunrays getting stronger by the minute, warming up the day. I opened the passenger side door of my car as Max and Charlie happily jumped out and ran toward the front door, with me following behind them. Hearing the jingle of my house keys, Charlie started to bark excessively. "Yes, I'm opening the door! You are so impatient!" I said to my little dog with a smile on my face. The front door opened, and the boys ran into the house and jumped into their oversized dog bed in the living room. Like typical pet parents, we had a dog bed in every room of the house, but the bed in my living room was their favorite. The soft, purple, and white fuzzy bed was made for a large dog. To them and their tiny build, it was the California king of dog beds.

I lay down on the floor next to them as the boys curled up in a ball. Petting them and scratching their bellies, I let their presence carry away my stress as my mind began floating away, wishing I could spend forever with them nestled up in their dog bed. Max and Charlie began to fall asleep as I fell into a peaceful sleep, lying halfway on their soft dog bed.

———

I WAS DEVELOPING my own rhythm at work. Getting into the flow of attending events and writing articles with one exception...*Jack*. A few days later, I was scheduled to attend an engineering event held at the University of Arizona and write an article about it. Knowing that my handsome colonel was in attendance, I carefully picked out my outfit. I selected a beautiful red pencil skirt with a seam going down the back and a dainty ruffle trim. I paired it with a black turtleneck top with the shoulders cut out and a pair of tall, sexy black heels. Standing in my room in front of my mirror, I thought, *Dang, I look hot!* I couldn't even believe what I was doing and what had come over me. This was something entirely out of character for me, especially since I was married. But I felt like a giddy schoolgirl getting ready to see her high school crush, and I enjoyed every minute of it.

As I walked up to the school carrying Jack's talking points in a professional white business binder, I realized I was nervous. *Calm down, Lillian!* I scolded myself. *Get it together.* I walked into the room and into a sea of kids. I saw the gorgeous colonel standing in front of the room. I confidently walked over to him and handed him the binder with his talking points. "Hi, I have your remarks for today's event," I said cheerfully.

Jack looked at me and replied, "You didn't have to do this for me, really, it's okay."

I looked at him, confused. "This is my job, sir. I have to print these for you."

He quickly replied, "I have a million of these binders. You really don't have to trouble yourself."

Not sure what to say, I replied, "Really, sir, it's okay."

He looked me straight in the eyes and said, "Thank you. I appreciate you." Immediately, my heart started to pulsate. I told him thank you, walked straight to my seat, and waited for the event to start.

As Jack stood in front of the room with the other speakers, I couldn't help but notice that he was nervous and starting to fidget! It was obvious he was trying not to look at me, but inside, it made me smile. As I sat there watching Jack make small talk with the other senior leaders in the room, I started to feel my passion for him slowly building deep down inside. Part of me wished that Jack would walk up to me, pluck me out of the audience, take my hand without a care in the world, and just leave the event. As he walked up to the podium to address the crowd of eager and bright-eyed college students with their parents, he opened the talking points but, as always, went a little off script. It made me smile because I knew he was speaking from his heart.

He started off his talk by discussing the important work that our brigade does to support the military and said, "I'm sure you don't want to hear about my time with NASA or even my work with the brigade, but if you want to join the Army, I will tell you why putting on this uniform is the best decision you will ever make."

I sat there fixated, unable to take my eyes off him. I had never heard anyone speak of serving their country with such conviction and passion. He loved it, and he loved his country. That much was obvious. It was then I knew I was falling in love with him.

Once the event concluded, I had to collect his talking points. Because the government is so tight with their funding, my boss stressed the importance of collecting the binders with the talking points to be reused for future events. It seemed ridiculous that the military was that tight with money, counting every cent spent, but I knew it meant big trouble if I didn't come back with that binder.

I stood up from my chair in a sea of students milling about the room with their proud parents, holding their certificates of achievement from the university's engineering program. I scanned the room, looking for Jack so I could retrieve the binder and return it to my office. I noticed one of the other senior leaders from our brigade, so I started to make small talk with him while glancing around the room out of the corner of my eye, trying to find Jack. After I was done talking, my heart unexpectedly started to dance. I looked behind me to see Jack casually leaning against the counter on his cell phone.

"Oh, There you are!" I said to him in a little too excited tone. "I'm sorry, but I have to get your binder from you and return it to the office." Jack leaned in super close to my face. We were only inches away from each other. I could see the softness behind his eyes as he said,

"It's okay. I have a million of these binders in my office."

Trying to slow my breathing, I said, "Sir, I have to take the binder back with me. It's my job." I felt the desire growing inside me even more, getting stronger like a volcano about to erupt.

He handed me the binder. As we stood inches away from each other, an awkward silence filled the air. My mind went blank. I had no clue what to say. A student walked up to him and started talking about how her dad worked for the Army. Thankful to the student who saved the day, I walked out of the building and back to my car.

Sitting in the parking lot in my car, I stopped to take in everything that just took place. My heart couldn't seem to calm down, and my mind flooded with thoughts that were never-ending. All the while, I was floating on a cloud with no interest in coming back down to earth. It all seemed so surreal, and I couldn't believe it was happening to me. Driving home with my notes from the event and tasked with writing an article once again, I found it harder and harder to concentrate.

Even as I sat in my weekly writers' meetings later on, my mind floated away in a wave of hearts and butterflies. I should have focused on what my boss was saying and the list of assignments at hand, but I felt so happy. I couldn't stop thinking about him. The smooth sound of his voice, the blue oceans of his eyes, and his strong body. I found myself going through my days with an extra skip in my step, feeling like I was the luckiest girl in the world. Here was this incredibly gorgeous man with his impressive military accolades and accomplishments, and he looked at me like nobody else in the world existed but us.

9

My creativity tank was running on fumes. It was desperately calling to be filled back up. Sitting at my desk at work one Friday afternoon, the day slowly crawled by, like watching paint dry. I mindlessly stared at my computer screen with another article staring back at me. Like a water faucet with no water coming out, my mind felt numb with no words left to write. Everyone left early from work for the day except for me. Every time I worked on post, I felt the Army's impending presence over me like I was being watched, so sneaking out early was out of the question. I glanced at the clock on the wall, moving at a snail's pace, wishing for time to move quicker. Once four o'clock came, I quickly packed up my laptop and notebook, shoving it into my bookbag as I flew home to get ready for my highly anticipated horseback riding lesson.

Walking briskly up my driveway, I hurriedly opened the front door and practically threw my bag on the sofa. Hearing my bookbag drop on the couch from the living room, Max and Charlie came running around the corner, talking up a storm.

"Hey guys! I have to get ready for my lesson before I'm late!" Seeing their treat jar in the living room, I snapped it open and fed them some bison dog treats to keep them happy while I was away.

Changing into my light blue riding jeans with my red and white plaid button-up shirt, I glanced in my closet and caught sight of my riding boots covered in thick dirt from last week's ride. "Crap. I forgot to clean off my boots." I grabbed the black knee-high riding boots and a towel from my laundry basket. I quickly dusted off the boots to prepare for today's ride. After getting dressed, I ran into the kitchen to grab water from the refrigerator. I glanced behind me and saw a confused look on Max and Charlie's faces like a tornado had ripped through our house. "I'm sorry, guys, for rushing, but I'll see you later!" I gave them each a kiss goodbye before flying out the front door.

While driving up the freeway toward the mountains, the sun was shining bright ahead with a slight breeze in the air as I saw trees slowly blowing in the wind. It was a perfect Friday afternoon for a horseback ride. I turned off the freeway and down a paved road that eventually led to a dirt road off the beaten path. I looked up ahead and saw a couple of chestnut Quarter horses. One horse was all chestnut with white socks, and the other majestic horse had a white painted face. The beautiful horses were galloping in the arena, getting warmed up and ready for their ride.

I slowly pulled into the dirt driveway and excitedly jumped out of my car, grabbing my water bottle. A younger girl named Ashley, about fourteen years old with honey-blonde hair and blue eyes, was wearing brown riding boots, black jeans, and a red polo shirt. She walked in front of my car, making her way to the barn to saddle her Boulonnais horse up for his ride. The white marble horse resembled a unicorn with his rainbow-colored mane and tail blowing in the wind and French braided into perfection.

Ashley spotted me and smiled. "Hi, Lily! Are you riding Cody or Sunshine today?"

I strolled over to Ashley and started petting her colorful horse as I felt my body start to relax. "I'm not quite sure today, actually. You know Cody is my favorite, but I may be riding Sunshine, which is fine as well," I responded.

"That sounds good," Ashley said in a bubbly tone. "I hope you have a great ride!"

"Thank you! I'm sure I will," I optimistically replied.

Being on the back of a horse was always my happy place. One of the great things about growing up in the Sierra Nevada mountains back home in California was having a horse. Wally was a Quarter horse that was taller than your average Quarter horse. We had a love-hate relationship, and his moments of testing me included him trying to buck me off when he didn't want to ride. On a hot summer day in July with the temperature hitting a balmy ninety degrees, a routine task of me spraying him with fly spray to keep the country flies off him almost ended with him kicking me in the face. Wally ran down the corral and back up in my direction, charging at me like a bull. He effortlessly flipped around and kicked the fly spray bottle out of my stunned teenage hand, only inches away from my face. Despite this unfortunate close encounter with my unruly horse, I still loved to ride.

I walked into the corral as Cody spotted me from around

the corner. The beautiful brown and white Paint horse trotted up to the opening of his stall and stuck his head out, knowing all too well that attention from me meant getting a vanilla cookie. "Hi, Cody! I know what you want, but you'll be getting your cookie after your ride," I laughed as I ruffled his bangs and ran my fingers down the side of his auburn mane. The horse huffed in frustration, almost as if he got the message. "Hey, don't be mad at me! You know the rules, and I don't make the rules," I lovingly told him.

I looked down at the corral and spotted a few horses sticking their head out of their stalls. Debbie, my horseback riding instructor, came walking down the aisle between the stalls. She was a tall, athletic woman in her early forties with light brunette hair pulled into a baseball cap. She was a professional barrel racer growing up but decided to retire early to open her own horseback riding school. Her soft brown eyes reflected her love for horses as I often spotted her spending time alone with them, just petting and talking to them. She caught sight of me talking to Cody.

"Hi, Lily. How do you feel about riding Cody today?"

I smiled at her. "That sounds great! I can start getting him saddled up."

Seeing me grab his turquoise halter and braided lead rope hanging up next to his stall door, Cody leaned his head in my direction. I carefully opened the stall door as I slid the halter on the happy horse, who was more than pleased to leave his stall for a nice ride and the opportunity to stretch his legs. The smell of hay and dirt filled the air as I led Cody from his stall to the hitching post situated outside the barn. Memories from my childhood riding Wally and learning how to barrel race filled my mind. In high school, I had to decide between joining the cheerleading squad or buying a horse since both were very expensive. I didn't even hesitate. I gladly chose my horse. I looked outside and saw Cody's grooming kit sitting next to his area, packed with his various brushes and a hoof pick.

After tying Cody to the hitching post, I grabbed the purple wire brush and started running it down his back and legs. Cody started to shake with excitement, enjoying the relaxing brushing like the gentle giant was getting a massage. I saw a cloud of dirt fly off his body and into the air which told me he must have enjoyed a good moment of rolling around in his pen just before the ride.

I finished his much-needed brushing and grabbed the hoof pick to clean out the bottom of his hooves. For some reason, Cody never liked this part of the grooming process, but it was very necessary. I ran my hand down his back leg and gently pinched the back of his leg, which was my signal for him to lift his leg. Cody whipped his head in my direction and shook his head vigorously. He quickly lifted his hoof and then firmly planted it back into the ground. I stood up and let out a small groan. "Cody! You do this every time! I can't ride you until I clean out your hoofs. Just please cooperate with me," I pleaded with the large horse. I slid my hand back down his leg for a second time, and this time, Cody lifted his leg. I then felt him putting all his weight into his leg and thus my poor hand holding up his leg. Like I was struggling to hold a seven-ton elephant, the pain started shooting up my arm. "Wow, Cody, you're not giving me any favors! I'm really working hard for this ride today!" I quickly finished cleaning out the rest of his hoofs as we were both thankful that part of the grooming process was over.

I grabbed Cody's small red and white saddle blanket and placed it on his back for extra padding. Seeing his saddle sitting next to his hitching post, I picked up the beautiful brown and turquoise saddle decorated with small white flowers and carefully placed it on Cody's back.

Debbie came up behind me and adjusted the saddle. "You need to bring it up just a little more and give him a pocket in the front for some air," she looked at me and smiled.

"Yes! I always forget to do that," I replied. "Thanks for doing that."

Debbie smiled at me as she handed me Cody's bridle to slide onto his face. I slid the bridle up in front of his face and put my hand on his bit, laying my hand flat so he wouldn't unintentionally bite one of my fingers. "Remember, it's like giving him a cookie," Debbie said gently as she guided my hand for Cody to put the bit in his mouth. Not fighting me, Cody let the bit slide into his mouth. "Perfect! Now buckle his bridle on the side, and he will be ready to go." Debbie instructed me. Seeing the silver buckle, I carefully slid it under his chin and buckled it. I felt a jolt of excitement run through my body. "Alright, Cody. Let's get going! Your girl needs some R&R time with her favorite horse." I ran my hand down his face and gave him a gentle kiss on his nose. His soft brown eyes looked at me as I fixed my gaze on the beautiful horse, drinking in the moment and wanting to never forget this feeling of gratitude.

With Cody's reins sitting on his neck, I reached up and grabbed the leather straps and led him to the open arena situated in the middle of the riding school surrounded by the desert mountain landscape. The warm sun was beaming down on the arena as I heard birds chirping off in the distance and saw ground squirrels running across the field. "Cody, don't get scared of the squirrels!" I cautiously told him. For some reason, the giant horse was scared of squirrels, like an elephant afraid of a tiny innocent mouse.

We made our way inside the arena and stood next to the steps so I could climb onto Cody's back. Because I'm short, getting on a horse doesn't come second nature, so I was always thankful to have a step stool to make it easier for me. I stomped onto the first step as dust went flying off my boot. Grabbing the front of the saddle and the back, I hoisted myself up onto the saddle with my feet firmly planted in the stirrups. I took a deep breath and exhaled a sigh of relief. "The hard part is over," I jokingly told Debbie.

"Yes, getting on the saddle always seems to be the most challenging part for everyone," Debbie replied. Moving the step stool out of my way, Debbie instructed me to walk Cody around the arena to get him warmed up.

With two small kicks, Cody started walking at a leisurely pace around the arena. I practiced moving my body to be in rhythm with Cody as he moved slowly around the small arena. I reached down and petted Cody under his mane as a thank you for being such a good boy. I took a deep breath as my eyes lit up, and a small smile started building across my face. My heart felt full of love. As Cody continued walking around the arena, my mind drifted away. The smell of horses combined with dirt and hay always reminded me of home. I longed to have a horse of my own but because of living on a military post, there was no way I could have a horse. I felt a little ping of sadness hit my heart as I started to reminisce about Wally. Even though he could be a pain in the butt at times, I still loved him.

Almost as if Debbie read my thoughts, she stated, "Cody's warmed up. Let's bring him to a trot." I smiled over at Debbie, looked at Cody, and gave him the command to trot as I lightly kicked his sides. Without a second thought, Cody began trotting around the arena. I gripped my legs as I did my best to coordinate my movements with Cody's to move with him. I learned the hard way that if I was out of sync with Cody, the ride was much bumpier and not as pleasant.

"Great job, Lily! Just relax your hands holding the reins." Debbie yelled out as I trotted around the arena. The minutes began to fly by without worry. Then a crazy thought hit me: *What if I just took off with Cody? Just rode away into the sunset and left everything behind? My problems with work, my inner love triangle with Jack and Aaron. What if I just rode away and didn't look back?* I sighed aloud. If only leaving my problems could be that easy. At that moment, a curious ground squirrel poked his head out from his hole in the ground not far from the arena. I immediately awoke from my trance.

"Cody, you're fine! Just keep going!" I kept my attention laser-focused in front of me, knowing all too well if I looked away, it could catch Cody's attention and thus spot the little troublemaker squirrel. Keeping my cool, we continued trotting around the corner as Cody didn't glance in the squirrel's direction.

Thank goodness he didn't see the squirrel! I breathed a sigh of relief as I remembered the last time Cody spotted a squirrel. Riding him one Saturday afternoon, I was completely oblivious to my surroundings when Cody saw a squirrel run across the field and into his line of vision. The giant horse leaped off the ground like the squirrel was charging in his direction and tried taking off with me on his back! My heart started racing as I grabbed the reins and pulled them back with every fiber in my body. Adrenaline was pumping through my chest like we were going to jump off a cliff. I vowed to be more observant the next time I rode Cody, and it paid off.

Before we knew it, time flew by in the blink of an eye, and the lesson was over. After trotting with Cody for about forty-five minutes, we slowed back down to a walk and a much-deserved cooldown. I reached down and gave Cody a big hug, wrapping my arms around his giant neck. "Thank you so much, Cody, for being a good boy today! You definitely earned your vanilla cookie today." I slowly hopped off Cody as the soreness from my legs ran through my body. "Riding horses never gets easy, does it, Debbie?" I asked her as I rubbed my legs.

Debbie laughed at me. "When you've been riding for as long as I have, it still has its challenging moments, but it's so good for our soul." I smiled. Deep down, I knew she was right. Riding horses was the perfect therapy for my soul.

———

MILITARY EVENTS no longer looked arduous and boring. With everything happening with Jack, I learned very quickly to expect the unexpected. He made work functions exciting. Shortly after writing about the engineering program ceremony, my next assignment consisted of writing about the grand opening of an operations center supporting one of the Army's technological advancements. Sandi, my co-worker and fellow Army ally, was assigned the talking points for the event and tagged along to bring the colonel his binder. Walking up to the event with Sandi, Jack calmly strolled up next to me. "So, we meet once again," he said cooly.

"I guess so," I chuckled to myself under my breath. Sandi stopped to hand him the talking points as I turned to Jack.

"I really like the changes you made to your speech at the pre-engineering graduation event," I told him.

"Oh, I very rarely follow talking points," he said jokingly.

I replied wholeheartedly, "Well, I liked your speech, nevertheless." He was unaware of the impact his words had on me. Flustered, he looked down at the ground.

"Thank you," he said sheepishly.

I walked into the super cold building and sat down in the uncomfortable plastic chairs, waiting for the event to start. I took off my face mask for the first time since joining the brigade. I looked over and watched as Jack made his way to the front of the room, sitting in a row of chairs facing the audience. I observed him from across the room, and once again, he was fidgeting in his seat, trying not to stare at me. I chuckled to myself, flattered at how timid I made this man who was larger than life.

I turned on my voice recorder and prepared to record the event. I wondered what lay in store, given everything that had happened between Jack and me, and what could it possibly lead to, if anything. A love affair was simply out of character for me. After the first person was done speaking at the podium and giving introductory remarks, Jack walked up with his talking points in hand. Once again, I don't think he gave them more than two looks, going off the cuff, talking about this amazing collaboration for the Army. He referenced an *AC/DC* song to drive the point home about the partnership. This made me laugh. He often seemed to have some sort of

AC/DC reference in his speeches, which told me he must really like their music. Even though I listened to mostly pop music, I played their music at times in my cycle class but clearly, I wasn't as big of a fan as he was.

As things wrapped up eventually, my cousin's daughter, Alice, called to talk about my Christmas gift. She was a beautiful, bubbly Puerto Rican girl in her early twenties with short, curly black hair that she inherited from her mom. Like her mom, she also had a sassy attitude that always made me smile. She studied at the university in the next town and wanted to give me my gift before she headed home to see her family. As I was on the phone talking to her, I couldn't help but notice Jack standing close by on his cell phone. Something told me he was just buying time, waiting for me to get off the phone.

Reading between the lines, I told Alice, "Let me call you back. I'm at work right now," and quickly hung up the phone.

I walked up to Jack, who was patiently waiting for me, all the while feeling my heart start to jump. "I see you didn't follow the talking points again, huh?" I said, poking a little light fun at him. He laughed under his breath.

"Yeah, I'm sorry about that." Abruptly, he looked down at the ground and said in a timid voice, "I was surprised to see you at that restaurant out in town. I've never seen you outside of work before." I had forgotten that I had run into him that night out to dinner with Aaron. He looked up and said in a lowered voice. "So why did you come to the event today?"

I smiled. "I am writing an article about it."

"Oh, I'm so sorry," he said apologetically. "Of course, with you being in Public Affairs, that would make sense."

The man oversees a brigade of more than two thousand soldiers and federal employees, not to mention contractors like me, so I didn't expect him to remember my job duties. As far as I was concerned, I was the Cinderella of the Army, but here I was lucky enough to be talking to my Prince Charming.

"That's okay," I told him softly.

He asked me about my job. "So, what do you think about working at the brigade?"

"I love it," I replied excitedly. A look of doubt came across his face.

"Really, you don't have to tell me that."

I quickly commented, "No, it's the truth. I really do love what I do. Especially when I get articles published externally, it's a great feeling." A big smile came across his face.

"It's like a little feather in your hat, isn't it?"

"Yes," I told him. "It really is."

"Why did you want to work for the Army?" he asked.

I replied, "Well, I really like contributing to a purpose bigger than me, and it's rewarding to see the ripple effect of my work." He looked at me, utterly astonished.

"Wow, that's really great to hear, but I wasn't expecting that. So how come you don't work onsite? I mean…I don't really see you very often on post." I smiled at his concern over not seeing me.

"Well, I work remotely from home," I told him.

A confused look flashed across his face. "Don't you want to come into work?"

He put me on the spot, and I hesitated a little. "Well…I really like working from home."

He sensed my hesitation and bluntly stated, "My wife just stays home. I even told her, why don't you leave the house once in a while, so the cats miss you…"

Completely shocked by his honesty, I remarked, "Well, I

do leave my house, but it's nice to have the flexibility to work from home." Just then, a soldier walked up to him and whispered in his ear. Jack looked over at him and nodded before turning back to face me.

"I'm sorry, but I have to go," he added in a flirty voice, "Maybe I'll see you around." My eyes must have been the size of gumballs because I felt my face flush, and my body started to get hot.

With my heart racing, I replied, "Okay, sounds good." I turned around and walked away.

As I got closer to my car, I excitedly ran the rest of the way and jumped inside. I immediately hopped on the phone to call my cousin Sophia, who also happens to be Alice's mom. We'd been close ever since her mom married my grandpa's brother while we were in high school. We bonded over the soap opera *Days of Our Lives* and have been inseparable since. "Sophia!" I yelled on the phone. "You won't believe what just happened!"

She started laughing. "What just happened?" she asked.

"He came up and talked to me for the first time, like really talked to me!"

She was quiet, then quickly remarked, "What?"

"Yes!" I squealed like a teenage girl in love. I told her the gist of the conversation and sat there quietly, waiting for a response.

"Well, I think you're right... He does like you," she hesitated.

"I think you're right, but this is crazy! I shouldn't be feeling this way because I'm married, and he's married," I said. She put her older sister thinking cap on.

"This is fun, but it's just flirting. It's nothing more than that." She quickly added, "It can't be anything more than that."

I sat in my car feeling like she had just popped my beautiful, happy balloon. "I know you're right," I said glumly. "But Sophia, he is *so* dreamy! He's literally the man of my dreams!"

She replied, "I know, but it's nothing more than flirting with a charming and good-looking guy... Just enjoy it for what it is."

"Okay," I sadly responded. Deep down, I knew she was right. It couldn't be anything more, even if we wanted it to be, because we were both married. To top it off, he was my boss... not just any boss—a colonel and the highest-ranking military person in my brigade. But I couldn't ignore my growing feelings for him that were bubbling under the surface, just wanting to come up and see the light of day. Feeling conflicted, I decided I needed to ignore my feelings for now. As hard as I tried, though, I just couldn't do it. They were growing, and they'd only continue to grow as time went on.

10

———

The tugging feeling inside my heart wouldn't go away. Another post event was happening the next day, but I wasn't scheduled to go.

Just quickly stop by and then leave. What harm could it do? The thought circled around in my mind. I wasn't writing about this latest brigade function, though, nor did I write the talking points. Something told me to go, so I went.

Since it was still cold, I wore my black-and-gray plaid skirt but paired it with thick black tights and a black top with my Italian black knee-high boots. I topped off the look with my vintage 1960s black school uniform blazer. Even though I was working for the military, my love for fashion was still very much intact and extended to my love for vintage coats. I owned a ton, and by a ton, I meant two closets full of coats ranging from the 1950s to the modern day. This is another aspect of my personality that made me stand out like a black sheep, whether I liked it or not. While some of the other civilian employees dressed very casually, wearing sneakers with jeans and a sweatshirt, I always put a lot of thought into my outfits. I was even dubbed a fashion chameleon by one of my co-workers because of my different outfit selections.

As I walked into the auditorium, my heart quivered, knowing I had to slide in discreetly. If either of my bosses saw me, they may wonder why I was there in person and not watching it online since I was not writing about the event. So, I planned to sit in the back of the auditorium, away from them. I quickly found an aisle seat, third row from the back on the right side of the room. As I quickly sat down, I started to scan the room, looking for Jack.

Like clockwork, he walked into the room with his binder and tablet in hand. He sat them down on the executive table in the front of the room, turned around, and started to scan the room, as well. I excitedly watched him from the back of the auditorium. Something in my heart told me he was looking for me. As he looked from right to left, he spotted me sitting in the audience. Even though he was wearing a face mask, it was obvious that he was smiling at me. Immediately, my face and body got hot.

After everyone found their seat, the event started, and Jack began speaking to the audience. Without thinking, I pulled my face mask down, boldly staring at him straight in the eyes and grinning at him. I could tell he was getting flustered as he started to adjust his face mask. I knew he was flattered by this beautiful woman who couldn't keep her eyes off him. He moved to the next part of the presentation, which was about sexual harassment. He began lecturing on the signs to look for and how to report it.

I giggled and thought to myself, *Oh wow, of all things he could be talking about in this moment.* After the event concluded, I decided to daringly pop down and say hello to my bosses. I walked over to where they were sitting in the front of the room, only feet away from Jack. "Hi everyone! I wanted to come by to collect the binder with the talking points." It was a flat-out lie, but I went with it. I bravely walked up to Jack, looking for the talking points. As I stood in front of him, we were mere inches from each other once again. I noticed my eyes were at his chest level. He towered over me since I was only five foot one. I looked up as my bright green eyes sparkled at him. I wondered if he knew what I was thinking. I saw his cheeks light up as I could feel him grinning under his face mask.

He said without hesitation, "So, are you coming to harass me?" Just then, my bosses were within earshot and quickly snapped their heads up. I'm sure they were horrified at what they just heard, and I'm surprised their heads didn't snap right off.

I stood there stunned and said hesitantly, "No…of course not. I'm just looking for the talking points."

I don't know why, but I lightly wrapped my petite hand around his strong bicep, touching his arm. He didn't pull away. All at once, I could feel the electricity pulsating throughout my body.

My co-worker, observing the situation, held up the white binder. "It's right here," he said in an annoyed tone. In other words, saying I needed to walk away from Jack. I walked over, utterly embarrassed, and grabbed the binder. Ryne happened to be standing close by. He overheard Jack's comment and was probably losing his mind. He told Jack that he wanted him to meet a new team member and introduced this young, bright-eyed kid who was the newest member of our team. Jack started to talk like nothing happened. Completely stunned, I grabbed the binder and said thank you. I made a beeline for the door and quickly walked out of the building.

What the heck just happened? I thought to myself as my blood pressure started to spike, and I felt my chest tighten. Jack obviously had no clue what had come out of his mouth. He also didn't realize that he unintentionally jeopardized my career with the Army.

After work, I went home and put together Aaron's last deployment care package before he was set to come home. I found joy in making his care packages, even drawing on the outside of his package with fun hearts and stickers while boxing up all his favorite munchies. For some reason, he never appreciated them. During the first year of our marriage, I excitedly sent out my very first deployment care package stuffed full of candies, socks and shirts. After Aaron received the package in the mail, he didn't hesitate to give me his thoughts. "Why would you send me these candies? I don't even eat them!" I felt instantly crushed. Since then, every package I sent was harshly critiqued, commenting about how they reflected what I liked versus what he liked. Nonetheless, I still enjoyed creating them and found it very therapeutic.

I walked into the house and was greeted by Max and Charlie, excitedly wanting their daily walk and dinner. "I know. I hear you, but Mom needs to run to the commissary to get more of your dad's goodies for his care package," I told them. After putting my work laptop away, I grabbed my purse and made the trek to the commissary.

Driving down the street in my neighborhood, I saw kids riding bikes outside with their friends as their parents watched close by with their neighbors. I reflected on Aaron and I never having kids, which was always surprising to the other military couples. With so many deployments and me working full time, kids were never really a realistic option for us. Hand-painted red, white, and blue welcome home banners with kids' handprints and hearts were proudly displayed outside their homes, which reminded me that I needed to pick up my custom signs for Aaron's homecoming. For the first time, I started to feel as if the life I had been living for the past four-teen years was foreign to me. Jack was lingering in the back of my mind. Even though I tried my best to push him away, like clockwork, he constantly came back to me.

I pulled up to the commissary, hoping that I didn't run into anyone from my husband's brigade. As I was walking down the candy aisle, thinking about what to get for Aaron's care package, I felt as if I was being tested. Whatever I picked out was going to be evaluated and judged by him. I could hear him in the back of my mind grilling me, saying, "We've been married this long, and you can't even pick out things that I like?" Part of me felt like a failure as a supportive military spouse, so I wound up picking out candy that I'd seen him munch on at home—Sour Patch Kids and Fruit Roll-Ups. *Oh well, at least it's something,* I thought to myself helplessly.

I drove home carefully, being mindful of my speed limit and setting the cruise control so I didn't unintentionally go even two miles over the speed limit. The military police seemed to constantly hunt for a reason to pull someone over on a post that didn't have much activity going on.

I walked into my bland military-style townhome with my custom Max and Charlie dog sign displayed in my front yard. While other people had proud Army life memorabilia outside of their homes, I preferred showing off my two adorable rescue dogs.

Opening the door, I was greeted by a chorus of barks from my vocal and very talkative little dogs. "Yes, I'm back! Let's get dinner, and we can go to the dog park." The one and only great thing about living on this post was having our very own private dog park. Even though the grass wasn't maintained very well, the boys still loved to have a place to socialize with other dogs, and I enjoyed meeting other dog parents on post as well. After feeding them, we started on our walk to the neighborhood dog park.

Walking down the sidewalk, the smell of freshly cut grass filled the air with the sun shining brightly overhead with a few white clouds lingering in the sky. We saw families outside also walking their dogs and I wondered if anyone was at the dog park as I was secretly hoping to have it to ourselves.

I opened the gate and entered the park and spotted another couple already inside with their little Bishon. Even though I didn't know them, I still wanted to be polite. "Hi! Your dog is so cute!" The wife, a short woman with light brown hair and pretty brown eyes, walked over to me. She looked down and saw Max and Charlie.

"Your little guys are cute as well. What are their names?" She asked.

"Max and Charlie," I said proudly. "They're seniors but still have a lot of energy left." She smiled as she bent down to pet Max.

"That's great! I'm hoping the same for my little girl one day." The Bishon excitedly approached Charlie, wanting to examine him. Charlie, wanting no part of this, reached around and unexpectedly bit the Bishon. I looked over, absolutely horrified.

"Oh, my goodness, I am so sorry! He normally doesn't do that! Is your dog okay?"

The husband, an intimidating man with a military buzz cut that told me he was the servicemember, walked over and bent down to examine his dog. "I think she's okay, but she's never been bit before," he said cautiously. He added, "What brigade is your husband with?"

My eyes grew large as a wave of nausea hit me. *Oh no, this isn't good,* I thought dreading having to respond. I slowly said, "He's with the brigade in Belgium right now. He's on deployment."

He looked at me and stated bluntly, "Okay, got it," like he had permanently memorized the details in his mind. As the man told me his name, I realized his name sounded familiar. I couldn't quite put my finger on it.

"I'm Lillian. It's nice to meet you. I can give you my phone number in case you need anything with your dog or if anything pops up after you get her home?" I gave the man my phone number. Taking that as my cue, I knew it was time for us to leave the dog park before any other unfortunate incidents took place.

Getting home, a feeling of dread hit me as I waited for Aaron to call. Right at 8 p.m., the phone rang, and it was Aaron. I realized I had to tell him what happened at the dog park.

"Hi babe, how's it going?" he said cheerfully.

I respond carefully. "It's going good, but I took the boys to the dog park after work, and there was an incident that took place that I think you need to know about."

Aaron responded anxiously. "What do you mean? Are the boys okay?"

I quickly replied. "Oh, no. The boys are okay, but… Charlie did bite another dog."

He frantically responded. "Is it serious? Is the dog okay?"

I reluctantly replied. "I think the dog is okay, but it's the owner of the dog that I'm worried about." I told Aaron the name of the dog's dad.

He responded angrily. "Are you serious? That guy's an officer, and he outranks me! Do you know how much trouble I can get into because of this? We better hope his dog is okay."

I felt awful for putting Aaron in that position. "I am so sorry. I'll be more careful the next time I take the boys to the dog park." I felt responsible for the incident. I just hoped the officer could forget all about his run-in with the ferocious, partially blind senior chihuahua at the post's dog park.

Winter 2020

11

———

Christmas decorations started popping up around the neighborhood as multi-colored lights twinkled and danced up and down the streets. Stores played festive Christmas music and filled their shelves with toys, gift baskets, and other gifts. The holidays were quickly approaching. The post was empty, with everyone taking leave to be home with their families. Since I decided to stay in the area for the holidays, I didn't take any time off work, nor did I really want to. Jack had turned my world upside down, but in the best possible way. My days at work became joyful, something I looked forward to. My time constantly led up to the next brigade event—where I excitedly picked out the cutest outfits possible. Since I was very feminine in nature, I loved wearing dresses and could easily wear a dress every day. But something I noticed over time was I went from wearing black slacks at the start of my job to now wearing adorable outfits. Three months of Jack's firm, intense eye contact on me made me feel desired and wanted for the first time in a very long time. But it was more than that. It was almost as if he could see past my beautiful dresses and perfectly styled hair. He saw beyond all that. He really *saw me.* He made me feel like the most beautiful woman in the world, and I was loving every second of it.

One particular Friday, everyone left early from work. I decided to go into the office, and since Jack's office building was across from mine, we shared the same parking lot. Pulling into the parking lot, I parked my car across from his parking spot. I always enjoyed doing that as a subtle way of letting him know that I was working on-site. I never knew if he noticed or not, but it made me feel good thinking that he did.

As I was getting ready to get out of my car, I looked across the parking lot and saw Jack walking out of the side door of his office. With my heart racing, I hopped out of my car and started walking over to him. His eyes suddenly grew large since he wasn't expecting me.

He quickly said, "And here comes Ryne coming out the side door behind me." I knew that was Jack's way of warning me that Ryne was also coming outside and could see us. Now, normally, the thought of my boss seeing me talking to our colonel out of the blue would have consequences. But for some reason, I didn't bat an eye. It could have been the Pope or the actual President walking by; I couldn't care less. My focus was one hundred percent on Jack. I didn't even glance at my boss as he walked past us, probably wondering what I was doing there.

Grinning, Jack anxiously adjusted his face mask. As Ryne passed into my office building, Jack's tone altogether changed. "Did you happen to write my blog article that just went out?" he asked. I must have had a deer-in-the-headlights look as I responded with concern.

"No, why do you ask?"

He stated, "Oh, I guess you're not to blame then for the mistake I saw." I stopped breathing. I was absolutely dumbfounded. *What?* He laughed, saying, "I'm just joking!" I started to laugh too and playfully hit his arm.

"You are such a brat!" He got me good. But it made me inwardly giggle that he had no idea who wrote his weekly blog articles.

"So, what are you doing for New Year's?" he asked in a flirty tone. I smiled, and since I wasn't wearing my face mask, he could see how flattered I was by his comment.

"Oh, not much," I said to him. "Since people will be setting off fireworks, I'll be home making sure my boys are calm and don't get upset." A look of surprise came across his face.

"You have boys? How old are they?"

"Oh no!" I replied. I realized he was thinking I had kids. "No, I have dogs, but they're like my kids."

"Oh," he said disappointingly. He continued, "Well, we have cats, but they hide under our bed when fireworks go off."

I noticed this was the second time he had mentioned his cats, so he must love animals, I thought to myself. Since I grew up with a love for animals, my family rescued just about anything that needed a home. This little interesting fact about him made my heart skip a beat. Realizing that he was off work, he said, "I'm sorry, but I should probably go." But he added a quick flirty comment. "Don't get into too much trouble on New Year's."

A huge smile flashed across my face. I bit my lower lip and replied in a coy tone, "I'll try not to." The handsome colonel got into his fancy sports car and drove away, leaving me floating in a cloud of love and pure bliss in the middle of the parking lot. After he left, I quickly returned to earth. I had to go into the office and face my boss, so it didn't look obvious that all I wanted to do was talk to Jack.

I walked into my office and found Ryne sitting upright at his desk, wearing a green button-up shirt with jeans and white sneakers. He had a serious look on his face. It was apparent that he was not too pleased with me. He looked over at me and said in an annoying, soft tone, "So you were talking to the colonel, huh?"

I could tell by his words that he was not too thrilled that I talked with Jack. "Oh, yeah," I said and quickly changed the subject. "I was coming in because I know we are moving offices and wanted to know if there's anything I can take over to the new space." A total lie, but I rolled with it.

"Umm, no," he said, looking around the office. "Nothing is ready to move quite yet. After the holidays, I think." A hint of suspicion laced his words.

"Oh, okay, got it," I quickly replied as my face flushed a bit. "I'll head back home and keep working but let me know when the time comes to pack up. I'm happy to help!" I hurriedly left the office as I felt Ryne's glaring eyes on me. I could tell by his comment about me talking to Jack that the underlying message was that I was *not* allowed to talk to him. However, I didn't care. The handsome colonel had my heart, and there was nothing anybody could do to take that away from me.

12

JACK

While driving home from work, Jack's mind floated away. A slow smile started to build across his face. He couldn't stop thinking about running into Lillian in the parking lot after work and their conversation about New Year's. He tried to remember the last time he had a fun New Year's, just letting himself have a little bit of pleasure for once. Demands at work and at home kept him up at night, but in the brief moments he talked with Lilian, those demands seemed to vanish at the sight of her warm and inviting presence.

Jack felt his body being flooded with warmth as his hands clenched the steering wheel briefly and then released. She was slowly becoming that little break in his structured military world that he didn't even know he needed. He had been immersed in that world for so many years. Before he knew it, he had lost that feeling of lightness and happiness in his heart. When did he lose it? Was it the moment he graduated from West Point and his expectations for always performing well kept looming over him like a dark cloud, or was it the moment his mother died? He wasn't quite sure.

Part of him knew that feeling this way for Lillian couldn't lead to anything. He was obviously married. Despite this fact, he couldn't ignore his surprising feelings for her growing in his heart as much as he wanted to. However, a small part of him also didn't want to ignore those feelings. He was starting to enjoy the subtle bursts of joy Lillian unexpectedly brought into his life.

13

———

Christmas and the New Year passed in a blur of small festive parties with friends and cold, spiritless evenings at home alone with my husband on deployment. With the holidays finally in the rearview mirror and Winter gone in the blink of an eye, a hopeful Spring was beginning to emerge on the horizon. Something told me this was more than just a crush on an amazingly gorgeous man. I continued to experience unusual events that took place anytime he was around. It seemed like the universe was trying to do its part to bring us together. As I drove to the gym one Thursday afternoon after work to teach my cycle class, I came to a stop at an intersection.

While I was waiting for the light to turn green, suddenly, my heart started to dance again! Something told me that Jack was coming. I turned and looked across the right side of the intersection, and there was Jack, driving up to the light in his sleek sports car. My mouth dropped open, and I was entirely stunned. How did I know he was coming at *that* moment? I couldn't believe this was happening for a second time as I reflected back on the time I knew Jack was coming into the same Italian restaurant Aaron and I were having dinner at. I had never seen Jack on my commute to the gym, and yet, my heart knew that he was nearby. As my light turned green, I drove through the intersection as my handsome colonel waited for his turn to go, unaware of my presence. My mind went into logic mode. For the life of me, I couldn't figure out how my heart knew when he was approaching. I initially thought it was a coincidence, but now it had happened for a second time.

I pulled up to the gym, and before my class started, I sent a quick text to my friend Julia. Julia and I had been friends for about twenty years, since my years in college. She was my go-to partner in crime as I navigated through my college dating journey, dating guys who always seemed to have some sort of issue with commitment. Their only goal in life was to bar hop and party, whereas I was fully committed to my job and studies in school. After I texted Julia about my surprising encounter, I wondered how in the world I was going to concentrate on teaching a cycle class. Somehow, I got through the class and switched open my messages to find Julia's response: "What! How did you know at that exact moment he was coming?" Of course, there was no way of knowing that, but somehow, my heart just knew.

"I don't know, Julia," was all I could manage to say because I really *didn't* know.

———

My Thursday commute to the gym went from being routine and dull to fun and exciting. No matter the time I left, even if I had to run an errand before leaving, I always saw him.

Like clockwork, my heart knew the exact moment he was driving up before I saw him with my actual eyes. Feeling myself start to giggle, I'd let out a little scream like a teenage girl at a boyband concert seeing her crush in person for the first time. I had no idea what was going on and what all of this meant, but I knew it had to mean something. Didn't it?

Even waiting for an event to start at work, with my back facing the door and dozens of people streaming in, I knew the exact moment Jack walked in because my heart started to flutter unexpectedly. *He's here*, I thought to myself. Not moving a muscle nor turning my head to see if I was right, I saw him walk past me out of the corner of my eye, and I thought, *Yep, I was right.*

These unusual experiences went on for months. The journalist in me wanted answers and explanations, but I simply couldn't comprehend what was happening. I also couldn't ignore the fact that I was falling deeper in love with him. He was very different from my husband and from other high-ranking military officers. He simply looked at the world in a different light and had the ability to make people feel worthy and appreciated. He was very down to earth, often letting his guard down when talking with me in a way that was different from everyone else. My heart felt safe with him, and I knew I could trust him.

I was also torn because I was married and knew that I was feeling things I didn't allow myself to feel in past relationships —and certainly not with my husband. It brought to light issues in my marriage that I had tried to face and work through over the years but just partly gave up, like open and honest communication about what I needed from him and from our relationship. Even being more supportive and attentive to my emotional needs and not just my physical needs or buying things for me. I realized that before Jack, I was sleepwalking through my life—doing what I thought a supportive wife was supposed to do but not feeling any love. It became more of an obligation, and even the times I tried to tell my husband what I needed in terms of love. It often fell on deaf ears. He had excuses from *that's just not the way he is* to *not being affectionate because of some ailing physical element that hurt him at the time.*

It all made sense when we decided to take a love languages test to find out about our unique love languages. When he learned one of my top love languages was physical touch his response was, "If I can go the rest of my life not hugging, I'm okay with that." That was the military person in him talking, and it absolutely alarmed me. It also made sense that over time, I got used to not being hugged, no cuddling, and no affection. Aaron's top love language was acts of service which in my mind, made perfect sense as I was constantly taking care of things around the house. But what I didn't realize is I had also given up on myself and the love I knew I deserved until now. I knew that what I felt for Jack, I *wanted* to feel for my husband. That was love, and I knew it. It made me wonder if I ever had been in love to begin with.

My friends picked up on my sadness and torn feelings between what I felt for Jack while being married to Aaron. As a surprise, Julia came into town to visit me and wanted to meet up for dinner. She called me out of the blue. "Hey, Lily, I'm in town and I thought we could have dinner tonight and catch up with everything going on in your life."

Excited by the distraction, I happily accepted and responded, "Oh my gosh, I love that idea. You have no idea how good it will be to see you and to catch up and get away from everything going on."

We made plans to meet for Mexican food, something Julia and I had enjoyed for years together. We had fond memories of going dancing in college. We'd start off our excursions with a delicious margarita before venturing out for the night.

I found a little hole-in-the-wall restaurant that had great reviews online. I walked in the door and was hit with the smell of sizzling fajitas and spicy beans with simmering meat. I looked across the restaurant, and there was Julia with our margaritas already in hand. Her beautiful black hair was up in a ponytail. She was wearing crop jeans with a fun, flowy red top with small white hearts.

"Hi!" I walked up to her and gave her a big hug.

She responded happily. "Hey Chica! I missed you so much! I'm so glad we could make this work…"

We sat down, and it was obvious she couldn't contain her excitement. "Okay, so tell me everything about Jack. What's been going on?"

I looked at her and took a deep breath. "Oh my gosh, girl, you have no idea. It's a total roller-coaster ride. I also feel so guilty about Aaron. At the same time, I can't seem to stop thinking about Jack, and we can't seem to stop flirting with each other! It's complete and total torture when all I want to do is run up to him and jump on him!" I also reflected on the conversation I overheard at Aaron's deployment meeting between the two military wives talking about their boyfriends and wondered if my conversation with Julia was unintentionally moving in that same direction.

Julia laughed and weighed in with her thoughts. "Wow.

This guy really has got your panties in a knot. Even Aaron never had this effect on you!"

I respond helplessly, "I know, and I don't know what to do . . ."

"Well, there's not much you can do since you're both married, right? I can't help but wonder if maybe you'll hear from him outside of work, though. I mean, look at you—your beautiful inside and out. He'd be crazy not to want to reach out to you. Not to mention, after that run-in with him and his wife at that Italian restaurant and the distance between them, all I can say is it's obvious the guy likes you." Julia was always brutally honest and was not one to hold back her thoughts about anyone or anything. I wondered if her brazen observation about Jack's marriage was something I had been thinking about all along but didn't have the nerve to admit.

"I don't want him to cheat on his wife, Julia, and I don't want to cheat on Aaron by any means. I just want to talk to him outside of work, you know?" The situation in my eyes looked so bleak that I couldn't think of a possible outcome that wouldn't end up with someone getting hurt.

"I think he's going to reach out to you," Julia said enthusiastically. "He'd be crazy not to reach out, but either way, this guy better do *something,* or he's going to have me to answer to!" In the back of my mind, I wondered if Jack would ever contact me outside of work. I had my doubts.

I started to feel torn about working there day in and day out and not being able to tell Jack about my growing feelings for him. It's not like I could walk up to him and talk to him. I couldn't even as much as send him a message on Microsoft Teams or send him an email. I was forbidden from interacting with him. I knew that Ryne had a watchful eye on everything I did ever since he heard Jack openly flirt with me and saw us talking that fateful day in the parking lot. It was obvious that I was on his radar, and I wasn't going to be leaving it anytime soon. I decided the best course of action was to start looking for another job. I also knew that if I took a leap of faith and left my job, at least I could give Jack the chance to decide what he wanted. But it also terrified me to leave because I was afraid of losing him and never seeing him again. I knew this was a risk that I had to take.

———

ON THE DAY that everything changed, I didn't see it coming at all. It started out like any other day. The post was buzzing about the upcoming Army promotion ceremony for the noncommissioned officers. The brigade planned a highly visible ceremony to mark the important milestone and recognize all the great accomplishments of the Army and its officers. Ethan tasked me with writing the talking points, and by fate, Jack was scheduled to lead the highly anticipated event. I felt a tremendous amount of pressure knowing how much weight the speech had not just for our brigade but for Jack as well. I happened to be working on-site in preparation for the big event when Ethan poked his head into my office.

"Are you working on the colonel's talking points for the Army promotion ceremony?" he asked me in a strident voice as he pushed his eyeglasses back.

"Yep! I'm working on them as we speak," I responded in an overly bubbly tone.

Not picking up on my sarcasm, Ethan replied flatly,

"Good. I'm glad to hear that. I don't think I need to tell you how important the colonel's speech is."

I did my best not to roll my eyes. *Of course, I know! If anyone knows how important this speech is, it's me!* I wanted to snap at him, but I held back.

"Yes, I understand how important it is to Colonel Cooper and the brigade. I will make sure they're up to Army standards."

Ethan managed a small condescending smile. "Good, that's what I want to hear." He turned around and left my office.

I sat at my computer and closed my eyes. I took a couple of deep breaths, trying to calm myself down from being chastised by Ethan before I even had a chance to write the speech. I imagined Jack standing proudly at the podium. As I reflected on the accomplishments of these noncommissioned Army officers, I started to write. The words flowed out of me like a beautiful waterfall. More than an hour went by and before I knew it, I had his speech written. I read the words I wrote about supporting the warfighter and our country with all the projects they worked on. I also highlighted the ripple effect these soldiers have, reaching far beyond the borders of our brigade. The speech was straight from my heart, and it was perfect. As I imagined Jack reading the words on that big day, a beaming smile came across my face. I hoped that he liked the speech as much as I did.

The next morning, I woke up feeling giddy and excited about the eagerly awaited event. As I sprang out of bed and stood in front of my closet, I speculated about what I was going to wear. After a few minutes, I finally decided on an elegant and professional ruby red knee-length lace dress. I paired it with my black closed-toed high-heeled loafers. I curled my long blonde hair and pulled the look together with a beautiful, beaded hair clip tucked just behind my ear with dainty pearl earrings. I smiled as I looked in the mirror at the beautiful woman looking back at me. I was on the heels of a transformation like a caterpillar turning into a beautiful monarch butterfly.

As I drove through post heading to the Army promotion ceremony, I passed by a large group of Army soldiers doing their daily morning physical training. I stopped at the crosswalk as they ran in formation in front of my car. I tried to time my daily commutes, so I missed them running, and they didn't make me late for work, but this time I wasn't so lucky. I looked at the clock as they continued running by like a train speeding efficiently down the track. After what felt like forever, they finally finished jogging. I did my best to rush to the event without speeding and catching the attention of the military police lurking on every other street.

I pulled into the parking lot and parked across from Jack's spot, my usual routine for when I worked on-site. I glanced at my reflection in the review mirror and pulled out my pink lip gloss, gently retouching my lips for a little extra glow. I got out of my car and straightened my dress as I held his freshly printed talking points neatly displayed in a white professional binder.

Since the event was taking place outside, I saw a podium set up in front of the flagpole with two soldiers waiting to raise the American flag. Jack stood to the side, talking to a couple of co-workers. My heartbeat and breathing increased as I started to feel anxious, like during the times I'd seen Jack at past Army events. Out of the corner of his eye, Jack spotted me walking, and an affectionate smile formed on his face. A feeling of nervousness hit me. I cleared my throat and closed my eyes, taking a calming, deep breath before I spoke. "Hi, I have your talking points for the event today," I told him in an unexpectedly shy voice. Looking at me, he gently grabbed the binder from my hands.

"Thank you for doing this for me. I really appreciate it." I smiled back up at him.

"It's no problem. I don't mind at all."

Reveille started playing on the loudspeakers. Jack set the binder on the ground and obediently turned to face the American flag as the two soldiers carefully unfolded the flag, attached it to the flagpole, and raised it into the sky.

I stood there next to Jack as he saluted. My hand was at my side when I felt this strong urge to touch his hand. With my heart pounding out of my chest, I slowly grazed his hand, gingerly touching his tight fist as he stood at attention. I looked up at him out of the corner of my eye. Not moving a muscle, he gazed down at me. We locked eyes as he slowly opened his tight fist and allowed my fingers to wrap around his. No words were needed. Our hearts were speaking a language nobody else was aware of. He was also falling in love with me.

After the song ended, Jack quickly pulled his hand back— probably hoping nobody else caught our special moment. He grabbed the talking points and walked up to the podium to kick off the event. I stood there with a thousand thoughts rushing through my mind like a roaring river, trying to wrap my mind around what had just happened. I was in complete shock that I had the boldness to hold his hand and that he actually held mine back.

Wow, I can't believe what we just did. I gazed at Jack as he started giving his speech. As he scanned the audience, his eyes caught mine. I could tell he was holding back a grin. I affectionately smiled at him as I looked down at the ground and back up at him. I knew what we did was risky, but it was almost as if our hearts didn't care. It was getting harder and harder for me to hide my growing feelings for him in the shadows. Lines had been blurred between us, and there was no going back.

14

JACK

The world he had known for so long was slowly changing for Jack. After the event, Jack felt the walls closing in all around him as the realization of his actions started setting in. As people came up to him, congratulating him on his speech, he felt the sudden urge to escape into his office. Adrenaline was shooting through his system—like someone was choking him in broad daylight. He needed to gather his thoughts after what had just happened with Lillian.

What were you thinking? He demanded to himself. His mind began fixating on the worst-case scenario. All it took was one look for someone to catch them holding hands, marking the end of his Army career. He politely smiled as he briskly walked through the double doors of his building and back to his office.

His assistant, Grace, caught sight of him walking in the front door. "Hello, sir. How did the speech go?"

Jack responded abruptly. "It went fine. I'll be in my office. If anyone asks for me, just tell them I stepped out."

"No problem, sir, I can do that." Grace politely replied.

She smiled, turned to face her computer, and continued typing up her email about the colonel's upcoming business trip.

Jack walked into his office and closed the door behind him. He closed his eyes and stood in the middle of the spinning room. He was trying to comprehend the situation but was unable to think coherently. Nothing made sense.

How in the world did I get here? He heard pinging noises coming from his computer. His Microsoft Teams program was open as people were sending him chat messages, needing to talk to him. *I have no time for this, and this isn't something I need in my life,* he thought to himself. He felt torn. What he felt for Lillian was fighting against his inherited military instincts and the commitments he made in his life—both professionally and personally.

She was starting to make him question all the decisions he made in his life up to this point. He wondered if maybe he got married too soon and if he had married the right person. He also loved the Army with its rules, structure, and giving back to his country, but now he was starting to question if maybe he had blinders on. Was he too focused on his Army career and ignoring his heart all these years without even realizing it? Whether he wanted to admit it or not, he had a feeling that maybe he was right. At this point, there was no ignoring his heart. It was expanding and growing whether he liked it or not.

15

———

"Did you hear about how Colonel Cooper *personally* reached out to that soldier whose wife is struggling with breast cancer? He actually offered to watch their kids so the soldier and his wife could have a date night . . ." I had started hearing office chatter about Jack's personality from people sharing stories about his love for the troops and our brigade while balancing the ever-growing list of responsibilities he carried on his strong shoulders. Everyone saw *Jack, the Army Colonel,* this powerful and worldly man with more than twenty years of experience in the military and so much authority at his fingertips. His ability to lead multiple brigades while being in the presence of Army generals and talking about conflicts abroad wasn't how I viewed him, though.

In my eyes, he was just Jack: The forty-five-year-old blonde-haired, blue-eyed, dapper man from a small town in Georgia. He grew up in a loving and supportive family with a mom who just adored him. She saw Jack as the keeper of her stars. They had a strong bond that kids nowadays don't have with their parents. The love he had for her was reflected strongly in his eyes as he often teared up when talking about her. She was so proud of him and all his incredible accomplishments and yet, Jack was never one to brag about himself. In my eyes, he was one of the last true Southern gentlemen.

But aside from what was happening with Jack, I saw signs that God was closing the door to my job at the brigade, and it was time to move on and find another job. A few months had passed since joining the Army, and by that time, I was really starting to feel the heat increasing from Ethan. It seemed like no matter what I was doing, my work was never good enough, even though I really enjoyed writing. He always had an issue with the way I set up quotes in an article and punctuation. Just a few weeks prior, he had begun to include Ryne in emails to me when he replied with edits to my work. My gut told me there was something going on, and I decided to face it head-on and talk to Ethan about the situation.

I went to work that day with "the conversation" looming over my head. As I walked into my musky old office building, I stopped right before entering his door. I listened as Ethan was typing away on his computer. An empty feeling formed in the pit of my stomach. I said a prayer for God to give me the words and the strength to get through this because I had no idea how it was going to go.

Stepping into Ethan's office, his back was to me as he busily worked. I took a deep breath and started to speak. "Ethan, can I speak with you for a minute?" He turned and looked at me.

"Sure, what's going on?"

I paused. "Well, I couldn't help but notice that you've been copying Ryne on your emails to me, and I just wanted to ask if there's anything that you want to discuss with me?" He looked at me from across the room. I could see the red glare in his eyes and the anger building up in his face. Like a tea kettle about to boil over, he began to unleash his frustration on me.

"I've tried to tell you about making certain corrections to your work and you haven't been doing it consistently . . ."

I remained calm. "Okay, can you show me an example of what you're talking about?" He proceeded with a laundry list of things that I was doing wrong. Some of the points he was making I didn't agree with. Others seemed a tad overexaggerated. Mainly, I think he was frustrated with repeating the same edits to my articles. I thought carefully about my words before responding, not reacting to his anger. "Okay, I understand. Well, are there any workshops or classes I can attend to work on what it is you're concerned about?"

A look of bewilderment came across his face as he let out a cackle.

"What are you talking about? The Army won't pay for anything like that!"

I was absolutely confused and pointed out, "That's not what I've heard from the colonel. He says that he supports us in improving and getting better."

Ethan scoffed at my comment. "Your incompetency as a writer is not the Army's issue. The Army won't support you taking any classes so don't bother asking. It's a waste of our time." I knew he was dead wrong. I also knew going against my boss wouldn't do anything, so I decided to just be upfront and address the elephant in the room.

"Do I need to worry about my future at the brigade?"

He didn't even hesitate. "Well, maybe not your immediate future." I couldn't believe what my own boss was saying. It was then I knew I needed to find another job because my future with the Army wasn't going to last for very long if my boss had his way.

In the meantime, Sandi and I decided to meet up and talk about the latest drama with Ethan. We were having lunch together, and I told her about the unexpected, explosive altercation with my Army career hanging on by a thread.

"This is crazy," she said with a look of shock on her face. "I have no idea why he's honed in on you, of all people, but we can't afford to lose any more writers."

Feeling stuck, I said, "I just don't know what to do, Sandi. I feel like nothing I do is right in his eyes, or it's just not good enough for his high standards."

Sandi came up with a solution as we sat outside eating our veggie burgers and fries. "Just send me all of your articles and let me look them over before sending them to Ethan." She was offering to be my personal Grammarly. I couldn't be more thankful.

"Thank you so much, Sandi! You don't have to do this for me," I told her. She looked at me with a sympathetic smile.

"You are an amazing writer, Lily. You don't deserve this, and I certainly don't want to see you get let go." We made a plan that anything I wrote, Sandi reviewed. She became my unofficial personal editor.

By the grace of God, a couple of days later, Ethan asked me to come into his office. Once again, I held my breath, not knowing what to expect. He said that it had come to his attention that the brigade didn't have a designated Public Affairs person to handle its media outreach. Since this was a strength of mine, he was changing my focus from writing articles and talking points to exclusively handling the brigade's publicity and securing press placements.

Inside, I breathed a sigh of relief. Working with the media and getting press placements was not only something I was passionate about, but I was very good at. I gladly accepted the challenge. Not to mention, I was already doing this work by pitching my stories to Ethan and advocating why they should get externally published. So now I was doing it officially and doing it for other members of my team. I finally started to feel valued for the work I was doing and thought my issues with Ethan were finally resolved and became a forgotten moment in time.

As I worked on a communications campaign for the brigade and pitched our articles to get externally published, I also attended the brigade's manager seminars. I had always found them particularly enjoyable and insightful. Even though they were mostly for federal employees, I gained some nuggets of wisdom attending them. While I could have attended them virtually, I went in person because it meant I had another opportunity to see Jack.

Walking up to the auditorium that day to attend another manager seminar, I saw Jack outside the building, trying to get in. His government ID wasn't working for some reason.

I walked up to the building smiling as I watched his frustration grow. "Are you sure you're allowed in this building?" I asked him jokingly.

He looked at me and said in a slightly sarcastic undertone, "Oh, I don't know if riffraff like me are allowed in here." I looked at him in disbelief. I wasn't sure if he was joking but I had a feeling there was an underline of truth in his comment.

"No, I wouldn't say that," I told him.

He looked at me straight in the eyes and replied, "Yes, I say that."

It dawned on me that he must be reflecting on how he sees himself in relation to me. If he could only see what I saw when I looked at him, he wouldn't say that at all. I wanted to tell him how amazing he was and that when I looked at him, I saw an incredibly strong man with a huge heart who could take on the world. In my eyes, he was a walking superhero. There was nothing he couldn't do. But I kept my thoughts to myself. I scanned my card and opened the door to let him into the building.

He walked up behind me to grab the door and gently put his hand over mine. My heart started to soar as I gazed up at him. I could feel the energy building between us like two magnets. I walked into the auditorium with him walking next to me. I sat down in my usual seat in the back row. My mind raced in a million directions as I reflected on our conversation and that brief, intimate moment in time when our hands tenderly touched. I watched him as he made his way up to the front and took his usual seat at the long executive table. Throughout the event, I did my best to pay attention to the speakers in the room. They were giving a presentation on becoming more effective leaders and ways to improve. After the event, I stood up from my chair and smiled down at Jack. I took a deep breath and walked out of the building feeling happy and guilty all at the same time.

Spring 2021

16

───────────

As things happened with Jack that I just couldn't explain, I knew I needed answers. Something told me this was all happening for a bigger reason than I could grasp. I knew talking to Jack was out of the question, given his high-ranking position in the military. Rather than talking to someone from my bible study group who I didn't think could understand my situation, I did something that was entirely out of character for me...I reached out to a psychic. After doing research, I discovered Margaret, a sweet but direct lady in her seventies who lived in the area. She had been a psychic for most of her life. After reading her website and doing some research, I figured I had nothing to lose, so I sent her a message. After getting a response from her, we scheduled a time on the phone to talk.

We started off our conversation with an open prayer. She explained about the session and asked if I had any questions that I wanted answers to. I was doubtful but went with it. I told her that I had a man in my life, and I wanted to know what he was to me. She asked me his name, and I told her.

That's when she got quiet. "He feels familiar. Have you had any interactions with him?"

I commented, "Yes, I have." She continued talking.

"Did you notice feeling a certain level of comfort between you two?"

"Yes," I said. Probably more so than I should have given his position, but yes, I did.

She said what I was feeling was due to a past life experience and that Jack and I had been together before. I was astonished, had no idea what to think, and was honestly skeptical. "So, what you're telling me is the colonel is my soulmate?"

I wanted to laugh like this was one big joke, and she said, "Your guides are telling me that you both have spent several lives together, and the connection you're feeling with him isn't imagined." She added, "He feels it as well."

I paused for a moment, and it dawned on me: The month prior to talking with Margaret, I remembered lying in bed thinking about Jack. Out of the blue, a song popped into my head. The lyrics were playing round and round like a record on a loop. Something told me to open iTunes on my phone, and I typed the lyrics into the search box. Out of the sea of songs in this long list, an album from the 1960s jumped out at me like a neon billboard.

"That's it!" I exclaimed. "That's the song." I played the song and suddenly, I started to sing the lyrics like I had heard it a hundred times, but I had never heard this song in my life. I don't listen to 1960s music, and that song was new to me. But in my heart, I knew this song very well. It reminded me heavily of Jack. The lyrics were so beautiful; they spoke about loving someone until the end of time.

Standing in the kitchen on the phone with Margaret, it

dawned on me that I never told her about that song. I had a feeling that she might be right.

She proceeded to tell me things about my marriage with Aaron that I had never told anyone. Without warning, my eyes filled with tears. "You've given up on the love train, and your marriage is something you and your husband have neglected," she told me. She added that I was sleepwalking through my life until I met Jack. "You woke him up as well because he's running on a similar track, reevaluating his marriage and life. But he must be older than you because he's handling this rather differently than you are. He is much more level-headed and measured than you." I laughed.

"Yeah, that sounds about right," I said to her. She continued to discuss my marriage.

"You need to figure out what you want to do with this marriage of yours. You need to think about what you want in a partner and what will make you happy. Whatever decision you make, you have to do it, with or without Jack. He's not going to rescue you, and you don't need rescuing." Margaret's tone was soft and yet blunt like a grandmother giving life advice to her lost granddaughter.

This was hard guidance for me to hear, but I knew I needed to hear it. I didn't need him to rescue me. I knew I had to figure things out for myself.

Margaret continued. "You also need to keep it separate from Jack because if something does grow between you two, you don't want to link issues. You will later regret it." I felt like I was in a therapy session and not talking to a psychic. I needed to clean my backyard first and figure out what I wanted in my life. She continued talking about Jack, explaining, "He's a very interesting man; there's a lot to him." Out of the blue, she said, "He also has a lot of artist in him, which has no place in the military." This was new to me. I'm assuming maybe Jack liked art, but I wasn't too sure.

"That's interesting," I said to her.

She went on to say, "I get the feeling that he's outgrown his marriage, and his wife feels it as well. They're very different from each other, and they argue at times. I see you two going out for coffee…but I'm not sure when—maybe this year." I froze. Margaret didn't know that I planned on asking Jack out for coffee sometime in the future once I left my job with the Army. Margaret continued to talk about my heart and what I deserved in a partner. "You need someone who will see you and love you for who you are because that's what you've delivered to other people. Jack also needs to step up to the plate and show you that he is worthy of you. You don't want to be with him if he isn't willing to step up to the plate."

Again, it was hard advice to hear, but I *needed* to hear it. Margaret advised, "Don't worry if you don't wind up hearing from Jack because I see another man coming into your life. He is a much better fit for you and will make you much happier than Jack." I found that hard to believe. But at the same time, I was also getting a small glimpse of a light at the end of a dark and very long tunnel.

Back at home, as I stood in the kitchen trying to digest this information, I realized I was standing at a crossroads. I could stay on my current path—married to my husband… maybe have kids in the future—or I could really sit down with myself, ask the hard questions, and not be afraid to face whatever answers arose. Then, I'd need to be brave enough to take the unknown path, knowing it may lead to happiness and a deeper fulfillment in life. Feeling disconnected, like I had one foot in my past and one foot in my future, I knew I had to pick my path very soon.

————

Hand-painted welcome home signs lined the post entrance and down the streets. Customized banners proudly hung outside military houses, welcoming the soldiers home. Aaron's homecoming from deployment quickly arrived. Normally, the house was decorated with bright, festive party decorations with streamers hanging from the living room ceiling and a large welcome home banner proudly hanging from our front porch, all in Army colors. However, this time was different. This was the first time I felt a huge disconnect from my husband. I had honestly gotten used to him being gone. I was in a rhythm at home and at work and found I didn't miss him much.

To me, this was a big red flag that something was wrong. I should have missed my husband…but I didn't. I felt guilt in my heart for feeling this way. At the same time, I was in love with Jack and wished more than anything that I could just tell him how I felt — but I couldn't talk to him without risking my job any more than what I had with our flirty interactions. After my husband came home from deployment, I did my best to put on a happy face, but he sensed my distance from him. One night as I was cooking dinner, I allowed myself to get lost in thought as I was sautéing meat with onions and bell peppers for him on the kitchen stove. The sizzle from the food not only filled the air but also the silence between us. Aaron stormed into the kitchen and glared at me from across the room. My chest tightened and my breathing increased as I kept my eyes fixated on the pan cooking his dinner.

"Are you cheating on me?" he growled. I looked at him out of the corner of my eye, his face red with anger and cold eyes fixated on me like a hunter aiming for its prey. My blood pressure started to spike. I said a silent prayer for God to help me in that moment. I felt helpless and terrified, like a trapped animal.

I took a deep breath as I felt my insides quivering. "No, I'm not cheating on you," I told him, trying to calm my voice.

"Well, I don't believe you," he spat out. His typical response as he never believed me anytime an argument ensued between us. "If you're not happy, then we can just get a divorce! I don't care!" I felt like he was testing me, but it also showed how little he thought of our marriage. Before I could think of a response, Aaron stormed out of the house and slammed the front door behind him, rattling the family photos framed on the wall nearby. I stood in the middle of the kitchen, holding my shoulders tight to try and still the quaking. Tears started flowing down my face. A voice inside told me this war was far from over. It was going to get worse before it got better.

As Aaron's suspicions about me grew, I found myself under surveillance in my own home as he randomly drove by to spy on me throughout the day. On a Monday afternoon during my lunch break from work, I got ready for my usual routine of walking Max and Charlie around the neighborhood before heading back to work. I stepped outside my front door with Max and Charlie barking excitedly, ready for their walk, when I looked across the street and saw Aaron slowly drive by with a look of suspicion laced across his face.

You've got to be kidding me! I stood in the front yard completely still as my mouth fell open. It happened again a couple of days later on another afternoon walk talking on the phone with Amelie. Aaron was circling the neighborhood like a vulture on the hunt. Our home had now become a battlefield as he continued to interrogate me like a cop drilling a potential suspect about my actions outside of our home. I couldn't even talk on the phone to my friends or go for a walk around my neighborhood without being accused of making a secret phone call. I technically wasn't seeing anyone, but in his mind, he was right, and I was wrong. I tried to defend myself time and time again, but it fell on deaf ears.

The cracks continued to show in my marriage, and things finally came to a breaking point with my husband. One night, while we were at the movies, he tried to hold my hand, but I just couldn't do it. He was never affectionate before and now he was trying to be. It just felt foreign to me. Yelling at me in the car on the drive back home, he growled, "Well, you may not be cheating on me, but you're thinking about someone else!" The truth was, he wasn't wrong about that.

The weeks slowly passed by, with each argument binding itself to me like a twelve-hundred-pound cement block tied to my ankles. I felt like I was in the middle of the ocean, paddling frantically, trying not to drown with nobody to help me in sight. Our marriage became a searing wildfire that scorched our more than decade-long union with our hands-on gasoline. With each passing day and one blow-up altercation feeding from the last one, I helplessly watched the inferno burn out of control, consuming everything in sight, including our marriage.

Eventually, my breaking point came when I was curled up on the floor crying while he was standing over me, yelling at me about things I was doing wrong in his eyes. All I wanted him to do was stop yelling at me. "I'm sorry! I'm sorry!" I pleaded as I covered my ears with my hands. "Just please stop screaming at me!" I knew what I was experiencing wasn't healthy, but this wasn't the first time I experienced this with him.

"You don't even know what you did wrong! You just want me to stop yelling at you, so you're saying sorry, but it doesn't mean anything!" He wasn't wrong about that, but the only thing I knew to do was to let him have his way.

After the yelling was over, I crawled into my bed and cried. I prayed to God to give me the strength to get through this season of my life. I knew the marriage was over. It wasn't healthy. This wasn't love, but I had a feeling this wouldn't be the last argument between us. There was no recovering from the trauma that had taken place since he came home from deployment. It was only a matter of time before our marriage self-imploded, but I also felt trapped with no way out.

17

Desperately searching for a light at the end of the tunnel, I continued to navigate through the drama of my marriage falling apart, combined with my conflicting feelings for Jack. Part of me felt like I was flying a plane by myself for the first time through the thick gray fog in the dead of winter with zero visibility and no instructions. I wanted more than anything to escape from my problems. The post was eagerly buzzing about the upcoming Army birthday marked by the annual Army Ball. I was always excited about the formal affair. Any opportunity to dress up was right up my alley. I also saw it as a way to make up for my disappointing high school prom, where my sad blue dress came from the clearance rack at JCPenney—I had also discovered a little too late that my date didn't know how to dance. Even though I looked forward to the yearly formal ball, Aaron never wanted to go. Each time I tried asking him, I was always immediately turned down.

"I don't feel like dressing up and besides, why do I want to see my co-workers when I have to see them every day at work?" he barked. Because of that, I only went once several years ago, but this year was different. Knowing our marriage was on the rocks and wanting to win me over, Aaron suggested we go to this year's Army Ball.

"My brigade is selling tickets for the ball, and I was thinking maybe we could attend this year. Do you want to go?" he asked me a little too enthusiastically.

Standing in our living room, I looked at him, stunned. Deep down, I didn't want to attend, given the circumstances. I also knew turning him down could spark another argument between us, like intentionally setting a wildfire in the forest of my life. Having no choice, I agreed to go.

"Sure, we can go to the ball," I said lifelessly.

"Great! I'll buy our tickets from work in the morning," he excitedly replied.

I went into our bedroom and closed the door. I plopped down onto my bed, where Max and Charlie were taking their afternoon nap. I wanted to be excited about the Army Ball, but I just couldn't make myself fake it. Trying to lift my mood, I opened my laptop to search for a gown to wear for the formal event.

The last time I attended, another woman had worn the same exact dress, and to make it even worse, she was sitting at the table right behind us. I told myself this fashion faux pas would never happen again. I decided to rent a designer gown instead. After browsing the internet, I discovered a floor-length forest green sequin strapless Badgley Mischka gown. The chances of anyone else wearing this gown were pretty slim, so I was in the clear. A small spark of joy unexpectedly flickered in my heart as I pictured myself wearing the formal dress and possibly seeing Jack.

The days leading up to the ball brought an excited skip in

Aaron's step. Out of the blue, Aaron offered to help with household chores, even offering to make dinner and wash the dishes. This was out of character for the man who said I never did enough to clean the house. He even tried to persuade me to clean more by offering to buy pink cleaning products, knowing pink was my favorite color. The memory was permanently branded in my mind.

Because of this, I was optimistically cautious about this sudden change in Aaron's personality. I had a feeling it wasn't going to last forever. On the day of the event, the beautiful dress arrived right on time. Opening the package, I pulled out the stunning gown. A little part of me started to come alive again with excitement for the big night. After carefully slipping it on, I examined myself in the mirror like Cinderella wearing her beautiful light blue dress. The strapless sequin evening dress sparkled when it subtly caught the light and hugged my body in all the right places. I smoothed out a few wrinkles while also smoothing out the negative thoughts brewing in my mind about the drama in my life. The gown was perfect.

Since I've always had a gift for doing formal hair and makeup, I applied my eyeshadow and touched my cheeks with a rosy pink blush, giving my face a subtle glow. I curled my long hair into beautiful waves that hung around my face, with part of my hair pulled back by a rhinestone hair clip that matched my gown perfectly.

Aaron walked into the bathroom wearing his blue Army service uniform with his ribbons measured to perfection on his chest and his black beret. "Are you ready to go?" He asked me. I took a deep breath and replied halfheartedly. "Sure, I'm ready to go." At this point, I wasn't even phased by his lack of acknowledgment regarding my beautiful formal gown. I grabbed my black sequin clutch, and we headed to the event.

We drove up a windy road lined with American and Army flags flying gently in the wind. The end of the road opened up to a beautiful military museum sitting on a hilltop overlooking the town. As we parked, I sat in the car, bracing myself like I was preparing for battle instead of going to a beautiful ball. *Just get through the night, and you will be fine,* I tried to tell myself.

I reluctantly got out of the car and felt the cool night air gently blowing all around me with the stars shining bright. I saw Aaron waiting for me with his arm out. I obediently locked my arm around his as we walked toward the museum. We stepped inside and were greeted by a spouse volunteer.

"Good evening, sir! Here is your program for the evening. Have a wonderful night!" Aaron grabbed the program as we walked arm in arm down the red carpet, making our way into the main ballroom.

Walking in, I saw a sea of tables with everyone's names on the plate settings. Spouses dressed up in their best formal attire, laughing and talking with their service members standing proudly by their sides. After finding our table, Aaron took a seat.

I decided I needed a drink to calm my nerves. "I'm going over to the bar to grab a drink," I told Aaron.

"Sounds good!" he exclaimed. "Get me a drink while you're at it."

"Sure," I flatly responded.

I walked over to the bar, where I was approached by a friendly bartender wearing a crisp black suit with a white button-up shirt and shiny gold cufflinks. "Hello, miss, what can I get you for tonight?" he asked me.

I ordered my usual drink. "I'll have a lemon drop with sugar on the rim, please," I told him.

As the bartender started making my drink, I stood at the bar and examined the room, seeing who was in attendance. My eyes caught sight of Jack talking to another senior Army officer. He started to laugh and then turned his head. He immediately caught sight of me standing at the bar. My heart began to race as his eyes slowly scanned my body from head to toe. His eyes locked on mine as I felt my body get hot. Finishing up his conversation, he made his way over to the bar and stood next to me. I felt my breathing increase, and my pulse quickened.

"Good evening, Lillian. You look beautiful tonight." He told me tenderly.

I looked up at him and stared into his soulful blue eyes, which made me feel like he could see my innermost thoughts.

"Thank you. You look very nice as well, but then again, you always look nice," I told him warmly. My eyes caught a glimpse of his various ribbons and medals proudly displayed on his uniform, reflecting his vast military career.

He smiled as he replied, "I don't look as nice as you but thank you."

An awkward silence filled the air as we both grew quiet while trying to ignore the fire between us.

"Where is your wife? Did she not attend?" I asked him curiously.

"No, she wanted to stay home. She wasn't interested in going," he said matter-of-factly.

The bartender approached with my drink. "Here you go,

miss." He then looked over at Jack. "What can I get for you, sir?"

"I'll have an Old Fashioned, please."

I looked at him and smiled. "Old Fashioned huh? That sounds like a pretty strong drink."

He laughed. "Yeah, it's one of my favorite go-to drinks."

I responded playfully. "I'll stick to my lemon drops and leave the Old Fashioned for you. I'm sure mine tastes better anyway."

He smiled. "Well, let's see. Why don't you try a little bit and tell me what you think?" As the bartender handed Jack the glass filled with his drink, he passed it over to me.

I slowly took the glass from him and took a big whiff of the drink. "Oh my gosh! That smells so strong!" I exclaimed.

Jack started laughing. "It's definitely stronger than your lemon drop that's for sure."

I slowly brought the glass to my lips and took a small sip of the drink. Unexpectedly, I felt a burning sensation traveling down my throat. "Wow. That is nasty! It tastes like rubbing alcohol—how can you drink that?"

Jack busted up laughing. "It's an acquired taste, but it's not for everyone."

I quickly responded. "That was a first for me and probably the last, but thanks for sharing it with me."

His endearing smile grew even bigger. "Anytime."

As we stood there gazing into each other's eyes, I realized I was getting caught up in the moment and broke our love spell. "I better get back to my table."

He responded. "That sounds good. I hope you have a wonderful evening."

I smiled at Jack as I turned and walked back to my table. I

looked across the room and saw my husband talking to one of his co-workers. I set my martini down on our table. He looked over at my drink and asked, "Where's my drink?"

Suddenly, I felt my anxiety start to spike up. *Oh no, I was so caught up with Jack that I forgot all about Aaron's drink!* I quickly thought.

"I am so sorry! I'll get that for you right now," I told him apologetically.

Aaron rolled his eyes. "Just get me any beer that's available."

I turned around and obediently made my way back to the bar as my mind wandered over to Jack once again. I had never seen him in his dress uniform. He looked so handsome, always dressed to perfection no matter the occasion.

The bartender saw me standing at the bar once again. "Back for another drink, I see. What can I get for you this time?"

I managed a small smile. "Any beer will do, thank you."

He walked away and came back, holding a Tombstone Brewing IPA. He cracked it open and poured it into a glass, handing it to me. "Here you go."

"Thank you," I told him as I walked away and back to my assigned table.

Sitting down, I gave Aaron the beer as he chatted away about some project he was working on with his second lieutenant. As I tuned them out, my gaze turned back to the open room. I spotted Jack sitting at his table in the front of the room with other senior leaders from my brigade. Suddenly, I felt a little ping of pain in my heart. I wished more than anything that I was sitting next to him and not with Aaron.

I glanced over a few tables away from Jack and spotted the

Fallen Soldier Table. A small table with a white tablecloth, a single chair, and one rose in a vase. The table was set for one, along with a lit candle. The table was a tribute to all the fallen soldiers who either died or didn't make it back home. Next to the plate setting were three small lemon slices, symbolizing the bitter fate of them not returning home. The table always made me stop and reflect. A reminder of the sacrifice service members made for our freedom that is often overlooked or taken for granted by the rest of the world. It made my problems look so small in comparison. I knew I had so much to be grateful for.

Just then, the opening speaker for the event walked up to the podium to give introductory remarks. "Ladies and gentlemen, please rise for the presentation of Colors and remain standing for the singing of the National Anthem, followed by the Pledge of Allegiance," He announced. *Oh my gosh, I totally forgot about this,* I thought to myself. I hadn't attended a military ball in quite a while and forgot about having to stand for Colors. I dutifully stood up from my seat as the Color Guard marched into the room with four soldiers marching in a row holding the American flag, the Army flag, and two rifles. I looked over at Aaron as he stood at attention, saluting the flags.

The soldiers carefully placed the flags in the front of the room and marched to the back of the room. A military spouse wearing a black strapless dress walked up to the podium and started to sing the National Anthem. I always felt so much pressure to not move a muscle during this part of the ceremony, and tonight was no exception.

After she was done singing, I obediently placed my right hand over my heart as the crowd recited the Pledge of Allegiance, taking me back to elementary school, where I performed it on a daily basis.

After we finished, I decided that I needed a break from the crowd. I quickly got up to use the restroom and freshen up my makeup.

Making my way across the ballroom, I walked into the vanity room leading into the bathroom. A large portrait of a beautiful pink and red rose bouquet hung over a small light pink velvet chaise lounge next to a vanity. In the bathroom were two spouses standing in front of the mirrors, talking as they freshened up their lipstick. I stood next to them using the other mirror and slowly pulled my lip gloss out of my clutch. I listened to their conversation and tried not to stare. One of the women wore a beautiful long pink satin gown with her jet-black hair pulled up into a bun. The other woman had honey blonde hair and was wearing a lilac purple strapless sequin gown. Her hair was pulled to the side with a stunning flower barrette. As I glanced at them, I realized I didn't recognize them. They must be from another brigade on post.

"Did you see Kristi is here with her husband? I was so shocked to see them! I heard they're having marriage issues," the blonde woman said to her friend.

"I know, right? I heard he's having a hard time at work but still works long hours just to avoid going home. I feel bad for her...who would put up with that kind of behavior unless they're desperate, right?" the other woman bluntly replied.

"Totally agree, and I mean, he is good-looking and all, but he's not worth *that*," the blonde woman remarked.

The woman wearing the pink dress turned to her friend and said, "Oh my gosh, so speaking of good-looking, did you see the gorgeous colonel in the front of the room?"

My heart stopped. I knew they were talking about Jack.

"You mean the freaking hot guy with the dreamy blue eyes and a body built like a superhero? Oh yeah, I totally noticed him. He looks like he stepped off the cover of a steamy romance novel. I heard that he's married but wow, his wife sure is lucky to have a piece of arm candy like him by her side."

With my shiny pink lip gloss in my hand, I slowly opened it and started to touch up my lipstick. Jealousy started to creep up inside my heart. Jack is good looking so I shouldn't be surprised that other women were also taking notice. The women continued chatting about Jack.

"But did you see that he's not wearing a wedding ring? I mean, it makes you wonder, right? A guy like that not wearing a ring usually spells trouble. If I had a guy like that, he better want to wear his ring."

What in the world are they implying? I thought angrily.

As if they were reading my thoughts, the other friend said, "Oh my gosh, yes! I couldn't agree with you more. It makes you wonder if he cheats on his wife. It happens so often nowadays in the military that I wouldn't be shocked, especially someone as hot as him . . ."

I was jumping out of my skin. *I can't imagine Jack doing anything like that!*

Sensing my anger starting to build, I needed to leave the bathroom before saying or doing something that I may later regret. I quickly finished touching up my lip gloss and left the bathroom, gladly leaving the gossipy women behind in my tracks.

I practically stormed back to my table with my heart still pumping with anger from overhearing the conversation about

Jack. *Just calm down, Lily. They're wrong about Jack. Just because he doesn't wear his wedding ring doesn't mean he's not trustworthy,* I convincingly told myself.

I sat down at our table as a waiter walked over with our dinner, serving baked salmon with grilled asparagus and mashed potatoes. The freshly cooked food smelled delicious, and I felt my stomach start to growl. With my nerves on edge getting ready for the ball, I realized I didn't eat lunch, so I was way overdue for a meal.

I looked up and smiled at the nice waiter. "Thank you so much." I ate my food in silence while Aaron was busy making his rounds talking to other people from his brigade. *Wow, for someone who never wants to attend an Army Ball, he sure is a social butterfly,* I thought sarcastically to myself.

———

As EVERYONE WAS busy chatting at their tables and enjoying their dinner, a tall white-haired man wearing a decorated Army uniform with more ribbons and medals than I could count walked to the stage. He was the guest speaker for the evening. Something told me he must be an Army general. I always found the speakers to be the highlight of the Army Ball. I enjoyed hearing about their time in the military and the experiences they went through. I opened the program on my lap and read that Thomas Gable was a retired Army general who served for more than forty years. I judged from his stern, dark brown eyes and sharp voice that he wasn't one to mess with.

Wow, if I were in a battle, I wouldn't want to have this guy as an enemy, I thought to myself. Retired General Gable served in the Vietnam War, the Gulf War, and the Iraq War. I could hear his passion for the Army and serving his country in his voice as he spoke about the troops he served with, sharing stories from being on the front lines and seeing things most people never dreamed of.

"During my time in the Vietnam War, I heard the last words of eighteen, nineteen, and twenty-year-old boys that will forever stay with me. There's simply nothing that prepares a person for that moment and what they're about to face when going into battle," Thomas said in a sobering voice that captured the attention of everyone in the room.

Thomas had served as a medic in Vietnam who refused to be evacuated and wouldn't leave his men behind.

"As much as I wanted to save them all, something told me most of these men wouldn't be returning home, but regardless, I made the decision to stay by their side for as long as I could," Thomas reflected honestly to the audience in a haunting voice that echoed in my mind.

As he continued sharing his story, it made me reflect on all the lives that were lost during the Vietnam War. Men with families, someone's husband, father, brother, or friend. Most of those men had left their pregnant wives at home to serve in the war. Many of them had small children and never returned home to see them grow up and live their lives. So many soldiers were forgotten over the years. Something told me Thomas remembered every person he served with not only during the Vietnam War but also other battles he faced throughout his distinguished Army career.

After Thomas wrapped up his speech, the crowd rose to their feet and applauded the military hero. Thomas politely smiled as he made his way off the stage and took his seat at

Jack's table. I looked to the side of the room and noticed a waiter from the kitchen approaching the stage with a multi-layered ceremonial Army birthday cake on a silver platter. It was a longstanding Army tradition for the oldest and youngest soldier with the Army to cut the cake with a large metal sword, as a symbol of the past and future linking together. A man and a woman approached the stage who were the oldest and youngest soldiers to serve in the Army at our post. The older man was surprisingly short, with thin brown hair neatly combed to the side. His dark chocolate eyes were behind gold-framed eyeglasses. The young woman towered over the older Army soldier with dark red hair and blue eyes. She had a look of discomfort on her face as she walked next to this soldier who clearly outranked her. The man grabbed the sword from the stage and with each having one hand on the sword, effort-lessly cut the black and gold cake. Everyone in the room erupted in applause and cheers.

The waiters then approached the stage, took the cake, and divided it up onto small saucer plates to hand out to the guests. A waiter approached me with a small slice of cake. "Would you like some cake, miss?" He politely asked me.

"No, thank you, I'll pass." I respectfully replied. As much as I enjoyed the general's speech, my encounter with the catty women in the bathroom made me lose my appetite.

Sensing my uncomfortableness, Aaron blurted out, "What's wrong with you? Why don't you want any cake?"

Another couple sitting at the table with us shot their heads up in shock. The husband, a young Army soldier in his early twenties with black hair and brown eyes, glanced at Aaron out of the corner of his eye, trying not to stare. *Great, I can only imagine what's going to be said around post after tonight,* I thought helplessly.

I glared at him from across the table. "I just don't want any, and besides, you know that I'm not much of a cake person." I always had ice cream cakes growing up for my birthday, so I wasn't missing out on much.

"Suit yourself!" He said as he shoved a large spoonful of cake into his mouth.

A wave of disgust washed over me. He had his Army weigh-in coming up, so cake was probably the last thing he needed, but I kept my fitness instructor critiques to myself.

I watched everyone socializing and enjoying the evening, but after more than fifteen minutes went by, a wave of boredom hit me. My mind was floating away, dreaming of being anywhere except where I was. After everyone finished eating, it was time to retire the Colors for the evening. Everyone rose to their feet as the same Army soldiers who brought the flags at the beginning of the event came and carefully took the flags from the front of the stage and exited the back of the room.

The master of ceremonies approached the stage for the last part of the evening. "Can everyone please continue standing as we sing the Army song?" *Oh my gosh, another part that I totally forgot about,* I thought dreadfully to myself. I forgot about having to sing like we were back in the high school choir. I dutifully picked up the program with the lyrics to *The Army Goes Rolling Along* printed on the back. I looked over at Aaron as he flashed a patronizing smile at me. He nodded his head as his way of saying, "You better sing." I took a deep breath as the crowd began to chant the song.

I'm not the best singer. Singing in public is not my forte,

but I humored my husband, who happily sang along with his work buddies.

After the song ended, I breathed a sigh of relief as the formal portion of the event came to a close. Everyone took their seats, and I heard loud music from the back of the room. People excitedly made their way over to the dance floor. It reminded me of all the times I asked Aaron to dance with me, whether it was at my favorite jazz restaurant or even on one of our dates. I got the same reply, "I don't dance. I only dance if I have alcohol in my system." I always found it to be a lame excuse, so I just stopped asking him.

About twenty minutes went by when I noticed the DJ started to play more romantic music for couples to slow dance. About two songs in, my ears picked up on a familiar song.

My heart started to race. It was *the* song from my past life with Jack. *It can't be! How can it be?* I thought to myself, rapidly blinking as I tried to process what I was hearing. I whipped my head around and looked at Jack from across the room. He slowly turned his head in my direction and looked directly at me. I saw his blue eyes grow large as his mouth slowly dropped open. *Oh, my goodness, does he know the song, too?*

My mind raced with a thousand thoughts flying at the speed of light. Jack got up from his seat and walked over to my table. I could feel my heart beating out of my chest, and my hands started to shake. He turned to Aaron, who rapidly stood up from his seat and saluted Jack.

"Sergeant White, do you mind if I have one dance with Lillian?"

Aaron looked up at him, quickly glanced at me, and replied, "Why no, of course not, sir! Besides I don't care for dancing anyways." With Jack outranking Aaron, I had a feeling Aaron wouldn't challenge the colonel by saying he couldn't dance with me.

Jack then turned to me with his arm out and said, "May I have this dance, Lillian?"

I looked up at him as my heart grew even more with love for him. "Of course you can, sir," I affectionately told him.

He gently led me to the dance floor as he took my petite hand in his and with his other strong hand, carefully placed it on my lower back.

I couldn't believe it. Here was the man of my dreams dancing with me to our song. The same song that defined our love decades ago in a past life.

He looked at me with such love in his eyes. I did my best to hold back the tears as he said, "This song is so beautiful. I just knew I had to dance with you."

The walls around us became blurry. Once again, nobody else existed but him and I. We had stepped back in time to the moment when we were together as a couple. The love I felt for him back then was the same love I felt for him now. Time wasn't standing in our way anymore. Time didn't exist. The only thing that existed was our unspoken love for one another. Our love had transcended time and space without even realizing it.

We danced in silence as we listened to the lyrics of the song. Our hearts were absorbing them like a sponge, taking in the moment.

I realized that no matter what happened between us, our lives were intertwined, always finding our way back to each other. Whether it was in this lifetime or in the next, just like a record on loop, playing the same beautiful love song over and over again.

Before I knew it, our song ended. We were back in the real world once again. Looking into his beautiful blue eyes, I could see the unspoken love he felt for me, even if he never said it out loud. "Thank you for dancing with me," he said softly.

I looked up at him and found myself saying, "Anytime."

He obediently held his arm out as I interlocked my arm with his, and he led me back to my table, where Aaron was waiting.

I sat down at the table as Jack turned to Aaron and politely said, "Thank you for allowing me to dance with Lillian. I hope you all have a wonderful evening." He turned around and walked back to his table.

Aaron turned to me and spat, "Why don't we call it a night? Besides, I don't need any other guys trying to steal you away from me. You belong to me and nobody else."

My blood ran cold as I caught myself mid-breath. Aaron had obviously picked up on the connection between Jack and I.

I got up from my seat and said, "Okay, we can get going."

As we started to leave the ballroom, I looked behind me at Jack, who was watching me walk away with a loving smile on his face. We danced to the song of our lives that night, always remembering that special moment and the love that will forever stay with us.

18

JACK

That night, as Jack drove home from the Army Ball, something inside him changed. He felt an unexpected shift inside his heart. Deep down, he knew that he was in love with Lillian. While the obedient military side of him wanted to stay committed to his marriage and the vows he made, his heart told him that he wasn't with the right person. He longed for a marriage like what his parents had but as hard as he tried, there was always something missing between him and his wife. A certain level of comfort that just wasn't there.

Lillian had awoken something in Jack's heart that, deep down, he didn't want to admit. *This was definitely not in my plans,* he thought hastily to himself. He was on a pre-planned path marked with success from the second he graduated from West Point. He was determined to stay on that path, but his heart yearned to go in a different direction. Day in and day out, as much as he tried to push Lilian out of his mind, she always found her way back into his thoughts. Now, tonight, with that dance they shared, he had done something completely out of character—especially since he was a married man. He felt drawn to her in a way that felt new and unknown. It was a feeling he never had even felt for his own wife.

He pulled up to his beautiful two-story home just outside of post and got out of his car. He walked silently through the side door into the kitchen, trying not to wake up his wife, who was sleeping in their bedroom. He slowly walked into the bedroom and saw her sound asleep with their two white Persian cats curled up at her feet. He felt a sting of guilt in his heart for what he was feeling for Lillian. But he also felt trapped. Even if he did want to leave, his wife would never let that happen. He had taken care of her throughout their entire marriage, with her never having to work full-time. He walked out into his office and gazed up at the awards hanging on the wall from his years of military service. A divorce meant turning their world upside down. She had the power to take away everything that he worked so hard for his entire military career.

He walked back into the bedroom and sat on the edge of his bed. He let out a sigh as he started undressing. His mind kept swirling with thoughts that if he had his way, he wouldn't even be thinking—all thoughts of Lillian. Whether he wanted to admit it or not, he loved her. He knew his time at the brigade wasn't going to last forever. But he was used to seeing her at events, smiling with that beautiful smile as she lovingly gazed at him from the audience. He was drawn to her. She was beautiful from the inside out, and it showed.

He was still shocked someone like her was working for the military. She didn't fit the mold of the typical government employee he was used to working with. He also knew that Ryne found her a threat to their structured military world. She didn't fit neatly into their way of life, and she didn't want to. With that thought, he smiled. She marched to the beat of her own bubbly, happy drum. It seemed like she lit up every room she walked into, and that light always caught his eye.

As he finished undressing, Jack neatly hung his uniform in his closet. He slid under the covers next to his wife. He turned off his light. He tried to sleep but his mind was busy with thoughts of Lillian. As much as he wanted to, he didn't have a solution to this problem. It was his job to always have a solution ready for any problem that would arise—no matter how big or small. Lillian was the one question mark that, for the first time in his life, he had no idea what to do about.

19

The next day, Aaron had the idea of taking a romantic train ride to a nearby town and grabbing dinner as a last-ditch effort in trying to save our marriage. Earlier that day, he ripped into me about my lack of effort in our marriage, making me feel guilty for not working hard enough in his eyes. I didn't agree with him and felt like our entire marriage consisted of paddling upstream against a strong current with no end in sight. Seeing no way out, I let him have his way. Putting on a friendly face and pretending to be happy was the last thing on my mind. He didn't know that earlier that afternoon, I had gone behind his back and had a birth control procedure done. Getting pregnant in the middle of this mess with my marriage falling apart was the last thing I needed. Even though we had stopped being intimate a long time ago, I didn't want to take the chance.

On the car ride to the train station, Aaron sensed my distance. "What's wrong with you? Why are you hardly talking?" He spat out. "Are you going through an early mid-life crisis or something?"

I shot back. "No, I'm fine! I'm just not feeling good." He didn't know that I was experiencing excruciating cramps as a side effect of the procedure. He suggested I take some ibuprofen.

"I have some medicine in the glove compartment. Take some and see if that helps." I highly doubted anything could help my pain, but I obediently reached over and took some of the medicine.

As we pulled up to the train station and got out of the car with people hurrying in and out of the station, he walked up next to me. He gently laid his hand on my back, something that was out of the ordinary for him. Being affectionate never came naturally to him, and it showed. It took every inch inside of me not to pull away, but I let him have his affectionate moment with me.

We walked inside the train station and Aaron found a café to order me some tea. I sat in the large plush purple armchair, trying to mask my pain as my arms were wrapped around my stomach. Stabbing pains shot inside me and down my back.

How in the world am I going to get through this day? I thought helplessly. I wanted so badly to just be home curled up in my bed with a heating pad on my stomach.

Aaron handed me the green tea latte, and before I knew it, the train was pulling up. It was time to board. We got inside, and I found the first seat closest to the window. Aaron sat down next to me with his hand on my leg, trying to hold my hand. I turned my gaze outside the train window, but I could feel the discomfort building inside my body, along with the pain from my birth control. I closed my eyes and pretended to sleep. All I wanted was to be left alone. I imagined Jack sitting next to me, holding my hand instead of Aaron. The pipe dream managed to put on a small smile.

The train stopped as we offboarded and found our way around a charming town just outside of the post. The real-life frontier town was straight out of the American Wild West. I almost expected gun-slinging cowboys to come walking down the main street as we passed historic brick buildings and an old saloon from the 1800s. We searched for a place to eat for about thirty minutes. I almost wanted to give up when we stumbled upon a small mom-and-pop restaurant in the middle of town with beautiful scenic photos of different places throughout Arizona. We sat down at the booth and didn't say more than two words as we looked over the menu. The conversation between us felt forced. I felt our likely separation looming over us like a dark storm cloud, ready to bring a massive downpour onto our marriage.

"So…what are you ordering?" Aaron asked me.

Not having much of an appetite, I ordered a salad. "I'll just get something light," I replied to him.

As we sat in uncomfortable silence with the painful battle raging inside my body, I decided I needed to get away. I asked Aaron to order my Caesar salad while I made my way to the bathroom.

Standing in the bathroom and looking at myself in the mirror, I wondered how in the world I got to this point in my life and how things were going to turn out. Even with the emotional and now physical pain that I was going through, I knew there was a light at the end of the tunnel. I started to feel the tears building up in my eyes. "Things will get better, Lily," I told myself. "Just get through this day, and you'll be back home before you know it." I reluctantly left the bathroom to find Aaron on his phone. I sat down and looked outside the window as we let the quiet surround us while waiting to eat. When our food finally arrived, I found myself taking tiny bites of my salad as the pain grew even louder in my body, demanding my attention.

After what felt like an eternity, we finished eating our meals and made our way back to the train station. Walking into the historic red brick train station with forest green trim around the windows, Aaron subtly reached over and grabbed my hand. My skin began to tingle with discomfort like a stranger was holding my hand. We walked outside to our stop as the sun was starting to set over the horizon, turning the sky into beautiful shades of pink and orange. I heard a loud whistle in the distance and saw the train pulling up to the station. We got onboard, and I found my seat once again. I allowed myself to get lost in the dreamy sunset as the train pulled away from the station. It was the silver lining that I needed, and I knew that I wasn't alone—God was with me the entire time.

But the war between Aaron and I raged on in the following weeks. The fighting seemed to only get increasingly worse, with Aaron accusing me of cheating on him because I was emotionally distant from him and me cowering and withdrawing like a scared little animal. I had never felt more terrified and alone in my life. It was March, and it happened to be Abbey's birthday. It soon became a day permanently fixated in my memory.

Aaron had stormed out of the house that morning, leaving for work after yelling at me because I wanted to give up on our marriage. He also left me in a puddle of tears as I sat on our living room couch hysterically crying. Not knowing who else to turn to, I managed to call Abbey to wish her a happy birthday.

As she was talking to me, he could tell something was terribly wrong. "What's wrong, Lily? What's going on?" In that instant, it was like a huge tsunami wave had broken through the levee of my life, and I couldn't keep it in any longer. I broke down and told her everything that had been happening since Aaron came home from deployment. As Abbey listened, I felt her anger building. "What the hell is wrong with him, treating you like this?" She said angrily. "Why is he accusing you of cheating on him? Did he cheat on you when he was in Belgium, and maybe he feels guilty and is taking it out on you?"

I quickly remarked. "No, that's not it. Aaron wouldn't cheat on me, that much I know for sure." Aaron had been cheated on by prior girlfriends before we got married. Though it seemed the ghosts of his past were coming back to haunt him, I wanted to believe that he didn't want to put me through the same heartache he experienced by cheating on me.

She continued talking. "What you're going through is not normal, and it's certainly not healthy. He shouldn't be treating you like this."

Even though Abbey was younger than me, I felt like she was so much older and wiser at that moment. Not knowing what to do, Abbey gave me the best advice I needed to hear. "You need to go home and be with your family. Get away from him and the situation. You need time alone to figure out what you want to do, but you can't stay there any longer." I knew she was right. I needed to go home, but I knew the timing wasn't right. I couldn't leave at that exact moment.

That night, after Aaron came home from work, I told him my plan to go home and spend some time with my family. "I want to go with you," he snapped.

Surprised by his response, I found myself reluctantly saying, "Sure…if you want to come, you can." It wasn't what I wanted, but I felt trapped and didn't see that I had any other choice. Immediately, I felt the strong need to call my good friend Audrey. She was one of the first friends I made when I moved to the area. She was also a fitness instructor and inspired me to become a cycle instructor.

"I'm going to take Max and Charlie for a quick walk, and I'll be right back." I grabbed their leashes and harnesses as they happily ran to the door, excitedly barking for their evening walk.

I waited until I was far away from my house before calling Audrey and telling her what had happened.

"What is it that you want?" She asked me in a resolute tone as she tried to pry my feelings open like a sealed can.

"Oh, I don't know. I guess if he wants to come, then he can."

She continued to pry further. "But what do *you* want?"

I knew what I was really feeling, but I was scared to admit it out loud. Thinking about it, I finally said, "Well, no, I don't want him to go, but I don't feel like I have much choice."

Audrey, being the voice of reason, replied, "You *always* have a choice. You need to be honest with Aaron about how you're feeling. If you don't want him to go, you need to tell him."

Ugh. I was so tired of arguing with him that I viewed this

as another battle to fight. But I knew she was right. She continued, "You need to be honest with yourself about how you're feeling. The sooner you're honest with yourself, the sooner you can start living the fabulous life that you were meant to live." *I wish it were that easy,* I thought to myself.

I finished my walk around the neighborhood with Max and Charlie in silence as Audrey's words marinated in my heart. As we approached my house, I felt my nerves rising inside me like I was slowly going underwater. I took a deep breath and said to myself, "Here we go." I opened the door and automatically took off Max and Charlie's harnesses and leashes. Hearing me walk back inside the house, Aaron walked into the living room. My eyes darted to the floor as I avoided making eye contact with him.

"I get the sense that you don't want me to go with you on your trip home. Is that right?" His passive-aggressive comment made me feel like I was being tested, and no matter the response, it wasn't what he wanted to hear. With that thought, I knew any answer I gave wouldn't be the right one. I decided to be honest.

I looked up at him and back down at the ground. "No, I prefer to go alone." I was trembling on the inside. I rarely spoke up against him.

He spat out. "Fine, go alone if that's what you want." I could tell by his comment that the underlying message was I was going to pay for this later. It was by far the scariest thing I had ever done, but my soul needed this time alone, away from the situation and his prying eyes.

———

MY BIRTHDAY quickly came the week after Abbey's birthday. To no surprise, Aaron and I had another fight. He accused me of going to a boyfriend's house when, in reality, I had gone to my acupuncturist appointment. I stood there absorbing his anger like a human sponge as I tried unsuccessfully to defend myself, but of course, in his mind, I was cheating on him.

He just wanted to catch me so he could say that he knew it. He was right, and I was wrong. I knew deep down Aaron could feel that something just wasn't right between us. Like most men in the military I had come across, Aaron didn't like change and even though he remained fixated with the notion I was unfaithful, he was comfortable in our marriage. Everything was handed to him on a silver platter—meals cooked daily, his work lunches ready before seven a.m., and his dirty laundry never sitting in the clothes hamper for more than a few days. Still, I wondered if Aaron had the nerve to pull the trigger on our marriage if I had been cheating on him.

I went to bed that night crying. I couldn't believe this was how I was spending my birthday. I lay there with tears streaming down my face, feeling so weak and exhausted from the emotional battle I was fighting. Then, I found myself getting out of bed. I got down on my knees, and there, kneeling beside my bed, I cried out to God. I wanted more than anything for God to bring *His* healing to this entire situation. I questioned why I was going through these trials, to begin with, and if there was a bigger meaning behind it all.

Of course, the dreaded *divorce* word loomed over me. I felt conflicted about what the Bible says about divorce, not to mention adultery. I knew my feelings for Jack were wrong on so many levels, not just spiritually. As hard as I tried to ignore them, they were always there and the spiritual battle inside my heart raged on. However, I also felt this was God's way of waking me up. There were serious issues with our marriage, and this was a symptom of a hidden cancer that had infiltrated our marriage many years ago.

It had reared its ugly head in different ways over the years, but now it was very apparent it wasn't going away. It needed to be addressed, and that meant starting with being honest with myself. I had suppressed the little voice inside me for so many years that now it was desperately fighting to get out and be heard like a bird trapped in a cage, wanting to be set free.

Realizing how long I had gone without love, I started to sob. Max, laying on his dog bed across the room, leaped to my rescue. He ran over, laid down next to my head, and buried himself in my hands. He gently nudged my palms with his snout. I looked up as he licked my face, gently kissing away my tears and trying his best to heal my pain. "Thank you so much for the love, Max. It's going to be okay; I promise." I got up, scooped him into my arms, and set him down on the bed next to Charlie as I crawled under the covers. Wanting to stay close to me, Max curled up next to my head on my pillow. I fell asleep while Aaron continued playing video games in the living room.

That night, I had a dream. I was driving in an executive town car and sitting in the front passenger seat. Jack was in the back seat with his parents, watching the ocean as we drove by. We were driving to the airport. He was flying out to another military post. As we pulled up to the pad where the helicopter was parked, Jack got out of the car and walked to my side. I rolled down my window. He took off his black beret, bent down, and gave me a kiss.

He lovingly looked into my eyes and said, "Happy birthday, baby. I love you."

After we drove away, I went out to dinner with his parents. It was an Italian restaurant, and I loved Italian food. We were in the middle of eating dinner when I looked down at my phone and saw I had a missed call from Jack. I remember feeling upset because I hated missing his calls, but he left me a message.

Sitting at the dinner table with his parents, I listened to the message: "Hey baby, it's me. I was just calling to tell you that I'm at post right now, and I'm listening to Frank Sinatra and thinking of you. Let my parents spoil you for your birthday. I love you."

I hung up the phone and woke up. Sitting in my bed with a smile on my face, I knew my angels wanted to make me feel better with that dream, and it certainly did. I also didn't understand the Frank Sinatra reference. Why him, of all people? I was puzzled, but I just let it go and continued with my day. My family was coming into town for my birthday. We were going to dinner that night at my favorite jazz restaurant, even though I wasn't up for celebrating, really. I felt like I was trapped in a real-life nightmare, and my birthday was the furthest thing from my mind. But for the sake of my parents, I forced myself to put on a happy face.

———

As MY PARENTS got into town, I told Aaron that I was going to escort them onto the post and take them to the Army lodge where they planned on staying. I sat alone in the parking lot, thinking about how I was going to break the news to them about my marriage. After thirty minutes, they finally arrived. I hopped out of my car and excitedly ran up to my mom and stepdad and gave them a long, overdue hug. It didn't take more than five seconds for them to see something was terribly wrong.

"What's going on, honey? Why do you look upset?" my mom asked. There, in the middle of the parking lot outside of post, I told them what had been happening between Aaron and me the past few months. They looked at me in total disbelief. "Why didn't you tell us this was happening?"

I didn't have a good answer. All I could say was, "Well, I just thought this was normal." "Oh my gosh, no, this isn't normal," my stepdad said with care in his voice. I told them my plan to ask Aaron for a divorce.

"I know this may seem sudden to you, but this is something I've thought about for a while now, and I'm just not happy."

They both looked at me. "Did you try everything? I mean, like therapy, praying to God, everything?" Since my stepdad is also religious, he said that Jesus could heal and fix just about anything. I sat there patiently listening to his insight and he wasn't wrong. Jesus could fix anything, but what if my marriage was something *He* didn't want to fix? He was allowing me to feel this way for a reason. He allowed Jack into my life for a reason.

In responding to my stepdad's question, I said, "Yes, we tried everything." Aaron and I took counseling off and on throughout the years, but nothing stuck. I prayed a ton as well, but in my heart, this was the right thing to do. The love wasn't there anymore, that much was obvious, and I was tired of living under constant surveillance and feeling like I was sacrificing and compromising more than he was.

"Yes, I respect what you're saying and no, I don't want a divorce, but I don't see there being any other options," I told them. My mom admitted to me the last time they came to visit they could tell that something was wrong because I wasn't happy. I couldn't believe it. They even saw something in my marriage that I couldn't see at the time.

Finally, my mom said, "Okay. We trust you, and we know that you will do what's best for your life. We will support you one hundred percent in whatever you decide."

As I stood there looking at my mom with a hopeful but sad smile on her face, I felt the weight of my impending divorce getting heavier in my heart. I also couldn't help but wonder if I was heading down the same path my parents took some fifteen years prior when they divorced while I was in college. Both my parents remarried to people who were a better fit than they were to each other. Even though no child wants to see their parents go through a divorce, it took a long time for me to see their happiness through their eyes.

Growing up, I've always been told that my mom, Rose, was my twin. I'm a spitting image of her—from the long blonde hair to our high-pitched laugh and sense of humor. My stepdad, Gabriel, a tall, heavy-set man with dark brown hair and chocolate brown eyes, brought out the best in my mom with his level-headed way of looking at the world and his fun sense of humor.

My dad, Wyatt, a tall herculean man with salt and pepper hair and chestnut eyes, had the spirit of an old cowboy who never went anywhere without his tan cowboy hat. He was never afraid of hard work and speaking his mind. He was also very loving, practical, and kind. He spoiled me like most fathers spoiled their daughters. At the same time, he instilled the importance of a strong work ethic which he always boasts that I got from him. He often let me ride on his backhoe growing up and watched him work on construction sites operating heavy equipment in and around Yosemite. They all played a role in molding and shaping me into the woman I had become. Deep down, I still wondered if I was making the right choice for my life.

———

THAT NIGHT at my birthday dinner, I did my best to put on a happy face, but in my heart, I was spending my birthday with the wrong person. I held back the tears while thinking about Jack. It was by far the worst birthday I ever had and not the way I wanted to spend my last birthday in my thirties. Even sitting at dinner, my stepdad tried to lighten the mood by complimenting me on how great of a cycling instructor I was and how proud he was of me.

Aaron looked at him and remarked rudely, "Well, at least somebody is getting something out of her because she's boring at home!" The comment upset my stepdad, but he held it together. I felt so hurt by his snide comment, but I knew it was just one more nail in the coffin of this marriage I planned on burying deep in the ground someday.

Later that evening, my stepdad told me in private how upset he was at Aaron for talking to me like that and that it wasn't okay for him to treat me like that. Deep down, I knew he was right, but I let him get away with it for so long. Over the years, even asking Aaron a question or seeking his help on something, it was met with a belittling comment. "What, are you stupid or something?" He would bark at me. "You have this thing in your pocket that's like a minicomputer called a cell phone. Just look it up and figure it out yourself. It's common sense."

Aaron consistently made jokes or snide comments at my expense, and before I knew it, I had lost my voice. But I was ready to take it back.

20

———————

H*ome. I'm going home.* The thought brought a spark of hope that I desperately hung onto. It was the week after my birthday. I decided to take Abbey's advice and visit home for a while. I needed to be with family, spend time with God in nature, and clear my head. It was exactly what the doctor ordered. My days were purposeful and filled with self-care. Meditating, praying, and taking long nature walks on my parent's property in the mountains. I let all that Yosemite had to offer, with its breathtaking towering mountains, beautiful snow, and luscious forest meadows, be the medicine for my life. It was the best time in Yosemite I had ever spent, and I absolutely needed it.

As my mom and I pulled up to the meadow in Yosemite Valley, we parked in front of the historic Yosemite Chapel on the valley floor. I got out of the car and put on my sweater in case the wind decided to kick up. The sky was a beautiful crystal blue, with the sun shining bright above us and nature in full bloom. I could still feel a slight chill in the air as the last of winter's snow still lay on the mountain tops in the higher elevations. We walked across the road to the vibrant green grassy meadow. I closed my eyes and just stood there in silence, letting nature give me a much-needed hug. My blood pressure slowly started to come down, and my breathing deepened. I filled my lungs with the fresh mountain air and finally felt at peace. I opened my eyes and looked around the beautiful meadow just below Yosemite Falls as a black and red hawk glided effortlessly across the sky.

I realized I was standing in the same place where my Native American ancestors lived some hundred-plus years ago and going through far worse trials than what I was experiencing now. The Southern Sierra Miwuk Nation was one of a handful of tribes that lived in Yosemite before it became a national park. I often heard stories growing up of my great-grandma and her relatives who fought for the land and their lives soon after gold was discovered in Yosemite. While many Native Americans lost their lives, my great-grandma and her family fought to live. She, along with her relatives, was forced to leave the only home they knew. Yet, they made it through. They survived. If they could survive, I could too. They were fighters, and so was I. I shared the same warrior blood running through my veins as them, and I seemed to have forgotten that. As I gazed up at the massive rocks towering above me, I realized that if God could create all of this and help my ancestors overcome the trials they faced, *He* could handle my situation. I also knew this life-changing moment would stay with me when I faced my upcoming trials back home.

After spending the day in Yosemite with my mom, I had lunch with my two aunts, who both happened to be named Victoria. I lovingly refer to them as my Aunt V's. Both my aunts were beautiful from the inside out. One of my Aunt

Victoria's was my dad's sister. She had long dark brown hair that always shined in the sun and piercing green eyes with hints of blue. Often, when visiting home, whether being in Yosemite or shopping in my hometown, people from the area could spot our resemblance and asked if I was related to her.

After learning she was my aunt, they lovingly shared stories about her growing up and how beautiful she was. My other Aunt Victoria was married to my uncle, but we remained close after they divorced. As far as I was concerned, she was the best thing to come out of that relationship. Even though we weren't related by blood, we also looked alike with our long blonde hair and our smile. I shared an unbreakable bond with both aunts. They'd been an intricate staple in my life since childhood, encouraging me as my parents went through their divorce and all through college. Time spent with them seemed to nourish my soul and they had the perfect advice I needed to hear. We were outside of Yosemite eating lunch. It was a beautiful sunny day with not a single cloud in the sky. I confided in them about what had been happening with my marriage. I could see the look of concern on their faces as they expressed how sorry they were for what I had been experiencing. They had lots of questions, and I did my best to answer them. Just then, my phone rang. A sudden tightness filled my chest as my muscles tensed up. It was Aaron calling. I decided not to answer it, which was out of the norm for me. I consistently answered his calls, but now I didn't care. I needed this time alone to think, so I let it go to voicemail. I put myself first for once.

After lunch, I stopped to chat some more with one of my Aunt V's. She lived in a refurbished country-chic barn house nestled in the countryside that looked like something out of

Town and Country Magazine. As she lay on the bed with her leg propped up, recovering from her leg surgery, I broke the news to her about Jack. She quietly listened as I spoke. I could tell she was deep in thought. I finally told her, "I don't know what to do about Aaron and my marriage." It was at that moment she asked me an unforgettable question.

"Do you miss him, honey?"

I answered, "Well, of course I do," and I added, "But I miss Jack more."

With love in her eyes, she gave me a big hug and said softly, "Well, I think you have your answer."

She was right; I needed to ask for a divorce, but I was terrified and had no idea what to expect from Aaron. I also was afraid of stepping into the unknown and being single for the first time in more than ten years.

That week, I felt myself getting stronger, more confident, and at peace with my decision to ask for a divorce. My chest was still a little tight from the stress. My heart felt heavy, but I needed to be honest with Aaron about my thoughts. I prayed during the last half of my drive back to the post. I also felt a newfound courage that I didn't have before. Even though it was only a week, I'd grown personally, emotionally, and spiritually. Having time to just think, be alone with my thoughts, and spend time with God gave me the confidence I needed with my decision. I had to stand my ground and not let Aaron sway me to his side or cast doubt on my feelings. What was in my heart was not wrong, and my feelings were valid. It was something I should have told myself a long time ago, but this time, I was stronger.

I walked into the door of my house as the tightness in my chest increased. Looking around the living room, I quickly picked up on the smell of salmon cooking in the kitchen. I looked in the kitchen and there was Aaron making dinner. He very rarely prepared dinner, so I was surprised to see that. Without saying a word, I started to help with dinner. I looked at him and said, "We need to talk," and walked into the living room. As he sat down, I could tell he knew what was coming. I don't know where it came from, but at the moment, I had so much peace. The words just flowed. For the first time since we got married, I was honest and transparent about our marriage.

"I love you, and I will always care about you, but it's not the same anymore." I sat there waiting for a response. I could see the tears building up in his eyes. The only time I had ever seen him cry was when his uncle died. I got up and sat on the couch next to him and gave him a big hug. "Everything is going to be okay," I told him with care, and I meant it. It just didn't look that way at that exact moment. Not saying a word, he got up from the couch and fell to his knees, sobbing in the hallway. There was nothing I could say to comfort him. For the first time in my life, I was honest with what I felt, and I wasn't ashamed. I wasn't going to hide it anymore. I knew that I deserved love and what I had experienced over the years wasn't love. At least, it wasn't the love that I wanted.

After less than a minute of crying, his military instincts kicked in. He got into sergeant mode and started to talk about dividing up the expenses. "I'm removing you from our joint cell phone plan," he said bluntly. Trying to persuade me to change my mind, he said, "You're going to have to pay for your own car insurance as well as your own cell phone plan." I didn't budge.

"Yes, I know, and I can handle it. I will be fine." I knew in the end this challenging season would make me stronger, but it was going to be tough for a while.

He confessed to me. "I knew when you started working at that brigade that you didn't want to be married to me anymore. You had changed, and you weren't the same person that I married."

He said it. The truth had finally come out. I realized that was why he wanted me to leave my job at the brigade and take orders elsewhere. He had seen a change in me that he didn't like. He wasn't wrong. I did change, but I changed for the better. I was growing personally and professionally. It was that growth that he found threatening. So, shortly after our conversation, I filed for divorce.

THAT SAME MONTH, Ryne notified the Public Affairs team that we were officially moving into a different office building after months of speculation and waiting. As he was talking to Ethan and me, he tried rather unsuccessfully to frame the move as an upgrade from where we were currently working.

"This building is much better than the one we are in now; with much more space…everyone will be much happier," Ryne said cheerfully. After hearing the news, my heart stopped. Moving buildings meant that I wouldn't be across from Jack's office anymore, which also meant moments of seeing him were cut down even more.

A feeling of dread washed over me. "Where is this building located?" I asked Ryne. He told me the building number.

"It's on the other end of the station," he stated.

"Where?" I asked him. I had no clue where this building

was located, and it might as well have been in the middle of a desert, but Ryne thought he had a great idea.

"How about we walk over to the building so we can see the space?" So, I, along with Ethan, Ryne, and a couple of my co-workers, made the trek across the post to see the new space.

Right as I walked through the rusty double doors and into the new space, I could see it was beyond outdated. A strong odor of muskiness hit me. The word "dungeon" popped into my mind. As I slowly walked through the building, I saw old pipes running throughout with small square windows at the top of the walls that reminded me of prison cell windows. Something about this building was very depressing, and I knew this was not a place I wanted to work. *I'm sorry, Jack, but your girl deserves better than this,* I thought to myself. As I was led to the open office space, I saw a sea of cubicles. This was my worst nightmare, especially as a writer. There's nothing more uninspiring than writing in a sad cubicle.

Ethan turned to me and said, "Lillian, let's take you to your space." I reluctantly followed him to my cubicle situated in the back of the room. "Oh, look, Lillian, you have half a window!" he said cheerfully. I quickly glanced at him and couldn't tell whether he was joking or serious. I realized that he was serious, like having half a window was a luxury I should be thankful for. I couldn't believe what I was facing. This was just another sign that God was closing the door to my job at the brigade.

As we strolled through the rest of the building, a feeling of dread hit me that I just couldn't shake off. After the tour, I ran into Sandi back in the office. She was sitting at her desk with her back facing the open door. She quickly whipped her head around when she heard me walking briskly down the hall.

"Hey, Lily! Did you see the new space?" I could tell from her voice that she was just as shocked as I was.

"Yes. There's just something about the building, Sandi, that I can't seem to shake off. Is it really creepy or is that just me?

Sandi leaned in close and whispered under her breath. "No, it's not you! I heard rumors that it was an old Army hospital that was built on an ancient Native American burial ground. Some of the people already working in the building said they experienced eerie things like chairs moving on their own and doors opening and closing . . ."

I confided in Sandi about my anxiety. "Sandi, I can't work in that building! Who wants to work in a building that's haunted?" The building was a walking OSHA violation, and I felt that working in a building that was haunted wasn't right and had to be some sort of health code issue.

"I know!" Sandi replied. "I was standing in the building next to my new desk talking to someone about it being haunted and rehashing some of the stories I heard when my tape recorder clicked on by itself and recorded my entire conversation."

The Native American in me kicked in. My intuition told me I needed to bless this building, and I needed to bless it fast. In the past, I'd blessed my apartment in college and even saw my grandma bless people with sage at Native American cere-monies. But blessing a building that was haunted was new territory for me. I told Sandi my idea.

"Yes, please come bless the building," she said pleadingly. So armed with my sage, I came the next day to bless my haunted office building. I waited until the end of the day when everyone was gone. I also knew I had to be quick in hopes of not setting off any fire alarms.

I started at my cubicle and opened my half window to let the bad energy out. I ignited the sage with my lighter when, out of thin air, a huge puff of black smoke combusted from the sage like a smoke bomb was set off. This was a first for me. Normally, when you light sage, you can hardly see the smoke. This was like a fire was set in the middle of my depressing office building that wouldn't be missed if it had burned down. I knew there was something in this building, and it didn't want me blessing it at all. I slowly walked the rooms with my sage stick, saying blessings of protection and peace for all the people in it. I even blessed Ethan's office, praying for him to just be a good boss and have peace. With each room I walked into with my sage, the more I could feel the space getting lighter. After I was done, I found Sandi in her cubicle. She decided to hang around for the show. "Okay, it's done," I told her.

"Thank you so much, Lillian!" she exclaimed. I decided working in this office was not for me. I needed to find another job before we moved into the haunted office building full-time.

21

Trapped with no way out. I endured an endless stream of berating from Ethan as things at work got more volatile. My life had turned into me walking on a very thin tightrope, knowing one wrong step could make things even worse. With my marriage falling apart and wanting so badly to turn to Jack for comfort or at least a listening ear, I felt more alone than ever. Going to work each day became increasingly difficult as I was a walking sea of emotions. I tried to hide my tears while sitting behind my laptop on the days I went into the office. Even though Jack was so close, his office was maybe a hundred yards away from mine; it felt like he was a thousand seas away from me and altogether out of reach.

On the days I was expected to work on-site, I found myself taking breaks and walking laps around the brigade to get some much-deserved fresh air and time to clear my head. Working on-site became something I dreaded because of my volatile boss, even though I was enjoying my new media pitching assignment. My work breaks seemed to bring unexpected surprises at the opportunity to see Jack once again. For me, these brief moments in time offered the chance to not feel so far away from him.

As I wandered throughout the station, I found myself mindlessly walking over to Jack's office building. His building had windows, but of course, nobody could look inside since they were too dark. I often wondered if one of those windows belonged to his office and if he could see me walking outside on my breaks. I reflected on the times I saw him walking to his car with my heart racing and trying not to stare at him too much. He left at the same time every day, so I knew that if I timed my breaks just right, I could catch him walking out to his car. Like clockwork, I saw Jack stroll out of his office building with his work binder in hand. He looked over at me and gave me that same subtle head nod and a hopeful smile. He got into his car and drove away.

What is wrong with me? I scolded myself once again. This man had me behaving in ways that were not normal for me. But I also felt happiness in a new way, even if those moments were quick and as evanescent as a beautiful rainbow.

That month, another Army brigade on the East Coast experienced an unexpected emergency, with their colonel having to temporarily step away from his duties. Jack decided to fill his role while he was away to help the colonel out. Sitting at my computer filling out paperwork to get approval for one of our articles, Ethan walked into my office.

He proceeded to update me on how Jack had been doing since he temporarily left our brigade for the East Coast. "Colonel Cooper doesn't have the same support he has here," Ethan explained bluntly with a smirk on his face. "I guess their public affairs team is run differently than ours, and they're more hands-off with their colonel."

A wave of concern hit me, and I felt worried for Jack. "What? Is he okay?" A look of bewilderment flashed across Ethan's face like I was speaking a foreign language.

"How am I supposed to know?" he spat out. I couldn't believe it. Was I the only one who cared how Jack was doing?

"Well, what does he need? How can I support him?" I asked with concern.

Ethan commented, "He does need someone to write his talking points for their Memorial Day Ceremony."

I quickly volunteered. "No problem, I can do that."

I gladly wrote his speech for their brigade's Memorial Day ceremony. At the end of the day, I met up for dinner with Audrey to tell her what happened. "Audrey! You wouldn't believe the look on Ethan's face. It never occurred to him to see how Jack was doing and if he was okay since he left for his trip . . ."

Audrey started to laugh. "Lily, you can't show that you care too much about Jack, or it's going to look too obvious that you're in love with him." I knew she was right. My feelings for Jack were starting to show, and I didn't know how much longer I could hide the fact that my care for him ran much deeper than making sure he had his talking points for upcoming events or that I was performing well at my job. Could Jack's trip and this time away from our brigade shift things between us? I couldn't help but wonder if the tide would turn and we would head in a new, unexpected direction.

Summer 2021

22

———

Like a bright red hermit crab on a white sandy beach leaving its shell behind and finding another one to grow in, I moved out of my house on post. For the first time in almost fifteen years, I was living on my own. Leaving my Army life behind. I rented a room from Aiden, a fifty-some-thing-year-old doctor with sensitive brown eyes and light black hair who was also going through a divorce. He was a father of four living in a beautiful two-story home in mid-town with three grown kids and one daughter graduating from high school. It was scary leaving my military way of life behind and venturing into uncharted territory. Living on an Army post was a huge part of my adult life. I felt somewhat sheltered as I learned new things all over again, like a little girl learning to ride her bike with training wheels. Aiden had a lot of patience with me and welcomed me into his home with open arms. He literally hugged me the first time I walked through his front door.

He looked at me with a caring smile and said in a calm voice, "It's going to be okay." I smiled back at him. Even though my situation looked rather bleak, I tried to keep my faith, knowing he was right.

As we talked, my mom and stepdad were busy outside unpacking the contents of my life in cardboard boxes from their truck to bring into my new home. My mom and stepdad were worried about me living on my own after almost fifteen years and in a home with someone who, in their eyes, was a stranger. I did my best to reassure them that everything was working out. I went back outside to help them with moving boxes.

"I don't know about this, honey; you don't even know him," my mom said with uncertainty.

"Mom, it's going to be okay, trust me. I even met him and his daughter before I agreed to move in, and I have a good feeling about this. If I didn't have a good feeling, I wouldn't be moving in."

As I carried boxes into my new room, my new hallmate Rafaela popped her head into my room. She was a nurse who was also renting a room from Aiden. Rafaela was taller than me, with light brown hair that hung loosely around her face and emerald, green eyes. Her soft voice reflected her gentle and caring spirit.

"Hi, I'm Rafaela. Welcome!" she said cheerfully and gave me a big hug. "This is the start of new beginnings for you. You know that, right?" I smiled at her.

"I do, yes. Scary but exciting as well."

She replied, "It's going to be fine. Aiden is great, and I've had nothing but great experiences since I moved in. I'm sure it will be the same for you."

I was still feeling a little nervous since this entire experience was outside of my comfort zone. At the same time, I was also at peace with where God had me at that stage in my life. I was adventuring into uncharted territory, finding support from strangers and a loving family in a way that I never had before.

A week later, Rafaela had the idea of us going out to dinner downtown. I was beyond excited for the opportunity to dress up, go out, and get away from my problems. We parked downtown and got out of the car. Rafaela spotted a friend across the street whom she used to work with at the hospital. We started walking across the street when I felt something sticky like I had stepped on a piece of gum. I looked down at my wedge sandal, and the sole had come right off! I stood there in the middle of the street, stunned at what had just happened. I called out to Rafela.

"Rafaela! The sole of my shoe just came off!" She turned around and looked at my shoe.

"Oh, my goodness! Are you okay?"

"Yes, just let me make it across the street." So, I hobbled across the street minus one sole. I didn't even make it across when the sole from my second shoe came off. "Oh my gosh! What is happening?" I said to Rafaela, dumbfounded. "What are the odds that the soles from both my shoes come right off seconds apart?" Rafaela looked down at my wedges that mysteriously turned into sandals.

Analyzing the situation, Rafaela exclaimed, "I think the universe is trying to tell you something. Literally off with the old and on with the new!"

I stared down at my feet and knew she was right. Aaron bought me those shoes years ago. It was almost as if God was telling me to let go of my past and make room for new things in my future. My soul was literally purging…starting with my shoes. Meantime, Rafaela's friend observed all of this taking place.

"Are you okay? Do you need shoes?" I looked at him, thoroughly embarrassed.

"No, I think I may have an extra pair of shoes in the trunk of my car."

He pointed out, "Okay, because my girlfriend and I live up the street, and she has shoes you can borrow."

I replied, "That's nice of you, but I will be okay."

The man extended his hand out. "Oh, I forgot to introduce myself. My name is Jack. It's nice to meet you." I froze. Wow, of all names for this guy to have, I thought to myself. It dawned on me. Maybe Rafaela was right. Maybe God was trying to send me a message to let go of the old and welcome the new, and maybe that new also included Jack.

———

THE BUTTERFLIES WERE BACK ONCE AGAIN. A few weeks later, I attended another All-Hands event at work. That same fluttery feeling formed in the pit of my stomach about seeing Jack once again, but also excited since I only saw him a couple of times each month. In my mind, it never seemed like enough time. Since I helped draft the script for this event and had to deliver the talking points, I was expected to attend. All the while, I couldn't stop thinking about what had happened a few weeks prior with my roommate and all the other unusual signs that seemed to be pointing back to Jack. I walked into the auditorium wearing a beautiful crisp white button-up t-shirt dress that was cut slightly above the knee, accented with a dainty brown and gold belt at the waist. I styled the dress with my tan Valentino kitten bow heels. Before, I was afraid to wear the beautiful high heels. It was almost as if I was waiting for some special occasion to wear them, like Cinderella wearing her glass slippers to the ball. I was beginning to feel like a completely new person, seeing myself in a different light. My inner confidence was starting to break through like a beautiful pink wildflower growing under concrete and finally pushing itself to the surface.

I walked in through the double doors of the auditorium holding the talking points for the senior leaders, all the while feeling butterflies fluttering around in my stomach. Walking down the aisle, I casually strolled past where Jack was standing only a few feet away from me. He glanced at me and quickly did a double-take. I had no idea what was going through his mind but a look of shock came across his face. I did my best to keep my composure and not giggle. After delivering the talking points, I turned around and took my seat in the back of the auditorium as Jack's eyes followed my every move. This caught the attention of Ryne, who got up from his seat in the front where he usually sat and walked to the back of the audi-torium. He conveniently sat in the seat right behind me. As the event started and Jack addressed the audience, I had the biggest smile on my face while looking at him without even giving a second thought to Ryne sitting right behind me. I could feel his presence lurking like a teacher keeping a sharp eye on his troublemaker pupil. I was sure it was hard for Jack not to smile back at me, but in his usual military way, he kept focused on the talking points at hand. But I knew I was on his mind. Ethan even told me prior to the event that Jack was in a bad mood, almost like a forewarning. If he was in a bad mood, I certainly didn't notice.

After the event concluded, I walked up to the podium to fetch the binder with the talking points to take back to my office. As I started to walk back up the aisle, I could see out of the corner of my eye that Jack was following closely behind me. I stepped outside and stopped to grab my sunglasses out of my purse. I looked across the parking lot and spotted Jack. He had stopped walking and was staring right at me. The world stopped moving. We stood there in the middle of the blacktop, absolutely paralyzed, our eyes locked on one another. My concerns and worries floated away. We were in our own private world once again. Nobody else existed but him and I. I realized that what was growing between us was so much bigger than just us. I was his forbidden fruit that he could never have, and he was my prince, my Sir Lancelot—that I also could never have. I'm sure when he decided to take orders at this brigade he never expected to meet this beautiful woman who stole his heart. I also never expected, when I took this job with the military, to meet this amazing man who perfectly captured what I wanted in a partner but didn't think I was good enough to have.

Suddenly, it became perfectly clear: I knew everything in my life had led me up to the moment I met Jack. He changed my world forever. Almost as if the clock struck midnight, our private bubble was popped by my co-worker Sandi. She came walking up behind me and had no clue what was happening between Jack and me.

"Lily, I didn't see you in the audience!" I quickly snapped out of my trance and looked behind me to see Sandi approaching. I glanced back over at Jack as he quickly turned his head and kept walking towards his office. We were back in the real world once again.

As I settled into my new single life, I found myself not watching TV very much but doing a lot more reading and meditating. It was just what the doctor ordered for this period in my life and was very soothing for my soul. One day, I was sitting on my couch reading a novel called *American Wife* and texting with my sister-in-law, Breanna. She was a petit woman with honey blonde hair, emerald green eyes, and a warm smile. As I explained what the book was about—a woman who winds up marrying a boy from her childhood who eventually becomes the President of the United States—Breanna told me about her love for period novels. She shared how her attraction to World War II stories must be a key that she lived during that period in a past life. I felt the strong urge to share the 1960s song that seemed to be a staple in my life and reminded me of Jack.

I had mentioned that I felt the same way as her, and as I sent her the song, I said, "I don't know why, but there's this beautiful love song that I've never heard before in my life, and yet, I know this song very well. It's very important to me."

After Breanna listened to the song, she commented, "Wow. This is a beautiful love song. It reminds me of when I used to listen to Frank Sinatra on my boombox as a child. I loved his music." It hit me. I realized from the dream I had the night before my birthday why Jack had mentioned Frank Sinatra: Frank Sinatra was known for love songs. I knew God was helping me to put the puzzle pieces together and using my family members to help. It was all starting to crystallize. I smiled at this thought and reflected,

"I know, Breanna, it is a beautiful love song. I couldn't agree with you more."

About a month into living in my new place and still

working remotely part of the time, I went to work for our weekly writers meeting to review our assignments for the next couple of weeks with my co-workers and my boss, Ethan.

The meetings currently had become boring, like watching paint dry, especially because I wasn't writing articles anymore. I was tuned out to what he was saying, especially since I wasn't doing any writing and had taken on a more active role in media pitching.

As I sat at the table with my co-workers, gazing off into the distance, suddenly, a demanding voice popped into my head: *Volunteer to do the talking points! Volunteer to do the talking points!* I practically jumped out of my seat. *Where was this voice coming from, and what talking points?* I thought to myself, totally confused. I looked at the list of assignments on the spreadsheet, and there was nothing mentioned about talking points. Without warning, Ethan said, "So the Pride Event is next week. Who wants to volunteer to do the talking points?"

Intuitively, I shot my hand up in the air. "'I'll do them!" I practically shouted. I didn't know why, but something told me that I had to write the talking points for this event. Regardless, I listened to the voice ordering me to write them, like a military officer giving an order to one of her troops. Later that afternoon, Ethan emailed me the details of the event, including the person giving the talking points. I smiled when I saw that Jack was going to be speaking at the event and that I was writing his talking points. Just then, it all made sense why the universe was so insistent upon me writing them. It was another opportunity to see him. As I soon discovered that little voice inside me was growing and wasn't so little anymore. I was learning to let go and trust

God that I wasn't alone on this journey. I was being guided all along.

After writing Jack's talking points for the Pride event, I drove to the auditorium focused on the assignment at hand, trying my best not to get distracted by Jack's presence. I spent an entire day writing the speech, which included highlighting the brigade's importance of being open to diversity. The speech also shared how listening and learning from gay and lesbian servicemembers benefits the Army. While getting out of the car, the sun was shining bright with only a few white clouds in sight. I walked up to the auditorium with a little bit of excitement in my heart at being able to see him once again. I entered the room, and he was already there, getting himself organized before the event started. I set my purse down in the auditorium and walked up to Jack.

"Hi! I have your talking points for today's event."

He looked at me and smiled. "Thank you, I appreciate you." A big grin formed across my face as I felt myself utterly present in the moment. I turned around and sat in the back of the auditorium, waiting for the event to start. My mind wandered to Jack, reflecting on our conversation. He never hesitated to say thank you anytime I wrote his speeches. I loved it when he said that because it's not very often that you're shown appreciation for the work you do, especially by the military. I noticed this was a trait that he had in common with the President, whom I was lucky enough to meet and spend time with while my husband and I were stationed on the East Coast. The President often took the time to thank everyone for their work, no matter how small the task.

One day, the President noticed a man raking up leaves outside. My husband observed him going out of his way to tell this man thank you for his hard work. Realizing this shared characteristic between two very powerful and special men, I smiled at Jack and took my seat in the middle of the auditorium, waiting for the event to start. As the technical director went up to the podium, Jack sat in the front row with his back to me. As I gazed down at him, it was almost as if he could *feel* me looking at him. Jack quickly turned around in his seat and stared directly at me. He did it several times. I felt myself stop mid-breath as my heart raced. At one point, I wanted to quietly mouth to him, "You need to turn around," but I was secretly flattered.

After the technical director finished speaking and went back to his seat, Jack walked up to the podium with his talking points ready to give his speech. As he spoke, I noticed he didn't veer too much from his talking points this time, which made me happy because I was particularly proud of this speech. My younger stepbrother Isaac was gay, so I had a personal tie-in with this topic. For me, letting Isaac know that he was loved no matter what was very important. As Jack gave his speech, there was one line in particular that I was proud of, and he delivered it perfectly.

"You shouldn't have to hide who you love to serve the country that you love."

It made my heart melt, and he said it with such care in his voice that I knew he really meant it. Diversity and inclusion were very important to Jack, going as far as implementing special emphasis groups at our brigade and reading books on the subject. I admired how that was one of the foundational pillars of his career with the brigade. Like a fascinating jewel, it was one of the many facets that made him not just a great person but an amazing leader.

After he was done giving his speech, Jack stepped off the stage, and instead of returning to his seat, he walked toward the back of the room where I was sitting. I sat there completely paralyzed with my heart racing.

What is he doing? Watching him out of the corner of my eye, I caught sight of a small smile. He then turned and walked past me as he made his way back to his seat in the front row. Something told me that was his subtle way of letting me know that he was thinking about me.

23

———

The post looked slightly different. There was a flurry of excitement in the air that broke up the humdrum of day-to-day job duties. Everyone at work was talking about the brigade's yearly anniversary coming up in June. Our team lined up daily events leading up to the big 5K run taking place on-site. I planned on participating in the run since I worked out just about every day as a fitness instructor. I was also excited about the opportunity since I had never participated in a 5K run before. Last minute, Sandi asked for my assistance holding the finish line ribbon and other administrative tasks for the run, which meant that I couldn't participate.

"Are you sure you're okay with this?" she asked me as we stood in her office discussing the logistics of the event.

"Of course, it's fine! Don't worry," I assured her. Again, I didn't mind helping out where I was needed.

On the day of the race, everyone chatted as they waited in front of the main building for the race to start. I was getting the ribbon ready with Sandi, when out came Jack. This was the second time that I had seen him not wearing his military uniform and in civilian clothes. I could tell everyone was surprised as well. He was wearing jeans with sneakers and a light blue and white French placket button-up shirt. He walked over to someone standing on the side of the group and was making small talk. I couldn't help but notice I was in his line of vision as I stood in the middle of the crowd. His eyes were fixated on me, and I was trying my best not to look over at him and smile.

Since it was getting close to race time, everyone was waiting in the middle of the road, getting ready to take off. Jack walked over and stood by the crowd only a few feet away. Everyone took off and started running, and I stood on the sidelines waiting for my cue to hold up the finish line ribbon. I looked over to my left and saw Jack standing close to me. We were both trying not to stare at each other. I was so flustered that my mind went blank. Again, I had no clue what to say, so I said the first thing that popped into my head.

"So why aren't you participating in the race?" I said jokingly to him. He looked down at the ground and then down at me.

"Well, why aren't you participating in the race?" he asked.

I remarked, "I taught my cycle class last night."

He said, "Oh, so this is your break day?"

I responded honestly. "No, I work out just about every day, so I don't really take break days."

"Oh," he replied.

Silence filled the air, so I did my best to continue the conversation with the shy colonel. "So…where do you work out?" I asked him.

"Life Time," he stated.

I smiled at him and said, "You should work out at my cycle studio; it's better," referring to the gym I taught at.

He said, "My sister works out at a cycle studio, but I do much better with someone telling me what to do, like working out with a personal trainer."

Without missing a beat, I replied, "You should come to my cycle class—I'll tell you what to do . . ."

He looked at me and remarked, "I know how to work the resistance knob."

I started to giggle. He was so adorable. "Well, that's good!" I said encouragingly. Without thinking, I gave him the details of my cycle class. "I teach Saturday mornings at nine-thirty a.m. at the cycle studio across from post. You should come…I promise not to pick on you too much." I was absolutely horrified. I couldn't believe what just came out of my mouth. Once again, awkward silence filled the air, and the conversation dropped. It was so obvious that I made him nervous. A flustered look flashed across Jack's face as he quickly turned his body to the side facing away from me.

Out of the corner of my eye, I noticed that he had a bandage on his elbow with a cut that looked like he had fallen.

"Oh, my gosh! What happened to your elbow?" I reached over with care as I gently touched his elbow.

"Oh, nothing. I just hurt it, but I'll be fine," he replied. I realized I had my hand on his arm once again.

I looked up at him and smiled. "You should put some tea tree oil on it. It helps with healing."

He looked at me and gave me a pleasant smile. "Thank you for the advice. I really appreciate it." Getting lost in the moment, I realized that I still had my hand on his arm.

Without warning, the runners came around the corner,

and it was time for me to do my job. I made myself walk away from Jack as I held up the ribbon with Sandi holding the other end, and the winners crossed the finish line. Jack congratulated the winners, and everyone posed for a group photo in front of the flagpole. I noticed he had a big smile on his face. He was so happy and proud of his brigade. I said my goodbyes to everyone, and Sandi thanked me for my help. As I left the event, I took in the conversation I had with Jack. *I can't believe I invited him to my cycle class!* I thought as a wave of dizziness hit me out of nowhere. I called Julia and told her what happened.

"Well, maybe you'll be in for a real surprise when he actually does show up to your cycle class, and you guys can finally have some alone time together. You can talk and tell him that you're getting divorced." Jack had no idea what had been happening in my life since the only time we seemed to see each other was during work events.

"Oh, I don't know Julia. He seemed pretty uncomfortable when I brought up my cycle class," I said helplessly.

"You never know!" Julia said in a cheerful voice. "He just may surprise you." Deep down, I was secretly hoping that she was right.

Later that month, we had our All-Hands event that I planned on attending in person. I helped write and gather the talking points for the speakers who were handing out awards recognizing the brigade's outstanding employees. So once again, I was required to print them off, have them in binders, and deliver them to the auditorium. But something unexpected happened the night before the event that at the time made absolutely no sense.

As I went to bed and fell asleep, I had a dream that was so

vivid and real. I was standing in the hallway of a house, wearing a brown corduroy dress. I automatically knew this was out of character for me because I don't wear brown, and I don't wear corduroy. I touched my stomach, and I was pregnant. Something told me I was having a boy and that it was Jack's baby. Just like watching a movie, in the next scene, I was sitting on a couch that was very low to the ground, which told me I must have been in a TV room in my home. I was folding laundry from a bright green vintage laundry basket with daisy cutouts. I was watching Elvis perform on TV. The program was in black and white. I woke up from my dream. Rubbing my eyes, I was trying to make sense of the dream I just had. It made no sense at all. I figured it was just one of many unusual experiences I've had since this man came into my life and I wondered if there was more to this dream than I realized.

24

It was hot and balmy, with the summer sun sweltering down day after day. It was triple digits today. I desperately was looking for an escape to get my mind off the sizzling Arizona sun, where I wouldn't be shocked to see an egg being cooked on the sidewalk. I figured Emilia was just the ticket. She was the first friend I made after my divorce from Aaron. After hearing my sad divorce story one day after my cycle class, she took me under her wing. Emilia's free-spirited personality taught me how to adventure outside of my comfort zone. Her beautiful dark blonde hair perfectly complemented her chocolate brown eyes, which had a glow of happiness behind them. She lived in the next town over about twenty minutes outside of post—a popular getaway spot nestled up in the mountains surrounded by fun mom-and-pop stores and scenic places to hike.

On this particular day, we stopped by a crystal shop. Anything sparkling and shiny was right up my alley, and this store was no exception. Walking around and touching all the beautiful multi-colored stones and reading about what they meant sparked my curiosity. The stones were displayed in beautiful gray marble bowls on an oak table situated in the middle of the store. Running my fingers over the stones, a cluster of rose-pink stones caught my eye. I reached down and picked up the tiny, beautiful stone and placed it in the palm of my hand. I carefully outlined the rough edges of the rose stone with my fingers. Standing behind the counter was a young guy in his late twenties named Dominic. For some reason, he and I just hit it off right away. We bonded over sharing about our recent break-ups. I looked down at his business card, which read *Certified Hypnotherapist and Past Life Regression.*

"Oh, interesting…what is that?" I asked him.

"It's a great way to really learn about yourself. For example, like any physical ailments and the reasons for them," he explained. "Or even deep connections you may feel with certain places. I pretty much put you in a hypnotic state to learn more about what you carried into this life."

I was intrigued. "I've never heard of that, but it sounds interesting!" I said.

I took his business card and gave him my phone number. He also expressed interest in working out more, so I invited him to my cycle class. "I'm having a theme ride next Thursday. You should come!"

Excited, he expressed, "That sounds great. Thanks for inviting me! I may take you up on that offer."

Emilia walked up to the counter and wasn't too impressed with the stones by the look on her face and was ready to go, so we said our goodbyes and left the store. Thursday came, and as I was getting ready for my class, I noticed that Dominic wasn't there. *Oh well, maybe he had something come up,* I thought to myself. The next day, I got a text message from Dominic.

He had a falling out with his roommate and was moving back to South Carolina. Before he left, he wanted to know if I was interested in meeting up at the local park in town and having a session with him. I was a little skeptical, but my curiosity was peaked so I agreed to meet him.

Sitting down on a soft pink furry blanket under a large green tree in the middle of a park, Dominic and I talked about his next move back home to the East Coast. Then, he gave me an overview of the session and what to expect. He asked me if there was anything specifically I wanted to know. I wasn't really sure since this was something new to me, which he said was okay. He instructed me to lie down and close my eyes. As I lay on the plush pink blanket in the middle of the park, he took me through a series of exercises to relax me and clear my mind. At one point, I saw myself lying in a field of grass surrounded by beautiful trees and a creek.

"I want you to imagine there's a huge movie screen in front of you, and it's playing all of your thoughts. Just let them run through and let me know when the screen is clear," Dominic instructed me. I saw thoughts about my insecurities playing in front of me, my fears and miscellaneous things happening in my life, things to do at work and at home. I let them all run their course until the screen was blank.

"The screen is blank," I informed him. I was instantly thoroughly relaxed. He said to imagine that I was at the top of a set of stairs. As I started to descend down the stairs, I felt even more relaxed. He took me down step by step; I felt very much at peace. My heart rate and breathing had slowed down, almost like I could fall asleep, but I was very much awake.

After I stepped down the stairs, he had me go back to various stages of my life. "I want you to imagine yourself as a teenager and tell me what you see." Unexpectedly, I saw myself sitting at a kitchen table with my mom and brother. We were eating pancakes and getting ready to catch the school bus and go to school. After explaining to him what I was seeing, he took me back even further in time.

"I want you to now imagine that you're a toddler and tell me what you see." As I looked around, I realized I was at my grandpa's house in Florida, standing in a glass gazebo with an indoor pool. Dominic took me back to when I was in my mother's womb, and a feeling of warmth and tingles traveled throughout my body, and I felt perfectly safe.

Finally, he said, "I want you to imagine you're standing in front of a door, and this door is a time machine, and once you step into that door and push the button, it's going to take you back before conception." I saw a beautiful brown door with a gold knob. I opened the door, walked inside, turned around, and saw buttons on the side. I pushed one of the buttons, and before I knew it, the door opened, and I stepped out.

Dominic said that there was a mirror in front of me and that I should describe what I was wearing. I looked in the mirror, and I was wearing a Pepto-Bismol pink-colored baby doll dress with pink ballerina flats and a pink hair band. The hairband stood out because I vaguely remember seeing something like it during my childhood years, but something told me it was much older. It was thick and ran across the top of my head.

As I described to Dominic what I was wearing, he asked, "What era are your clothes from?" I wasn't really sure, but I got the feeling it was the 1950s or 1960s. He asked me to look around and describe where I was. I looked around and was standing in the front yard of a neighborhood, but the lawns stood out. They were pristine and perfect. Not a blade of grass nor a leaf from the hedges were out of place. No cars were in the driveways, and all the homes looked the same.

As I described to Dominic where I was, he asked, "Are one of these homes yours?"

I noted. "Yes, I think so." He instructed me to find my home. I turned around and saw a beautiful white home with an attached garage. There were three cobblestone steps with an iron railing leading up to the front door. The door was also white and had three small square windows at the top. "I found my home," I told Dominic.

He stated, "I want you to walk inside."

As I slowly walked up the steps and opened the door. I looked in the house, and the first thing that stood out was the brown living room furniture with clear plastic covers. This made me giggle because this was something new to me. I looked across the living room and saw the dining room with a light fixture that told me it was vintage and not modern. Dominic asked me who was in the house. I looked in the kitchen and saw Jack standing there. Dominic instructed me to walk up to him. At first glance, I noticed he was wearing brown polyester pants and a nice tan polo shirt. His blonde hair was combed neatly to the side. He looked so nice. I remember walking up to him and giving him a big hug. I realized how much I really missed him.

Dominic said that he was going to ask me a series of questions that he wanted me to ask Jack, and I said okay. "I want you to ask Jack what he does for a living." As I asked the question to Jack, the words "construction" and "engineering" kept flashing in my mind; I said I think he does something with construction and engineering. He had me ask Jack what I did for a living. Before I could even ask the question, an image of a children's book flashed in my mind—it was green and yellow with a dinosaur on the cover. When I asked Jack the question, he said I was a children's author, and I wrote children's books. Dominic had me ask Jack if we were married, and he said yes, we were married.

Dominic continued with his questioning. "I want you to ask Jack if he has any wise words or advice that he wants to tell you."

Jack commented softly, "I love you, and I will be with you. Just know that everything is going to be okay."

At the time, I wanted to believe him, but it was just so hard. It seemed like the odds were stacked so high against us. Dominic asked me if anyone else was in the house. Suddenly, I heard what sounded like kids playing down the hall, and I didn't even hesitate. I just knew.

"Yes, we have two boys. They're ten and twelve years old." He asked me what year it was, and without missing a beat, I said, "It's 1967."

For his last question, Dominic softly asked, "Do you know where you live?"

Out of nowhere, I found myself stating, "We live in Monterey." As I stood there with Jack in the middle of our kitchen, looking into his soulful blue eyes filled with trust and love, I knew that he really loved me. But then Dominic said it was time to go. I gave Jack a big hug and started to cry. I didn't want to leave him. I felt so much happiness and love in that house, but I also knew that I didn't belong there anymore.

As Dominic gently brought me back from my trip in time, I opened my eyes and looked up at the large green tree I was lying under in the middle of the park. As I focused on the tree and the white dainty flowers growing on the tree, I noticed they looked 3-D, almost like I could reach up and touch them. I slowly sat up and looked across the park. The grass was a bright, vibrant green. I gazed up at the sky, and it was a beautiful bright blue. It was almost like someone had turned this invisible knob from low to super high, and it magnified the colors in my world. Rubbing my eyes, I was shocked. "What is going on, Dominic? Everything is super bright!"

He looked at me and smiled. "Sometimes that happens when someone has a very intense experience like you just had. It will alter how you see things." I sat there trying to comprehend what had just happened. I saw the cars driving by and the birds flying in the sky. I couldn't get over how clear they were. I also felt peace in a way that I never felt before in my life. This lasted only a few minutes, and it went away. Everything was back to normal.

Talking with Dominic after the session, he said most people need healing from their past lives, and sometimes they will bring their past pains into this life, but in my case, he said I had a beautiful life with a loving family. I didn't need any healing. I couldn't believe what I had just experienced. Trying to let all the details sink in from my trip back in time, I remembered my dream from the month before, where I saw myself pregnant, folding laundry in the TV room, and watching Elvis perform on TV. I realized that must have been a past life memory, a snapshot in time.

I also remembered a moment when I was meditating at home. My mind was clear, and I was not thinking of a single thing when I saw a fog…and Jack walking out with two boys. I was entirely confused at the time because I thought maybe he had kids, but I wasn't sure. I noticed the boys were very young, around five years of age or a little older. The one boy he was holding was wearing all white and was sleeping in his arms. I remember thinking white is not a good color for a little boy to wear in case he gets stains. The other boy, on the other hand, was standing next to Jack, holding his hand. The little boy was wearing a red and white nautical shirt that reminded me of the Cracker Jack Boy. Like watching a movie, I saw myself walk up to Jack, and he handed me the little sleeping boy. I tried to think about something else, but my mind didn't want to change the channel.

I remember feeling so confused, wondering where this vision had come from. *Was this something I was hoping for in my future? Did Jack have kids in real life?* After my session with Dominic, it dawned on me that what I could have seen that day in my vision was our kids from this past life we shared together.

After my session with Dominic, we sat in my car and chatted while I drove him back to his hotel. In the car, I had mentioned the 1960s song that reminded me so heavily of Jack. I told him that I knew the words, and yet I had never heard the song in my life. Something told me to look at when the song came out. That was when I pulled the song up on my phone and saw that it came out in 1966, which happened to line up with the vision I had in my session earlier that afternoon. As we both sat in silence, I played the song for him, almost as if we were both taking in the lyrics.

After the song ended, he finally spoke. "Wow, that is a beautiful song, and it's very powerful too." I agreed with him. As we pulled into the parking lot of the hotel, I gave him a big hug and thanked him for everything. "I didn't do anything; you did it all," he said with a smile.

Later that evening, I drove to pick up Emilia since we had plans to go wine tasting at a small winery nestled in the beautiful countryside just outside of town. As we sat in the back patio with a wine glass in our hands, I told her about my session. She was amazed.

"Oh my gosh, Lily, that's crazy . . ."

"I know, it really is," I reflected.

"So, what are you going to do?" She asked me.

"What do you mean? There is nothing for me to do. I can't live in the past; I have to live in the present, so all I can do is just wait and see what happens."

She responded. "I mean, yeah, I get that, but it's not every day that people learn about a past life they had, let alone meet the person that they shared that life with."

She was absolutely right. I got to peek behind the curtain of what I had once before with Jack. Part of me wished that I could relive that life again. It was the love and support that I had longed for in my marriage but never had. I then remembered something Aaron told me during one of our arguments toward the end of our marriage that really upset me. In the middle of our living room, he was grilling me on what he called my "unrealistic expectations of a spouse." His angry voice cut deep as he taunted, "Life isn't a Hallmark movie. Not everyone gets their happily ever after." Now, here I was, lucky enough to get a glimpse of my happily ever after. I had it once before, and my heart longed to have it again.

In the midst of our conversation, Emilia got up to use the restroom. I walked around the vineyard, taking in the sights. I gently touched the grapes hanging on the vines as I enjoyed the beautiful evening with soft music playing in the background. Suddenly, that same 1960s song started playing throughout the vineyard. I stood there, unable to move a muscle. I noticed there were no words but just the melody playing. As my mind was trying to make sense of this, a group of people sitting at a picnic table next to me recognized the song.

One woman sitting at the table said, "Oh, I know this song!" She started to sing the song, and the rest of the people sitting at her table joined her and started to sing. My mind went blank. Tears started to build up in my eyes. I felt God was validating that the experience I had with Dominic was, in fact, real and that I was on the right path. As Emilia came back from the bathroom, I kept the experience to myself.

After the wine tasting, I dropped off Emilia and headed back home. On my drive back home, Dominic called me.

"Hi, Lily, it's Dominic."

"Hey, Dominic. What's going on?"

He started to speak. "Well, you remember that song that you just played for me in the car earlier?"

"Yeah, what about it?" I asked him.

He confessed. "Well, I didn't want to tell you this before, but that was my roommate's favorite song."

"Really? Of all songs?" I asked.

"Yes!" he exclaimed. "I think I was meant to help you."

I agreed. "I think you're right."

25

———

My face beamed with excitement. Sitting at my desk and looking at my inbox, my eyes began to grow wide and glow. I could have easily run a victory lap around post. Positive responses were rolling in from the articles I was pitching to the media about my brigade. They were getting published left and right, which meant Ethan was happy for the moment and not hyper-focused on my every move.

In addition to pitching our articles to the media, I also had the opportunity to get involved with our brigade's American Indian heritage group. Since I'm part Native American from Yosemite, the fact that I was able to get involved with my Native American heritage at my work and be a part of this group was a very big deal. I also thought it was another great way to be involved with the brigade. For my role in the group, I was asked to help organize my brigade's annual American Indian heritage event, but this also meant going outside of my lane—something that wasn't very welcomed by the military. I wondered in the back of my mind if my new role would have dire consequences.

I happily walked into the front office for my first meeting with the American Indian heritage group, thoroughly excited about sharing my family history, including my involvement with my Native American heritage growing up. Since my grandma taught me tribal dancing, I occasionally performed at my hometown's Heritage Day parades. Once I started freelancing in high school, I wrote articles covering my tribe's activities for our hometown newspaper. One of the leaders of our group happened to be a senior leader of the brigade: Noah, a civilian. He was a short, balding man with a happy-go-lucky personality and a big dimple smile. Surprisingly, he and I got along very well. He was also excited to be taking on a new role as part of the group.

Since I was emailing our group about solidifying the details for our event, including the location and the guest speakers coming to post, this involved coordinating with our public affairs office. Since Ryne was the senior public affairs officer, he was looped in on the email. Sitting at my desk one day, I was working with one of our graphic designers to create the tribal flyer for the event, and I saw an email from Ryne pop into my inbox. Normally he doesn't email me and usually goes through Ethan. A pit formed in my stomach. I nervously opened the email as Ryne stated bluntly that I was not allowed to talk to Noah—I had to go through him, Ryne, first. My eyes remained fixated on the email as I felt my face grow hot. *What? I had no idea I was doing anything wrong!* I angrily thought to myself. Seeing this as his way to control me, I confided in Sandi about the situation and vented my frustration.

"How am I supposed to coordinate an event if I have to go

through him to talk to anyone who's part of this group?" Sandi nodded in agreement.

"I agree with you—this just doesn't work." She had a suggestion. "Why don't you explain to Ryne that you're part of this group? Maybe he doesn't know . . ."

I didn't think much of it, but maybe she was right. I responded to Ryne's email explaining to him my involvement with the American Indian heritage group. He shot back a rude email. "Yes, I know, but if anyone should know about following the chain of command, it's you." I knew he was referencing me being a former spouse to an active-duty soldier.

Responding to his degrading comment was pointless. I had to let it go. I was on his radar—that much was obvious—so I decided to drop it and continue with my work, trying to keep my head down and stay out of trouble.

A week later, I was asked by my American Indian heritage group to make Indian tacos for one of our meetings. This is something they were particularly excited about because not all Native Americans knew how to make these. It's an art that was handed down to me by my grandma and great grandma. I still remember standing in my grandma's kitchen in her log cabin outside of Yosemite as she showed me how to make fry bread when I was fresh out of college. I was so proud of myself for following the recipe perfectly. With the dough fresh in my hands, my grandma walked up to me and closely examined it. She picked up the dough and said bluntly, "The dough doesn't feel right!" And without giving it a second thought, she threw it away. I felt blindsided.

"Grandma! I followed the recipe exactly. What do you mean it doesn't feel right?"

She laughed at my response and said, "It doesn't feel right.

It will take you a few times, and you will understand." She was right. I now know how the dough must feel and have a certain texture for it to come out right. She also told me that what you feel in that moment will come out in the fry bread—it always does. I also learned that cooking from a place of love and gratitude in my heart not only makes cooking that much more enjoyable, but I can really appreciate the person I'm making it for. They can taste and feel my love for them through my meals.

As I made a fresh batch of tacos for my American Indian heritage group, I also made a fresh pot of pinto beans, which is the foundation of the Indian taco. I layered it with meat, lettuce, tomatoes, onions, salsa, and sour cream. As I proudly brought my batch of tacos into work for our latest American Indian heritage group meeting, everyone was impressed.

"These are delicious!" My senior leader said with delight. Other people echoed the same sentiment. Having a few left-over tacos, I thought it was a good idea to take one to Jack. I figured that he probably never had the Native American dish before, and something told me he might enjoy it.

I was so nervous walking into his office to deliver the taco. I was greeted by his receptionist, Grace, at her desk. I stopped to introduce myself.

"Hi, I'm Lily. I work in Public Affairs, but I'm also part of the American Indian heritage group. We made Indian tacos for our meeting, and we had some left over. I wanted the colonel to have one, if possible." She smiled at me.

"That is so nice of you but unfortunately, he's out traveling for the week, but he'll be back on Monday. Why don't you come back and bring him one, and I'll let him know that someone is bringing him lunch." My heart got excited and skipped a beat.

"Okay," I said excitedly. "That sounds great!"

I walked out of the office beyond giddy for the opportunity to share my Native American heritage with Jack. I had a feeling that this was his first Native American dish, so I wanted to make it extra special. That weekend, I went to the grocery store and picked up all the fresh food. I made sure everything, from the lettuce to the tomatoes, was organic. I also picked up sparkling water to accompany his lunch and nice clear plasticware for his plate. I even used my roommate's personal silverware from home for his utensils. To hold his silverware, I carefully folded a napkin and tied it all together with a bright gold ribbon in a beautiful bow that I hand-picked from the local craft store just for this occasion. I texted Julia to tell her all about my latest development with Jack. She responded in her usual sassy Julia way.

"I think you need to dress up as a sexy Pocahontas when you take him your cooking!" I started to laugh.

Julia was like the bad angel that sat on my shoulder, giving me inappropriate advice like leaving my underwear on Jack's car as a calling card (something that I would *never* do). In her mind, it was a brilliant idea. Her colorful comments make me laugh.

"You're just asking for me to get arrested by the military police if I do that, Julia!"

She stated, "If you get arrested, I will gladly bail you out of military jail." I laughed at her comment, but there was no way that I was going to test her and see if she was true to her word.

Monday morning came as the sunrise peaked through my bedroom blinds. I excitedly popped out of bed, waking up early to make Jack's Indian taco from scratch. I called my grandma, frantic about keeping the fry bread fresh for the afternoon. "Grandma, I need your help."

"What's going on granddaughter?" she asked.

"I'm making fry bread, but it needs to stay fresh until eleven a.m. What do I do?"

She laughed at me, "Who in the world are you making this taco for?"

I quickly remarked, "Someone at work . . ."

"Okay, just keep the fry bread in the oven on low."

"Got it," I exclaimed. "Thank you!" I hung up the phone.

As I put all the ingredients in the bowl, the dough started to form. I carefully grabbed a bunch of dough and rolled it out on the cutting board with my rolling pin. I kneaded the dough with my fingers and dropped my first batch in the hot oil. As the bread cooked, it turned a beautiful golden tan color. I pulled out my first piece of fry bread and couldn't believe what I was seeing: the fry bread had formed into the shape of a heart. My grandma was right. Whatever you put in the fry bread will come out. It was obvious I made this one with love because of who I was making it for.

Wanting everything to look perfect, I decided to wait until I got to work to assemble this special taco. I was thankful nobody saw me that day in the parking lot as they probably wondered what in the world this girl was doing dressed in high heels and a light blue dress, carefully making a meal from the passenger seat of her car. I was determined not to spill anything, so I brought all the toppings with me in separate containers. I tried my best to calm my breathing as a wave of nervousness came over me. My pulse started to pick up as a small sparkle and gleam formed in my eyes. I had an excited bounce in my step as I walked up to his office with his drink and food made to culinary perfection, along with his perfectly wrapped utensils accented with a beautiful bow.

As I walked down the hallway, I entered his front office and saw Grace manning the front desk. "Hi, Grace. I have the colonel's lunch, freshly homemade." She looked at me and at the perfectly crafted Native American taco.

"Wow, that looks delicious!"

"It is," I said excitedly. I explained to her how he should eat it. "It's like a tostada but better," I said. As I continued to talk to her about Native American food, she stopped me midway through my sentence.

"Why don't you go into his office and give it to him?" I froze.

"Is that okay?" I asked her with concern.

"Of course it is," she said. "Besides, you'll be better off explaining it to him than me anyway." I paused.

"Okay, that sounds good." I turned away from her desk with Jack's food, drink, and utensils in my shaky hands. I was about to enter the office of the *Great and Powerful Oz*, and I was beyond terrified. I gave myself a little pep talk. *Don't trip, Lily. Just put one foot in front of the other, and you'll be fine.*

I slowly walked into Jack's office. I quickly glanced around, and in the middle of his bookshelf, I caught sight of a framed photo of him with the President. Achievements of his military accolades covered the office walls. He was standing at a white desk with leadership books next to his computer. I was stunned. *I can't believe that I'm here*, I thought to myself. He turned and looked at me. I was sure he was just as shocked that I was standing in his office as I was.

Not missing a beat, a small, playful smile formed across his face. "Hi, what's up?" he said. My heart was racing. I tried to calm my voice and remember the statement I rehearsed in my drive.

"I'm part of the American Indian heritage group, and I made Indian tacos for our meeting last week, and I wanted to bring you one." I set the plate on his desk, along with the sparkling water, utensils, and a side of sour cream and salsa.

He looked at me as his smile grew and asked jokingly, "It isn't old, is it?"

I shot back. "Of course, it's not! I made everything fresh this morning." He had no idea how much work I had put into this, making an entire batch of eight pieces of fry bread just to bring him one taco.

I explained to him how to eat the authentic Native American dish. I could feel the glow from his beaming smile, but he was also careful about keeping eye contact with his computer. I was sure he didn't want to make it too obvious how happy he was that I brought him lunch.

"So, what you're saying is this is going to get messy."

"Yes," I proudly responded.

"Well, thank you for bringing this to me." A beaming smile swept across my face as I left his office. As I walked out to my car, my mind was flooding with thoughts. *What if Ryne finds out? What will happen to me?*

Knowing that I was probably in so much trouble for bringing Jack lunch, I came to the realization that I didn't care. I got to see the man of my dreams and share my Native American heritage with him. The action was worth the consequences. It was also a monumental moment that remained with me for the rest of my life.

Shortly after delivering the most important taco I had ever

made, I went into my office to work for the day since I was already on-site. In the hallway, I ran into Ryne, who was talking to one of my co-workers. He had just come back from the front office. It dawned on me that I missed him by a matter of minutes. He had no idea that I had just delivered something personal to Jack. Thanking God for watching over me, I thought I was in the clear.

A couple of days later, I received an email from Grace saying that she had my utensils that I brought Jack and asked if I could swing by her office to pick them up. I had forgotten all about them and made my way over to the front office to grab them. I walked into the office and approached her desk but noticed she was on the phone. She pointed to the desk next to her, and there, sitting on the desk, along with the silverware, was a handwritten note from Jack. A big smile came across my face. This was so unexpected. I tried my best to contain my excitement. I looked over at Grace, who was still on the phone, and thanked her. I turned to the desk carefully, grabbed the utensils with the handwritten note, and left the office.

Sitting in my car, I set the silverware and the note down in the passenger seat. I looked at it for a few seconds. Then, I gently picked up the handwritten note from Jack. It was on his personalized stationery with his initials at the top. It read:

DEAR LILY, *Thank you for thinking of me with the delicious Indian taco. Fry bread was a first for me. Thank you again for the delicious lunch treat. Best, Jack.*

• • •

A TINGLING SURGE shot from my head and spread throughout my body. I looked up from the note as I felt myself being blissfully carried away. Judging from the way he wrote fry bread instead of fried bread told me that he must have researched it online. I felt so special that he took the time to write me a thank you note for making him lunch. All the work I went through to make it, even risking getting into trouble with my boss, was worth it. I sat in my car without a care in the world as all concerns and worries escaped from my mind. At that moment, I felt capable of doing anything.

26

———

Life looked bright again. I felt as if my luck was starting to change. A couple of days later, we had a brigade event that I was writing about. The Army had successfully completed a high-profile project, and the senior leaders wanted to share the good news with the rest of the brigade. I decided to wear the same gold ribbon that I had used for Jack's silverware from his lunch in my hair, wondering if it caught his attention. I wore a beautiful black dress with ruffles on the trim and around the arms. The dress came together with a perfect bow tied to the side.

Sitting in the audience in the auditorium, waiting for the event to start, I looked to the side of the room and saw Jack strolling in. He made his way to the front side of the room, where my boss handed him his microphone piece to attach to his belt. As he adjusted the microphone, he looked up at me. With a big grin on his face, he quickly winked at me.

Automatically, I could feel myself getting flustered. *Did he just wink at me in front of everyone?* He was so quick that nobody noticed it, which I was thankful for. We were in our own little private world with just him and me. As things got ready to start, he walked to the front of the auditorium. We began staring directly at each other, almost as if nobody else was in the room.

I felt the desire building up inside my body as I bit my lower lip. He started licking his lips, just staring at me. Meanwhile, everyone was unaware of what was happening between us, except for my boss, Ryne. I looked over at him and saw he was watching me like a vulture stalking its prey. As Jack started to go into his presentation to the workforce, he kept glancing at me but kept his composure.

After the presentation was over, everyone started to leave the room. I turned to walk out and noticed Jack following closely behind me with his entourage of people like he was Elvis Presley. He caught up to me and casually brushed my hand as he continued walking by. I quickly shot my head in his direction as my heart started pounding. He looked down at the ground and was grinning. I knew he didn't want to make it obvious by making eye contact. I walked to my car, trying my best not to stare at him as my mind became hyper-focused on my surroundings. As I drove away and looked over at him, a charming smile formed across his face. A lightness filled my chest, and my heart skipped a beat once again.

On my way home, I called Amelie. I told her everything that had just happened. "I can't believe he did that!" she said in disbelief.

"Oh, I can," I told her without hesitation. As I drove home floating on a cloud, I was in a heavenly bliss.

When I was with Jack, I felt seen in a new way, and yet, Jack and I had never actually talked about our feelings for each other. But at the same time, it was almost as if our hearts knew what to say and were talking to each other. No words were needed. It was a strong connection that was new for me and honestly, I had no idea what to do with it. My heart hoped that our perfect picturesque world wouldn't come crashing down anytime soon.

Autumn 2021

27

The temperature finally started to drop. Pumpkin patches with fun hayrides and corn mazes were starting to sprout up. Everyone in town was also buzzing about the upcoming state fair. October had finally arrived as our brigade held its annual Hispanic Heritage event. Wanting a break from attending in-person events, I didn't plan on attending initially. But for some reason, this voice told me that I needed to go. I decided to ignore the feeling until Sandi messaged our department on Teams:

HEY EVERYONE! *My Hispanic Heritage event is happening tomorrow, and anyone attending the event to show their support would be greatly welcomed.*

I LOOKED AT THE MESSAGE. *Well, I guess I'm going,* I thought reluctantly. I responded to her message: "I will be there."

"Yay! Thank you, Lily!" she replied.

Walking up to the outdoor event, I noticed there were food trucks, a mariachi band, and colorful festive decorations all around. I glanced around the crowd and didn't see Jack right away. I decided to take a seat at one of the tables next to Ethan. Making small talk with him, I looked across the quad and saw Jack walk out of the side door of his office building and past the taco truck. He casually made his way over to the designated table for the senior leaders attending the event.

Even though he wore the same military uniform every day, I still couldn't get over how good-looking he was and the way he carried himself. He wore that uniform very well, and it suited him perfectly. He sat down at the head of the adjacent table with the other senior leaders. He looked across the quad with an affectionate smile on his face. I knew he was smiling at me. I looked over at him and smiled back. I was sure he could see me out of the corner of his eye.

After introductory remarks, Jack walked up to the podium and presented awards to some of the people who organized the event and to other federal employees. One of the employees who led the Hispanic Heritage group shared her long-standing history with the Army. Her parents met at the brigade with her mom being a secretary and her dad working for the Army as an engineer in the 1960s. After he pursued her for about a year, they fell in love and got married. Now, their daughter was working at the same place her parents met some sixty years later. The heartwarming story brought a smile to my face. I looked at Jack out of the corner of my eye as he quickly glanced in my direction with a small smile on his face. I couldn't help but wonder if maybe this place had a history of people unexpectedly falling in love. Once the woman wrapped up her story, everyone happily clapped as she politely smiled and made her way to the table in the back row.

Two gray-haired men wearing jeans and button-up shirts accompanied a blonde curly-haired woman wearing a zebra print shirt and jeans to the podium. They shared about their involvement with a non-profit that helps to remove barriers Latinos face in employment, education, housing, and health care.

After the event, Jack stood to the side on his phone. Without warning, Noah walked up to me and started talking about our upcoming American Indian heritage event. He was anxious about the high-profile event taking place in less than a month. I reassured him everything was going well and that he had nothing to worry about. I had already completed our flyer and secured the speakers for the day, along with their transportation to and from post. As I was talking, I looked out of the corner of my eye and saw Jack still on his phone. Something told me he was buying time so I could talk to him. I quickly wrapped up my conversation with Noah and walked over to Jack.

"Well, hey there, handsome! Always on your phone, I see," I playfully told him. I then touched his hand that was holding the phone.

He looked up at me and smiled. "I know, I'm always busy. It seems like I have something to do all the time."

I responded lightheartedly. "You are the brigade's colonel, after all, so you must be the busiest person on this post."

"I know, it does seem that way, doesn't it?"

I smiled at him as I said, "You are so good at what you do.

I hope that you are proud of all that you've accomplished at this brigade. You really are doing a great job."

He looked down at the ground and over at me, "Oh, I don't know about that, but that's nice of you to say." He continued talking. "Speaking of accomplishments, I've read one of your past articles, and I wanted to tell you how great it was."

A big smile formed across my face. I was so flattered that someone in his position took the time to read one of *my* articles. "Wow, thank you so much! I really appreciate you saying that. I meant what I told you before. I really do enjoy working at the brigade, so I'm glad it shows." Aside from the drama I was having with Ethan and Ryne, I really did enjoy doing my job. I also pondered which article of mine had caught Jack's eye.

Jack looked at me straight in the eyes, and a big smile flashed across his face. I could feel my heart exploding in my chest. He had me wrapped around his finger and didn't even know it. More than anything, I wanted to tell him that he was the silver lining for all the trials that I'd been going through in my life. He meant more to me than he could ever know.

"Well, I better get going. Duty calls as they say," he said in a lackluster voice. He quickly added, "But I'm sure I'll see you again soon."

I bit my lower lip as I smiled at him. "That sounds good; I'm looking forward to it." He walked away and once again left me floating on cloud nine.

As I was getting ready to leave the event, our photographer, Daniel, walked up to me. He normally didn't talk to me while he was photographing, so I found this rather odd, but I went with it.

"Hi Daniel, what's up?" I said to him.

He stated, "Well, I wanted to ask you about something that I wasn't sure about. I'm assigned to photograph a change of command ceremony, but I don't know who it is for." My heart stopped and sank in my chest. It *couldn't* be Jack's ceremony.

I told him, "Well, it can't be our colonel because he's not leaving until June."

He answered, "Yes, you're probably right. It's probably some other event on post since I get assigned those. I figured I'd ask you in case you knew anything." I looked at him, trying to hide my concern.

"Yeah, Daniel, I'm sorry. I don't know anything about it, but it could really be any event since we have so many happening on post." I told him goodbye, and as I left the event, my mind was going in a thousand directions.

It can't be Jack's event, I told myself. *It's too soon, it just can't be.* I felt like I was racing against the clock trying to find another job…thinking I had until June, which is when Jack's rotation at the brigade would come to an end. November, on the other hand, was right around the corner.

I went home and started my work, but a nagging feeling wouldn't leave me. Something told me to check the photographer's schedule. I had no idea where it was kept, so after thirty minutes of hunting through random files on Microsoft Teams, I finally found it. I looked through the Excel spreadsheet and saw it. It read: *November 2, location: Courtyard.*

"That's our courtyard," I told myself. My blood ran cold as I stared at the computer screen, feeling completely numb. How was I going to find out if this was Jack's event and if he was, in fact, leaving the brigade early? It was not like I could send him an email, let alone walk up to his office and ask, "So, are you leaving the brigade early?" I felt so helpless—like I might never know until the ceremony actually took place. I just hoped the answer I was seeking was finding its way to me.

28

───────

The bright morning sun pierced through my blinds and lit up my bedroom as I slowly emerged from my bed. Rubbing my eyes, I sluggishly made my way downstairs, feeling the morning coffee calling my name. I hunted around the kitchen and quickly realized I was out of coffee.

Darn! I can't believe I'm out of coffee! I thought to myself helplessly. I made a plan to stop at Starbucks to grab some coffee before heading to my usual cycle class that I taught at nine-thirty a.m. Normally, I don't stop for coffee, but that day, I decided to since I was adamant about not teaching a cycle class without some sort of caffeine boost. With my coffee in my hand, I walked out of the shop and headed to my car. I looked across the parking lot and saw Jack walking in the opposite direction toward his gym. My eyes grew large with shock. Suddenly, I heard this unexpected voice say, *Well, you wanted to know…here's your chance! Go ask him.*

I was beyond terrified. Calling out his name, I felt like I was in a dream where I was trying to yell but couldn't get my voice out. I probably sounded like a terrified little mouse as I called his name from across the parking lot.

"Jack!"

He looked over at me and walked across the parking lot to where I was standing.

"Hi! This is a little early for you, isn't it?" He knew I taught my cycling class at nine-thirty, and he was right—it was early for me.

"Yeah, I was just stopping for coffee," I told him.

He mentioned the food I had made for him that day. "Thank you so much again for bringing me the taco—are you part of the American Indian heritage group?" he asked me.

"Yes, I am," I told him. "I grew up in the Yosemite area."

Not being able to hold back my anticipation, I jumped straight to the point. "So, Daniel came up to me after the Hispanic Heritage event saying that he's photographing a change of command ceremony. That's not your event, is it?"

"Yes, it is," he noted. "I'm leaving the brigade in November." He stood there facing me with a blank look on his face. Almost as if his leaving the brigade was no big deal. I looked at him in disbelief.

"What? What do you mean?" It was quite obvious that I was upset by the news.

He looked at me with concern. "It's just…my time to go. I've accepted orders in Virginia—I'll be moving to the East Coast. I've accepted an executive officer position working for a two-star general at the Pentagon." The job was an amazing opportunity for Jack and a very coveted position for someone in his rank. He asked me curiously, "Why? What's going on? Is everything okay?"

I stood there frozen. My mind went blank. The moment

had finally come. I knew I had to tell him what I'd been feeling for the past year. Memories of our time together, brigade events, random instants when we talked, and the special dance we shared at the Army ball came rushing back into my mind.

I nervously looked down at the ground and back up at him. A slow grin formed across his face. He knew what I was about to say. I slowly started to speak.

"Well, Jack, there's something that I've been wanting to tell you." I looked down at the ground again and said, "Honestly, I didn't think about telling you this soon, but..." I looked up at him, took a deep breath, and with my heart beating out of control, I said, "I really like you." I paused. I couldn't believe the words that had just come out of my mouth.

"Ah," he said, obviously flattered.

"There's a possibility I may be leaving the brigade in the near future, too."

A shocked look flashed across his face. Now, he was upset. "What do you mean? Where are you going?"

I told him that I had a few opportunities, but I hadn't decided yet. It was a total lie, but something told me job opportunities were coming soon.

"Oh," he remarked disappointingly. I looked up at him and couldn't believe what I was about to say.

"But when I do leave, I was going to see if you wanted to maybe have coffee sometime." There. I said it. It was now all out in the open. Now, he looked down at the ground.

"Oh..." he replied, astounded. I could tell he wasn't expecting this at all, and honestly, neither was I. "I don't think that's a good idea," he said with softness in his voice.

"Of course, I understand," I replied. And I did understand. I'm not sure what I was expecting, but I felt like I was saying the first thing that came to my mind.

He looked at me and said, "I'm sorry, but I better go."

"Okay," I told him. He turned around and walked into his gym.

As I walked across the parking lot and got into my car, tears streamed down my face. *I can't believe what I just did!* I thought to myself. With one short conversation, I managed to ruin the perfect fantasy world that we'd been living in for the past year. It all came crashing down like a roaring waterfall that ripped through my life. I called Audrey and told her what happened, repeatedly beating myself up for what I had just done.

"Oh my gosh! I am so sorry. I can't imagine how hard this must be for you, Lily." Audrey had her therapist hat on. She was a program manager at a mental health hospital and continued speaking, "But I am so proud of you for being honest with him about your feelings. I know it may not seem like it now, but what you did was very brave. You should be proud of that." I could barely speak because I was crying so hard.

"I don't feel brave, Audrey," I told her helplessly as I sat sobbing in my car. "I feel like I made a total mess of things, and now I have no clue what is going to happen." There was nothing anyone could say to bring me peace as I drove away, leaving Jack behind to work out at his gym.

A FEW DAYS after dropping the biggest bombshell of my life, I saw Jack at another brigade gathering. The mood had changed. We went from flirty, fun looks at each other to him going out of his way to avoid me altogether. He didn't even want to look at me. I was absolutely heartbroken and couldn't believe what I had done. With just one conversation, I had destroyed our perfect little world. I regretted telling him about my feelings. He was going to leave the brigade in less than a month, and a new colonel would take over. In past events, Jack didn't want to talk about leaving his job, but this time was different. As I sat in the auditorium next to Ethan, the event started. Jack addressed the group and said without any hesitation that he was leaving the brigade. Everyone looked around, startled.

Ethan whispered to me, "Wow, I wasn't expecting him to say that!"

In my heart and soul, I knew why he said it. It had to do with the conversation we had a few days before. He was sending me a clear message that he was leaving and wasn't coming back. I felt blindsided by his words, which I knew were directly aimed at me. The comment pierced through my heart like an arrow.

After things wrapped up, he purposely had his back turned to me and was talking to the new colonel. As everyone left out the front door and across the parking lot, I noticed he left out the side door. I knew he was doing his best to avoid running into me. I got in my car to drive away but looked over at him as he walked back to his office with the new colonel. He caught a glimpse of me and quickly turned his head downward to avoid eye contact. He had a serious and ashamed look on his face. Tears started to build up in my eyes. He didn't know it, but he had my heart in the palm of his hands and was crushing it into a million pieces.

I texted Amelie to tell her what happened. "You can't take it personally," Amelie advised. "He's reacting out of fear for his job and marriage. It's nothing personal against you." But it was personal. It was very personal. I stepped outside of my comfort zone and allowed myself to be vulnerable with him, and this was how he responded.

29

JACK

Jack's mind was spinning out of control as he tried to focus on his workout. He tried making small talk with other people at his gym, but his mind was not there. It was like he had gotten hit over the head with a bat that practically knocked him out.

I can't believe she just admitted that she has feelings for me, he thought, astonished. Part of him wanted to confess his feelings for her but instinctively held them back. Deep down, his heart was beaming with the news that she had feelings for him. She had confirmed what he had been feeling for her that past year as well. On the other hand, his perfect, military-structured world was crumbling before his very eyes. With his move coming up and getting ready for his last set of military orders, he knew something like this could ruin his military career.

What in the world am I going to do? He didn't want to hurt her but at the same time, he had to think about his marriage and his career. With him being so close to retirement, he knew he couldn't risk it all. The gamble was dangerous, and the stakes too high. His head took over and was overriding his heart. He knew what he had to do, whether he wanted to or not. He needed to find a way to get rid of Lillian, so this didn't turn into a bigger situation than what it already was and potentially ruin his life.

30

Just when things were going well, it seemed my life was once again being uprooted and ripped apart. I tip-toed on eggshells and anxiously held my breath, not knowing what to expect next. Shortly after the brigade gathering with Jack, Ethan notified everyone in the department that we were to work on-site at our new location four days a week. That same day, I also found out that Charlie, my fifteen-year-old chihuahua, was diagnosed with heart failure and had to be watched pretty much around the clock. I wondered how in the world I was going to care for my senior dog when I had to work onsite just about every day. I felt like my world was crashing down around me, and there was nothing I could do. I felt so helpless and hated it.

As I drove to the office for my first day working in my haunted decrepit office space, I was surprised to still be working for the military and not in a new job after spending most of my free time job hunting. Regardless, I believed I was still here for a reason. Maybe God had a thousand reasons with one of them being Jack. I saw his car parked in his parking spot as I drove to my sad office building on the other side of the post.

Things had shifted between us. It was no longer flirting, fun, and excitement. It was now avoiding me, not looking at me, and pretending that I was not in the room. It hurt. The man of my dreams, the man who held my heart, was breaking it, and he didn't even care. Our world looked entirely different now. It was broken beyond repair like a beautiful snow globe that once housed our perfect, untouched world. I threw it on the ground as I watched the glass violently shatter on the floor. Now, I was left to pick up the pieces. It was our own private, make-believe world, but I wanted to be with him in real life and not just a fantasy in our minds.

I also knew that in order for our world to be better, it had to be broken first so it could become something even more beautiful and real than ever before. But I was also afraid of losing him once he moved away and that he wouldn't want to be with me—sailing right out of my life like a ship in the night and taking my heart with him.

I vented to Julia about how things unfolded and how frustrated and angry I was. She said soothingly, "Don't be too down, Lily. You have good, positive things happening in your life. This door closing was a huge window letting the breeze blow through your hair."

She was absolutely right. Jack was that breeze blowing through my hair, showing me how to live my life again and how to love again. He also showed me the way I deserve to be loved. Jack brought hope and joy in the midst of a dark time in my life as I navigated my divorce. He also taught me to love myself again. Even though it seemed like doors were closing all around me, the door to my marriage, my job, and now even Jack, I knew I had so much to be grateful for. I just needed to keep persevering and believing in Jack to follow his heart back to me.

31

—————

I tried to conjure some excitement for my job and push Jack out of my mind. Two weeks had gone by, and I was in the office preparing the talking points for our Native American Heritage event. I was also tasked with printing up all the press placements I earned for the brigade and displaying them in a white binder for the new colonel to read. I was in the middle of printing off more than ninety articles when I got a phone call from my boss, Tim, a tall man with black hair and a commanding voice. He was in charge of the contracting office that hired me to work for the Army. Since my daily direct contact was with Army personnel, I never heard much from him.

"Hey Tim, what's going on?"

He stated bluntly. "Lillian, I've got some bad news. I'm letting you go today." My heart started hammering from the unexpected news. A wave of lightheadedness hit me as I tried desperately to catch my breath.

"What?" I managed to say. "But why?" My mind was reeling. I felt like I couldn't think straight.

"Ryne called us and said you broke protocol by walking straight into the colonel's office to bring him lunch." My mind frantically scanned, trying to pinpoint what exactly he was talking about. As if I got hit over the head with a brick I didn't see coming, it hit me: He was talking about the taco I had made. That single taco.

"You mean the American Indian food I gave him?" I asked him.

"Yes, that must be it," he said.

I was thoroughly confused. "But I didn't burst into his office…I made them for my heritage group, and I had some left over. I took one to him, but his assistant said he was out of town and to bring him one on Monday, so I did," I told him angrily. "She said it was okay for me to go into his office to take him the food…"

Without reacting to my anger, Tim calmly commented. "Well, Lilian, that's not what your boss is saying happened. I'm sorry, but you have to leave the post right away and leave your computer and government ID at your desk. If you try to come back, they can arrest you." As the words started to sink in, I realized that I hadn't taken a breath during the entire conversation and was having a panic attack.

Tim continued, "Lilian, I am so sorry. Honestly, I didn't even sleep last night because I was so upset. I have no idea why they're doing this to you when they've been so happy with your work, but you have to leave right now." I could tell by the care in his voice that he was sincere in how he felt about the situation. Despite this, it didn't soften the blow of being fired.

I found myself hysterically crying. I couldn't believe all my hard work over the past year was now washed away. I was being disposed of like yesterday's trash and treated like a criminal. I hung up the phone and slumped at my desk in disbelief. My heart was racing. I was having pain in my chest, and I couldn't seem to get myself to calm down. Sandi ran up to me. She sat in the cubicle next to me and heard the entire conversation.

"What just happened?" She was appalled. "I can't believe they just let you go out of nowhere!"

Somehow, I managed to say, "Sandi, I wrote the colonel's talking points for the Native American heritage event. Can you please make sure he gets them?" I don't know why I cared, but I did.

"Of course I can," she said without hesitation. "Don't worry about it."

It dawned on me why they wanted all my press placements printed and documented; they knew I was going to be let go. I went into Ethan's office in tears. He was standing at his desk wearing an unflattering mustard yellow polo shirt that didn't even match his black pants. His greasy red hair made me briefly wonder the last time he washed it.

He stated matter-of-factly with no care in his voice, "I'm sorry this happened to you, but this is just the way it is in the Army."

"I just don't know why I'm getting let go—his secretary said it was okay to go into his office and bring him the food!"

Ethan stated coldly, "I don't know either, Lilian, but I am sorry." It was obvious that he wasn't sorry for me being let go. If anything, he was probably elated and happy to see me leave.

I walked back to my desk with my head hanging down low and tears streaming down my face. Sandi grabbed a nearby empty cardboard box and helped me pack my desk.

As we walked outside to my car, she said, "Lilian, I can't

believe they did this to you. If they can let you go for something as small as bringing the colonel lunch, how do I know I won't be next?"

I wanted to tell her, *Well, don't ever bring the colonel lunch*, but I kept my thoughts to myself. Instead, I told her, "Sandi, stay in your lane, and you will be fine. I didn't stay in my lane, and this is what happened."

She reached over and gave me a big, warm hug. She hugged me tightly, almost as if she wanted to shield me from all the hurt I was feeling, like someone who was just in a car accident. She promised to call soon and talk more. I got into my car dazed, as my mind tried to absorb something that I just hadn't seen coming. I sat for what felt like minutes. I couldn't believe that I had been fired from my job and gone through a divorce, all within months. Finally, I called my now ex-husband and explained what happened.

"What?" he said. "Are you fucking kidding me?"

"Yep," I told him.

He replied bluntly, "This shouldn't come as a shock, you know, but this is how the military is. You're just another cog in the wheel." That was his favorite saying for describing the military. He added, "Come over to my office, and I'll give you some money to help you with your bills."

I couldn't turn down free money and said, "Sure, thank you, I really appreciate it." I drove over to his office on post to gather the money that I needed to pay my bills for that month.

After picking up the money, I drove back home with my office supplies sitting in a sad cardboard box in the backseat. I quickly sent my roommate, Aiden, a brief text message telling him I had been let go.

He was shocked. "I'll be home tonight, and we can talk about it," he stated. I made the dreaded phone call to my mom and told her what happened.

"What?" She was just as surprised as I was. "All because you brought your colonel lunch? Honey, that just doesn't seem right." Oh, but it was, and this was the way the military operated.

I also heard rumors shortly after I started my job that the public affairs department at my brigade had a reputation for just letting people go for no apparent reason. I didn't want to believe it was true, but it even happened with a former co-worker who started at the same time I did. She was still recovering, and it had been a little over a year since she was let go.

Making my way down the family phone tree, I texted one of my Aunt V's to tell her what happened. "Can they legally do that to you?" I had no clue, but regardless, this was now the reality I was living in. She speculated, "Well, that was one expensive Indian taco you made for your colonel…" I let out a small laugh, knowing she was right. It was by far the most expensive food I'd ever made.

With the news of my firing still sinking in, I sent Abbey a text message telling her what happened. Not even two minutes went by before she called my phone. She was yelling and clearly upset. I could hear her pacing back and forth in her kitchen as she was preparing her lunch.

"I just can't believe it! How can they do that to someone…" She was angrier about me getting let go than I was.

"Abbey, I don't know. I honestly don't have a good explanation for what happened." She continued angrily.

"I looked up to Ryne, too! I said such great things about

him, and I can't believe he did this to you, and he's a father! I never expected him to do anything like this!"

I weighed in, "Abbey, it's just the way the military is." Her anger dropped down into sadness. "I feel responsible for this. I'm the one who told you to take the job in the first place," she recalled.

"Abbey, you can't put this on yourself. You had no idea this was coming," I pointed out.

She remarked with irritation in her voice. "Well, they don't deserve you, Lilian. They were lucky to have you, given the amount of press hits you got for them. I could only hope to have someone like you on our team." I managed a small smile.

"Thank you, Abbey, for saying that, but honestly, I was just thinking this morning that maybe I'm not a good fit working for the military. It looks like God heard my thoughts because He slammed that door right in my face."

She quickly noted, "Well, I have no doubt that you're going to get an incredible job, and if you need anything, and I mean *anything*, please don't hesitate to call me. If you need a reference, I can be that for you."

I respond defeatedly. "Thank you for that, Abbey. It really means a lot."

After getting off the phone with Abbey, I decided to take a relaxing bath in an attempt to wash the day away. I lit some lavender and eucalyptus candles to help ease my stress and carefully placed them around the bathroom. After pouring a cup of lavender salt under the warm running water, I stepped into the bathtub as the clear water continued to fill the tub. I did my best to calm my mind, but it was racing out of control as I kept replaying the unfortunate day in my mind.

I stepped out of the bathroom, soaked and wet, looking

like a drowned rat, when Aiden got home. He walked up the stairs and gave me a warm hug. He told me to come downstairs when I was ready to talk things over. I put on some comfortable clothes and went downstairs where I saw Aiden sitting at our kitchen table. I sat down next to him.

With care in his eyes, he said, "This is not your fault. You are not a bad person, and you didn't do anything wrong. I just want to tell you that in case you need to hear it."

I commented half-heartedly. "Thank you, Aiden, I appreciate it."

He got into dad mode. "Okay, so we need to come up with a plan for how we're going to find you another job." I had no energy, and he could read it on my face.

"I know this isn't something you want to do right now but trust me; you need to do it. Spend a day, or however long you need to grieve this loss and get back to it," he added. "Believe me when I tell you it's going to be okay." Even though my situation looked and felt hopeless, I held onto the hope that this was all happening for a reason.

<h1 style="text-align:center">32</h1>

The rain came down slow and steady at first. Dark clouds covered the sky as the drops got bigger. The continuous stream of pelting against my bedroom window sounded like someone shooting a bb gun. It instantly woke me up. I faced my first official day of unemployment, and it was raining. The first rain of the fall season. I lay in bed watching the rain come down outside my window. I tried to figure out if the heavens were crying for me or if this was God's way of washing away the old things in my life, making room for the new things to come and grow. I knew I was in the middle of a metaphorical rainy season, but I also knew my sunshine was coming soon. I closed my eyes and imagined the rain erasing everything that happened the day before. I also allowed myself to feel all the hurt, frustration, and anger from being let go from my job.

The next day, I decided to pick myself up from this setback and get back into the world. Being productive, I knew, was key to my healing. The first thing I did was email Jack. This terrified me, but I knew it was something I had to do. I had the email already saved in my drafts folder from a few months prior. I had thought about sending it after I left the brigade for another job. Never in my wildest dreams did I imagine sending it under these grim circumstances. Opening my personal email, I had saved his work email address in my phone, knowing I wouldn't have access to my work email anymore. I drafted an email thanking him for everything he did for me while I was working for the military. I ended it by asking him out for coffee again and giving him my phone number.

Here I was, risking rejection for a second time, but something in my heart told me that I was doing the right thing. Now that I wasn't working for the brigade anymore, we could at least talk without anybody lurking around. I felt excited. I had so many things I wanted to tell him about: My first big press placement I got for the brigade, the ninety-plus press hits that I got in total for them, and other things that had been happening in my life. But in the back of my mind, a small part of me had my doubts of that time coming to pass.

As the days went by, I did my best to keep my mind busy. I applied for jobs every day and continued to teach my cycle classes while spending time with my friends and dogs. All the while, I just kept thinking, *Any day now, he's going to call Lily…just hang on a little longer.* Before I knew it, a month had gone by, and my hope dwindled down. By this time, it was November. I knew Jack's change of command ceremony was quickly approaching and would be streamed online by my old brigade. I told myself that I didn't want to watch it. I couldn't take any more pain.

But as fate had it, I woke up that morning at five minutes till nine with his ceremony starting at nine a.m. My heart told me to watch the ceremony, so I did. It turned out beautifully. I watched from my tiny laptop screen as he confidently walked into the auditorium, saluting with a serious but proud look on his face. I listened to heartfelt speeches from his troops about the impact Jack had on them during his time at the brigade. Among the various awards and plaques Jack received commemorating his time with the Army, he was presented with the Distinguished Service Medal for leading the brigade during the Covid pandemic. During his closing speech, Jack said all the perfect things, reflecting on his time at the brigade and all the people who touched his life. In my mind, I imagined myself sitting in the audience at his ceremony, supporting him in person. Instead, I was watching it from my bedroom on a computer screen.

His time at the brigade was a fleeting moment in time—two years gone in the blink of an eye. The brief moments we spent together were now gone as well. He was closing this chapter of his life and starting a new one. I wondered if the chapter of our story was closing as well—if it was ending before it ever had a chance to begin and see what could have fully grown between us. While he was surely excited and anxious to start the final chapter of his military career, did he know he was leaving me behind as well—or did he not really care? In between the memories of all his amazing accomplishments with the Army and his time at the brigade, I wondered if I flashed across his mind—the times he saw me sitting in the audience at our many military events…the briefest of moments when our eyes met, and our hearts acknowledged what we felt for each other. The times his hand discreetly touched mine and made my heart soar, or was he looking to leave me behind as well? Did he want to forget that he ever met me? I just didn't know.

As I sat there in my cold bedroom, watching him leave the auditorium at the end of his ceremony, I questioned if he'd ever come for me or if I was another princess hoping for her prince to come for her.

A voice inside me said he was permanently leaving my life. I started to cry. My biggest fear was coming to pass—that I'd lose him and never see him again. I decided to write him one final letter laying it all out and telling him everything—from the day we met to how I felt now. He needed to know how he changed my life because he had no idea. At least I could reflect on this period of my life and know that I tried everything to be with this man. I could look back with no regrets. I also knew that this was the last time I'd reach out to him.

Sitting in bed fresh from watching Jack's ceremony online, I closed my eyes. I said a prayer for God to give me the words to say what I needed to say but, most importantly, the words Jack needed to hear. I took a deep breath, and with my laptop sitting on my lap, I opened my eyes. I started to free-write and allowed the emotions to pour out of the depths of my soul. I wrote for what felt like forever. When I had no words left to say, I stopped. I took another deep breath and read what I had written. As I was reading the letter, re-living our story one word at a time, I knew in all my years of writing that this letter was by far the best thing I had ever written. The words flowed and took on a life of their own. I just let my heart say what it needed to say. I didn't edit a single word from that letter. I decided to send the letter as is because it was perfect. Knowing he was moving back to the East Coast, I made the decision to send it after the holidays, even though I was still partially in denial about him leaving. It didn't seem real.

I called my Aunt Victoria and told her about everything

that happened, including the letter, and that Jack was moving soon. "You're going to find out when he's gone," she said matter-of-factly.

"What? That's impossible, Aunt Victoria. We don't even have any of the same friends, so how can I find out when he's leaving?" I said, confused.

"Trust me, your auntie knows these things. The universe will have a way of letting you know when he's gone. When you do, I don't want you to be alone. You need to have someone with you." I dismissed her comment.

"Aunt Victoria, even if I do happen to find out when he's leaving, I'll be fine. I don't need anyone with me." She insisted.

"Please, just for me, find a friend or someone who won't judge you and will just listen and be there for you because this is going to be very hard for you." I thanked her for her concern but again repeated that I was going to be fine.

"Really, Aunt Victoria, it's going to be okay."

———

THINGS WERE MOVING ALONG RATHER WELL with my job search. I had three job interviews lined up that I was particularly excited about. Two of the jobs fit with my background and passion for mission-driven work that I discovered after working for the military. The third was a wild card with a marketing agency that I wasn't too sure about, but I still decided to do the interview anyway. Sitting in the third job interview at a table of about five people from this marketing agency, one of the men asked me what it was like working for the military and if there was a hierarchy system. I wanted to say, *"Yes, and if you don't fall in love with your colonel, you'll be fine.*" But of course, I didn't.

After thinking carefully about my response, I said, "Yes, there is a hierarchy system. For example, you're not allowed to email the colonel or message him on Microsoft Teams. When you talk to him, you have to address him in a certain way and others in the military as well."

Obviously, my track record for staying within this hierarchy system was not so good and cost me my job. I was never one who followed the rules very well to begin with. That should have been my first sign that maybe working for the military wasn't a good fit for me. I could see Jack in the job interview sitting at the table across from me with a big grin on his face, saying, "Yeah, you don't follow protocol very well," referencing the one time I messaged him on Microsoft Teams knowing I wasn't allowed to but did it anyway.

I guess I was a rebel at heart, but despite that, I did enjoy working for the military. I continued with my response. "If it wasn't for my job with the Army, I wouldn't have discovered my passion for mission-driven work and wanting to make a difference. So, if I could go back, I wouldn't change anything." And I meant it. I wouldn't change a single thing. If it wasn't for the military and marrying my ex-husband, Jack and I wouldn't have crossed paths. I knew it was all cosmically inter-related and happened for a reason.

Leaving the job interview, I gave Margaret, the psychic, a call. It had been a while since we last talked. I wanted to touch base with her and give her an update on everything happening in my life. Things sure did look different from the last time we talked.

"You're doing great," she said cheerfully. "Everything is

falling into place just as it should. I wasn't worried about you one bit and knew you had great things coming into your life." I mentioned the three job interviews to her. "The first two look the strongest, and you can't go wrong with either one. Both are great opportunities, but the third one I'm not too sure about. In the end, you're going to pick the one that is the best fit for you."

A wave of peace came over me. I was learning to trust God and that He was guiding my steps. I knew it was all coming together. Feeling like Jack was lingering in my mind, I decided to ask about him. I didn't want to, but I also hadn't heard from him. Doubt was growing in my mind if he'd ever contact me. She opined bluntly. "He's moving on. He's preparing for retirement and wants to leave you and his life here behind."

Wow. I couldn't believe it. Just like that, he wanted to forget all about me like he was holding a pencil and, at the other end, erasing me from the story of his life. She continued talking.

"He had his mind made up about you, though, even before you brought him that fated lunch."

Confused, I said, "What do you mean?"

She replied. "He talked to someone about you. I'm not sure who, maybe a boss, but the words your guides are saying is, *broke protocol.*" I froze. My mind flashed back to when Tim called me to deliver the horrible news about my job. Ryne had echoed those same exact words to him. It then hit me. Jack had talked to Ryne about me.

Angry tears built up in my eyes. It was like I was getting let go from my job and losing Jack all over again. I said angrily, "How could he do this to me? I trusted him! I even defended him to my friends when they speculated if Jack had anything to do with me getting let go…I said no, he wouldn't do that!" He threw the first punch, and it was a punch right to my gut. Margaret commented softly.

"You needed to get away from that job. They were holding you back. Your life has blossomed ever since. Jack won't forget you, and he will think of you with fondness, but he's able to compartmentalize and ignore his feelings for you. That's the military person in him." I couldn't believe what I was hearing. At the same time, I shouldn't have been surprised. In my mind, Jack was like a walking transformer, built by the military piece by piece. They had molded and shaped him into the invincible machine he is today. Like a robot, he could turn off his feelings, so he didn't feel anything for me and continued to operate and keep moving forward with his life. Meanwhile, here I was…feeling stuck and dealing with all these feelings that I didn't know what to do with. But unlike him, I was not able to ignore them. I just wasn't built like him.

33

JACK

Jack sat at his desk with a sober look in his eyes. His hand partially covered his mouth. It had been more than a week since Lily was let go from the brigade. He had tried to focus on work, but his heart felt heavy, knowing she was no longer part of his world. At Army events, he automatically scanned the room looking for her but quickly reminded himself that she was gone. He was faced with the realization of never seeing her smile at him from the audience with that glimmer of admiration in her eyes. Never seeing her walk around post on her lunch breaks. Never talking to her at work gatherings. Was confiding in Ryne about what had been happening between him and Lily a good idea? He questioned if letting her go was the right decision. His head told him yes, but his heart said he made a mistake. Lily brought a glow, a sense of joy, to his world that he didn't fully appreciate until it was too late.

The words from Lily's email asking him out for coffee kept replaying in his mind like a constant hum that he couldn't shut off. What if they did go out for coffee and just talked?

The battle raged in his mind. He knew because he was married, meeting her was a bad idea. Especially if they were seen by anyone from post with the possibility of gossip spreading rampant about his personal life was the last thing he needed. He also realized that when Lily left the brigade, she unknowingly took his heart with her. He felt torn. Now he was having to live with the consequences of his actions whether he liked it or not. There was no going back.

34

―――――

Time flew by—first days, then weeks. I invited Sandi over to my house for dinner so we could catch up since we didn't get the chance to talk after I left the Army. I couldn't be more thrilled for her to finally visit. As I danced in the kitchen, enjoying the jazz music playing in the background, I put the finishing touches on our vegetable lasagna. I heard playful squeaks in the living room and peeked my head around the corner to see Max and Charlie playing with their new stuffed animals.

When it came to them owning dog toys, they're like their mama with shoes: they couldn't have just one. I got lost in the moment, watching them play, until the doorbell rang. The boys suddenly jumped up and automatically sounded off the little dog alarm, barking like a pack of wild dogs. "It's okay, you guys! It's just Sandi," I reassured them. I opened the front door to find Sandi standing on my front porch with a big smile on her face. She was wearing light blue jeans and a floral pink top that matched her flower earrings and necklace perfectly. She was holding an exquisite bottle of white wine in her hands. I felt myself tear up as I realized how much I missed seeing her on a daily basis.

"Hey, Lily! Oh my gosh, it's so good to see you!" She gave me a long overdue big hug.

"It's nice to see you again, too, and under better circumstances. Come inside!" I grabbed the bottle of wine and led her into the dining room. I popped the cork open and poured us each a glass. She looked affectionately at me as she sipped her wine.

"You look great—more relaxed and happy…"

I laughed. "That's nice of you to say. I guess getting fired can do that to a person."

She laughed at my comment. "No! I'm being serious. You look like a weight has been lifted off your shoulders, and your face is glowing."

I stopped to reflect on her words. "I didn't think about that, but I guess you're right. It really does feel like a weight has been lifted off my shoulders. I'd wanted to leave my job with the Army for a while now. I just hadn't planned on getting fired."

She quickly replied. "Well, yeah…who plans on getting fired? Nobody does!"

"Touche," I tell her. "How has it been since I left?"

She sat down at the dining room table and started to snack on some chips and hummus. "Well, nobody's really talked much. It was brought up at a recent staff meeting that you were no longer with the brigade, but other than that, nobody's said anything else since."

"I guess I shouldn't be shocked. I'm sure they would love more than anything to forget that I was ever there under the circumstances." I murmured.

She responded softly. "It is unfortunate, and I so wished that it never happened to you. I just wish there was something I could do. Is there?"

I responded wholeheartedly. "This is for the best, Sandi. There was nothing you could do. Besides, if it wasn't for you editing my articles, I honestly would have been fired a long time ago if Ryne and Ethan had their way."

Sandi replied with sincerity. "That's nice of you to say, Lily, but I don't think I did very much. If anything, I've been trying to figure out why you were let go, to begin with, for something as small as bringing the colonel lunch. It's insane, and a small part of me is wondering if I could get let go as well for such a minor infraction."

The last thing I wanted was for Sandi to have any worries about her job security. I decided it was best to tell her the real reason why I was let go.

"Sandi, there's something I have to tell you, and it's probably going to come as a shock. This is what I believe to be the actual reason for me getting let go…"

Her eyes grew large. "Oh my gosh! What is it?"

I took a deep breath. "I had feelings for Colonel Cooper."

Sandi's eyes grew even larger. "What!"

I calmly responded. "Yes, I had feelings for him, and that's why I believe I was let go. It wasn't for bringing him lunch, so you don't need to worry about losing your job. Honestly, the Army can't afford to lose any more writers now that I'm gone."

She sat there, taking in my words. "This makes so much sense now, but it's not an excuse to let you go. How is it your fault that you developed feelings for him? You couldn't help that!"

I then confided. "That is true. I'm not going into the

details, but I believe that he had feelings for me as well. I think that much was obvious the times we talked or just were present in the same room."

She reflected. "Now that I think of it, I remember when you and I attended a brigade event…I don't remember which one…maybe an All Hands? Anyway, I remember when we walked into the auditorium, Colonel Cooper was standing in the front talking to someone. He stopped mid-conversation when he saw you and gave you this head tilt. I looked over at you, and you smiled at him. I knew he wasn't looking at me, so I figured he had to be looking at you."

I laughed as I reached over and refilled our wine glasses. "Yeah, that's happened quite a few times."

She angrily replied. "He's partially to blame as well, then. He knew what he was doing, and you shouldn't have been fired over it."

"I appreciate that, Sandi, but please don't be mad at him. We were both to blame, and I think everything played out like it did for a reason. Looking back, I can see why God allowed Jack into my life. I don't have any regrets."

Sandi quickly responded. "If I were you, I would be angry. If anything, I'm angry for you!"

I said kindly, "Sandi, I was angry at first, but since I've had time to reflect on the situation and really pray about it, I knew Jack was divinely planted in my life. I was in an unhealthy marriage that I didn't see until he came into my life. That's a blessing, isn't it?"

Sandi admitted. "I can see a change in you, that's for sure. You seem much happier. I'm glad you're in a better place."

I gave her a loving smile. "I really am. I believe things will only get better from here. Trust me, I'll be okay. Actually, I'll be better than okay. I really do believe that with all my heart."

Sandi reached over and touched my hand. "I believe that too, and I'm glad that you took the job working for the Army because if you hadn't, then we wouldn't have met!"

"I totally agree! See? God lets everything happen for a reason." I smiled at her as she patted my hand.

Just then, the oven timer went off. It was time to grab the lasagna. I felt my stomach growl as the smell of freshly cooked lasagna filled the air. I stood up and said, "I am starving. I can't wait for you to try some of this vegetable lasagna. I've been experimenting with making new recipes, and so far, this one is my favorite."

Sandi stood up and smiled as she walked over to the kitchen. "It smells great. I'm excited to try it! Ever since you made those Indian tacos for our American Indian heritage group, I've been wanting to try more of your cooking. I still can't get over how delicious those tacos were..."

I exclaimed, "Nothing beats Indian tacos in my book! I'll have to make them for you again soon, I promise."

———

That month, Audrey, the first friend I made when Aaron and I got stationed in Arizona, was on a quest to find the perfect gym. With her passion for fitness and being very fit, she had a hard time finding a gym. One day, she called me and told me about her idea of checking out Life Time.

"Audrey, you do know that's where Jack works out, right?" She wasn't bothered by that in the slightest.

"Yeah, but what are the odds of me seeing him? I mean, there are a ton of classes. There's no way I'll see him."

Hoping she was right, I said, "Okay, well, check it out and let me know what you think. I've never been, but I've heard it's a great place to work out."

"Sounds good! I will keep you posted. See ya, Lily." She hung up.

The following Saturday, Audrey called me after taking her first Life Time class.

"Lilian, you were right!" She practically yelled.

"About what?" I asked her.

She continued. "You said I wouldn't see Jack, and I didn't think so, but I actually saw him in my first class!" My heart sped up.

"Audrey, are you serious?!"

"Yes!" She yelled. "It was so crazy because I've heard about this guy for almost a year, and now, I'm seeing him in the flesh." I felt a pit form in my stomach.

"I knew this was coming," I told her. She started chatting away about her first class at the gym.

"Lilian, I love it. The music is the bomb, the people are so nice, and the workouts are fun." I was shocked.

"Audrey, are you kidding me?"

"No!" she said excitedly. "I signed up for a membership on the spot."

"You did?" I couldn't believe what I was hearing. "Audrey, you won't even pay thirty dollars to take my cycle class because you say it's too expensive, but you signed up for a membership with Life Time—that's a lot more expensive than my cycle class!"

She quickly reiterated, "I love it, Lilian! It's exactly what I've been looking for."

"Okay, well, I'm happy for you, but I have a feeling this isn't the first time that you're going to run into Jack." She once again didn't believe me.

"There are so many classes, and with my work schedule, I don't think I'll see him. I think it was just a coincidence that I saw him this one time." I had a feeling she was wrong.

The next week, Audrey took her first official class since signing up for her Life Time membership. As I was about to start my Saturday morning cycle class, she texted me. "You won't believe it, but he's here!" *Here we go*, I thought helplessly. As she was waiting in line, she kept texting me. "He seems very nice. He's talking to everyone."

I weighed in. "I know Audrey, he really is a nice guy." The last thing I needed to hear from my friend was how great Jack was, knowing how in love I was with him. After my cycling class, Audrey called me.

"Well, you were right," she said. I didn't want to be right, but given there was only one Life Time in town, the chances of them seeing each other were very high. She started to talk about her workout. "I kept watching the screen in the workout room and was competing with him as I was working out. I just kept celebrating that I was beating him!" I let out a small laugh under my breath. She's super fit, and so this comes as no surprise to me. She said jokingly, "It's like I'm your unofficial spy..." I got quiet.

"I suppose that's true, Audrey."

It had been over a month since I emailed Jack asking him out for coffee, and I still hadn't heard from him. My heart started to feel heavier and heavier to the point where I told

Audrey to stop talking about seeing him at the gym because it was just getting too difficult for me. She wholeheartedly understood and respected my wishes.

Two weeks went by, and on that fateful Saturday morning, I woke up and just knew he was gone. The next thought that entered my mind was *Audrey was going to text me.* Without giving it any more thought, I left my phone upstairs in my room. I went downstairs to fix my breakfast. After I finished eating, I went back upstairs and looked down at my phone. I had a missed text message from Audrey. It read, *Jack hasn't been here for a while. I think he may be gone.* I just knew it. I don't know how, but it was almost as if my soul knew he had moved.

On my way to the gym, Audrey called me and explained what happened while she was waiting for her gym class to start. "It's so strange because I was at the gym this morning, and I happened to be standing next to these two women who were talking about Jack. One had asked the other when he left, and the other woman said he left on Friday. What a strange coincidence that I was standing there at the same time." There it was. The catastrophic bomb in my life had dropped. It was official. He was gone. My aunt was right. I knew this wasn't a coincidence. God wanted me to find out that he was gone.

Tears started building up in my eyes. I couldn't hear this, not right now. "Audrey, I have to teach my cycle class, but I'll call you later."

Somehow, I managed to get through my cycle class that morning without crying. My heart felt so heavy from hearing the news. At the end of class, we went into stretching. I could feel the tears starting to stream down my face. Since I was also sweating from working out, it wasn't as noticeable—which I was thankful for. After leaving the gym, I called Audrey and burst into tears.

"Oh, Lillian, I am so sorry things didn't turn out how you hoped," she compassionately told me. "I know this is hard, but you will get through this, I promise. I know it doesn't seem like it right now, but believe me when I say you will overcome this."

I somehow managed to make it home. I walked upstairs into my bedroom and threw my gym bag on the ground. I stood in the middle of my bedroom with my arms hanging at my sides and my shoulders lowered. A feeling of helplessness washed over me. I was drowning in sadness that I wished more than anything not to be feeling. I took off my gym clothes and stood in the middle of the shower. My body was drained of its energy.

With the hot water running down my head, I started to cry. *How in the world did my life turn out this way?* I thought helplessly to myself. I closed my eyes and allowed the water to refresh my soul, making it anew.

As I stepped out of the shower, I grabbed my journal. I needed to write and get my feelings out on paper. I opened the journal, and before the pen hit the paper, I burst into tears again. I lay on my bed, curled up in a ball, and sobbed. I felt like someone was grabbing my heart and squeezing it. I had never felt pain like this before in my entire life. I knew the tears were from loss—a loss that I never experienced before and didn't see coming. After crying for what felt like an eternity, my face was red and puffy. I called my Aunt Victoria. "You were right, Aunt Victoria, I found out."

"Oh, baby girl, I am so sorry! I wanted to be wrong, but my gut feeling just knew this was the outcome."

In between the tears, I said, "Aunt Victoria, I've never felt pain like this before… We've lost family members to death, but this pain that I'm feeling hurts much worse."

Empathy coated her words as she replied, "Honey, you loved this man from deep down in your soul with all your heart. This is going to hurt much worse than death because this is the man that you love, and you can't be with him. Believe me when I tell you, you will get through this. You will be stronger on the other side, but you have to allow yourself to feel all these feelings. It won't be fun, but you have to do it."

"But I don't want to…it hurts too much," I cried.

"I know," she said soothingly. "This is why I didn't want you to be alone. Do you have anyone you can call who can be there with you in person?"

"I do, but honestly, I just want to be alone right now, Aunt Victoria."

"Well then, you'll just have to stay on the phone with me. Let me tell you a story…" I sat on my bed, wiping the tears from my face and listened as my Aunt Victoria shared the story about how she met her now husband after divorcing my uncle. I realized that even through heartbreak, love can find its way back into our lives when we least expect it. Eventually, we can learn to love again.

Winter 2021

35

———

The days and nights started to blur together. It was the constant dark storm cloud plaguing my life that wouldn't go away. I woke up one morning looking and feeling like death after crying most of the night. I wanted to get away and take a day trip to get my mind off Jack. With it being Christmas, I got in my car and let the open road dictate my direction. Driving into a nearby town that was decorated for the Christmas holiday with holiday lights shining bright, I strolled thoughtlessly past the stores and let the Christmas season lift my spirits. Each building looked like a whimsical gingerbread house from my childhood and brought back memories of making them during Christmas every year with my family. Each store displayed a beautiful Christmas tree glowing in green, red, and gold lights. Christmas ornaments and other holiday trinkets filled the window fronts as Jingle Bells echoed up and down the streets. In the main town square stood a tall blue spruce Christmas tree lit up in multicolored lights with glass gold snowflakes. The bright lights from the tree could be seen for miles. In exploring downtown, I spotted a bookstore and museum.

As I ventured up the stairs, I noticed the museum was dedicated to the work of Hans Christian Anderson, the fairy-tale author who wrote *The Little Mermaid* and *Princess and the Pea*. I paced myself slowly through the museum, seeing his handwritten notes, original books, and other mementos from his life. I spotted a glass case with small, doll-size mattresses inside and the story of *Princess and a Pea* displayed below it. The story was one of my favorite childhood fairytales. My mom read it often to me before bedtime, but I had forgotten about it until now.

I read the story as tears started streaming down my face. The story was about a prince in search of his princess. One night, a girl was outside his castle, soaked from the rain. She claimed to be a princess but didn't look like typical royalty. In the end, the prince discovered that she was, in fact, a princess. It was just so reminiscent of my and Jack's story: Him looking for his princess and me, not looking like a princess, but in fact being one. I was that girl soaked from the rain, looking disheveled but trying to tell Jack, "I am a real princess! I know I may not look like one, and I know that we come from different worlds, but I'm telling you the truth…I am a real princess." Here I was, standing in front of Jack, but he didn't see what I saw. So, I had to let him go down the path he'd chosen until he realized the princess he'd been looking for was here all along.

Going into the Christmas holiday, celebrating was the last thing on my mind, let alone going home to see family. All I wanted to do was stay curled up on my bed at home, but I made myself go home anyway. Driving back to my hometown,

I was stopped at a light when I noticed a truck in front of me in the next lane. Displayed on the back of the tailgate in huge letters were three words. It read: *Love is Patient.*

Now, patience was the one thing that I didn't have—it was not part of my nature. I'd always been the type of person that if I wanted something I worked hard to get it. But Jack was the one thing that no matter how hard I worked, nothing happened. I knew that God was teaching me patience because *He* knew it was practically non-existent in my life. *He* was showing me that love is indeed patient. I knew that I had to be patient to wait for Jack and see how this all unfolded. I didn't have much choice, did I? It had been almost two months since I left the Army. I decided to wait for him, but not forever.

That same week that I went home for Christmas, I accepted a new job. It was the glimmer of hope I needed that told me the tide was turning in my life for the better. The job lined up with my passion for mission-driven work, which I enjoyed while working for the military. It was also a higher position working for a public affairs firm supporting the federal government. I pulled over on the side of the road in the middle of nowhere while driving home. I excitedly filled out my new hire paperwork on my cell phone, all the while thinking how proud I was and how far I'd come in my professional journey. I also couldn't wait to share this exciting news with Jack when the right moment came—along with everything else that I accomplished while working for the military that he probably had no idea about. It was a small light at the end of the tunnel, but I hung onto it like my North Star. Even though I wanted to believe in my heart that our time was coming soon, doubts slowly started to seep into my mind and were taking root.

As I spent time with my family for Christmas, my mom and I were putting the final touches on the tall white pine Christmas tree in our living room. I slowly handed her the hand-painted silver and red glass ball ornaments as she carefully placed them around the tree. My body was cold, and I felt the tightness in my chest increase. Not even the festive tree decorated with glittery gold garlands and beautiful Christmas decorations from my childhood could lift my spirits. Moving slowly, with my face turned downward, my mom could tell something was up. I wasn't acting like myself. She could tell that something was bothering me.

"What is going on with you?" my mom asked me as we sat in the living room, visiting after decorating the tree. She handed me a cup of warm hot chocolate in a bright red mug. "You're not yourself, and I know something is wrong." I decided the time had finally come to tell my mom what had happened the past year.

"Okay, Mom, I'm going to tell you what's been going on," and like I was giving a presentation on my love life, I said, "I need you to hold all your questions until the end after I'm done speaking, okay?"

"I can do that," she said. So, I started from the beginning. I told her about the day I saw Jack for the first time and how I was struck with a ton of emotions like a bolt of lightning. The odd events that took place anytime he was close to the past life memories I was having and him leaving out of my life.

After I was done with my verbal presentation, I said, "Okay, I'm done."

"Okay, good, because I have a million questions." I laughed.

"Of course you do," I said. "So, let's hear them." In true

mom fashion, she had a lot of questions. Everything from wanting to know what he was like, where he grew up, did he like animals because she knew I loved animals, what he did for the military, how long he had been married, and the list went on.

After addressing her endless questions, I finally said, "I wrote a letter to him, and I'm going to send it after the holidays." She looked at me with concern in her eyes.

"Lily, that's not a good idea. What if he calls?"

"If he calls, he calls, but he needs to know Mom because he has no idea what's been going on and that he changed my life." I had my mind made up, and there was nothing anyone could say to change it.

"Okay, but I just don't want you to get hurt," my mom said softly. The truth was I was already hurt. This man had unintentionally hurt me and broken my heart, so really, I had nothing left to lose.

"It's going to be fine, Mom, trust me," I told her. As soon as the words escaped my lips, they echoed in my mind. Was everything going to be fine? My life was unraveling before my very eyes, and I was beginning to wonder how my outlook on life may change after this chapter was over.

36

After coming home from the holidays and celebrating what must have been the saddest New Year of my life, I handpicked the date to send the letter of my life to the man of my dreams. Going to bed the night before, I couldn't sleep at all. I set my alarm for a quarter to four in the morning, knowing that he was on the East Coast, and started work in true military fashion at seven a.m.

When my alarm went off the next morning, I woke up feeling anxious. My mind was afraid, but my soul was at peace. The moment that I had waited for all this time had finally arrived. I opened my email and carefully inserted the letter in the message box with his email address. I closed my eyes and said a prayer over my letter—hoping the words stirred something unexpected within his heart. With my heart racing, I bravely hit the send button. It was finished. It had been sent.

Staring at the computer screen, I couldn't believe what I just did. Still reeling from shock, I got an auto-response from him saying he was out for the holiday and no longer with the brigade. At least I knew that my email made it through. With adrenaline still pumping like I had jumped off a cliff, I took a few deep breaths to slow my heart. I started to feel relaxed and laid down to go back to sleep. About twenty minutes later, I was almost asleep when my heart started to dance once again! My eyes popped open. I knew he was reading my letter. I smiled and fell back into a dreamless sleep.

The next morning, I woke up, and my world looked brighter. It was almost as if the heavy weight I had been carrying on my shoulders for the past year had finally been lifted. I felt free. I knew I'd done the right thing, and from here on out, there was no going back. Now, it was his weight to carry and to do with it what he felt was right. I believed in my heart that he'd do some soul searching as I had and really stop to think about his life and his happiness. I just hoped that when reaching his final conclusions, I was somehow part of that answer, and he'd call me.

———

TIME WENT ON, and it seemed the more days that were crossed off the calendar of my life, the less hopeful I became at the thought of Jack reaching out. Even my Aunt Victoria, in her loving but blunt way, said, "Honey, you have to accept the fact that he may not call. His silence by not even responding to your email is your answer. It means he's not interested."

I didn't want to believe it, but I knew she was right. I didn't understand why he wouldn't respond when I poured my heart out to him. I'm sure my letter was like getting hit unexpectedly with a curveball, but still, it just didn't make sense. It had been almost a month with no response—no call, no email. Nothing but silence.

I finally came to the realization that he wasn't going to contact me. It was like I was starring in a bad country song where the girl waits for the man of her dreams, but he never comes for her. I replayed the past year repeatedly in my mind, trying to figure out if I had missed something or if maybe I had been wrong about him after all. I felt led on by him, toying with my heart for the past year when he knew it wasn't going to be anything more than fun flirting with a beautiful woman. Yet, it didn't have to end this way. I knew that he was missing out on something that could have been amazing and life-changing if he had allowed it to be. Unfortunately, because he couldn't see past his current situation and being so rigid and immutable in nature, it was his loss. Regardless, I didn't have any regrets. I trusted my heart, and I knew it wouldn't lead me astray. I had to believe that in the end, even though I didn't get the fairytale ending I had pictured in my mind, eventually, I'd find my storybook ending.

37

JACK

Jack felt the blood rush from his body as the words from Lily's letter kept replaying like sparks shooting around in his mind. He couldn't believe that she had made such a big life-changing decision all because of him and how strongly she felt for him. It was obvious that she loved him. The decision spoke volumes—for her to leave her marriage without talking to Jack about it. She followed her heart and did something that he didn't think was possible. She risked it all for him. Part of him wanted to call her, but he also knew that if he did, what could it possibly lead to? His hands were tied. He couldn't imagine a life with her without it getting messy. His entire life was all about order and structure.

As he sat in front of his work computer at his desk, the smell of bacon and eggs cooked in the kitchen by his wife lingered in the air.

She peeked her head into his office and stood in the doorway with her arms crossed in front of her chest. "All you do is work! Your food is ready. Tear yourself away from your work computer for once and come eat your breakfast," she said impatiently. Jack quickly whipped his head around.

"Just give me a minute. I'm in the middle of something important," he said bluntly. Jack's wife rolled her eyes as she let out a huff in frustration. She vigorously shook her head and left the room. He turned around as his eyes fixed on Lillian's letter sitting in his inbox amid other emails about his upcoming responsibilities at his new duty station. *I can't call her, I just can't,* he scolded himself.

It took all the willpower he had not to pick up the phone and tell her what he had been feeling for her that past year. That she wasn't imagining their connection; he had, in fact, felt it too. He realized that what he felt in his heart for Lillian *was* love—the type of love that you only see in movies or read about in books. His practical mind told him that kind of love didn't exist. It was a thing of fantasies, not rooted in reality. Now, here he was, he had found that fairytale love without even looking for it. But it was too late. He had made his bed, and he was going to lie in it whether he wanted to or not. He didn't have any choice but to push his feelings for Lillian as far away from his mind and heart as possible. He decided the best course of action was to stay on his pre-planned military path and stay with his wife.

I'm going to lock up my feelings for Lillian and throw away the key, he thought matter-of-factly. *As long as I keep my mind focused on the mission at hand and making it through my last set of orders, I can retire and before I know it, I'll forget all about Lillian.* Besides, he figured it would only be a matter of time before she'd forget about him and move on with someone else… But would she?

38

Driving Saturday morning to teach my regularly scheduled cycle class was no longer routine for me. My world looked completely different. I sat at the light with my playlist for the class playing on low. I blindly stared at the traffic light but couldn't care less when it turned green. My heart and mind felt numb. Learning to navigate this new normal was scary and unchartered territory for me.

As time went on, I started to see more and more each day why I was alone during this period of my life. I was on a path of spiritual growth and enlightenment, figuring out who I was on a soul level. I found myself spending more time horseback riding in the mountains and journaling any and all feelings that bubbled to the surface. Horses and journaling became my much-needed therapy. Allowing myself to find peace either on the back of a horse or getting lost writing in the pages of my journal. I realized I needed to learn how to openly and honestly love myself and put myself first. This time, I told myself to choose to love not out of obligation but from my soul and following my heart's compass. If I allowed a new man, whoever he may be, into my life, he would help me grow and become the person I was meant to be. I didn't need a man to complete me; I was complete just the way I was. Instead, he should complement me and highlight all the wonderful and amazing qualities that made me who I was.

I was beginning to enjoy this journey of creating and getting to know who I was on my own: the amazing, beautiful, special, and so very talented woman God created me to be. Realizing that each and every day, I was unique and one-of-a-kind. I started to see that in myself, and the right man, the one I was meant to be with, he'd see that in me as well. But I knew that until he came into my life, I'd continue to let my light shine bright until he came along and wanted to shine bright alongside me.

With that said, I knew that I had to put myself back out there and date again. Part of me was naturally terrified of getting my heart broken again. I also knew that keeping it behind a cement wall after what happened to me wouldn't be a good idea. There was someone out there for me. There was a man worthy of the love I had to give. I also didn't want to deprive myself of the chance to be loved again. I was lucky enough to find that big love in my life once, and I knew I could find it again. I just had to trust God that I was being guided.

After I was done teaching my cycle class, one of my regular cycle members, Bethany, came up to me. She had a ticket to a contemporary Christian concert with one of my favorite artists. She was unable to attend and offered to pass it on to me. I jumped at the chance. Later that evening, I was standing in a long line waiting to get into the concert. The line wrapped around the side of the building and down the parking lot. The impatient girl in me didn't want to wait.

Is this going to be worth it? I thought. Well, it turns out it was worth the wait.

As I was standing in the middle of a huge church auditorium at the concert, surrounded by loud praise music, I allowed my heart to absorb the lyrics as people were singing and clapping in the audience. My spirit was exhausted with the trials taking place in my life like I was running a marathon with no end in sight. I slowly closed my eyes. With my hands folded, I felt compelled to have an honest conversation with God about everything that had been happening in my life. I laid it all out and didn't hold back. I expressed my frustration at how everything had turned out with Jack. I told God exactly what I was looking for in the perfect partner for me. I prayed for a man who loved God just like I did and who had a good and kind heart. A partner I could pray with and talk openly about God and any other issues. This man would understand the importance of making God the center of our relationship because I had one where God wasn't the center, and it didn't turn out so well. I said that whoever that man was, that was the person I wanted on my arm, holding my hand through life. I didn't need him to make me happy but to learn from him and grow, while he felt the same way about me. I wanted someone I could be vulnerable with and, at the same time, feel safe and secure. I finally knew what I deserved: A man who saw me as the precious jewel of his eye and never took me or my love for granted.

After I finished my list, I ended my prayer with: *Don't waste my time with anyone who doesn't fit this bill! If it's not Jack, keep him away from me, but if it is him, bring him back to me. Either way, I just want you to bring me someone you want me to be with.* I was done. I had let go of the steering wheel of my life and was handing it over to God. No more looking for Jack, no more chasing a ghost. I was going to let God play matchmaker for me and do all the heavy lifting, knowing that the right man was coming into my life when the time was right.

Well, as it turned out, God worked pretty fast. A month after I prayed that prayer, I met a handsome but shy man name Anthony. He was tall with dark hair and striking hazel eyes that seemed to complement his adorable dimple smile. His eyes had a warmth and gentleness behind them that told me I could trust him. He answered my prayer to a *T*, but I didn't realize it at first. I noticed Anthony had started attending my cycle class back in December but was absent for a couple of weeks.

"Hey!" I told him as he came back to my class. "I noticed you were gone. Where did you go?" He smiled at me.

"I went to Israel on a mission trip with my church." Something inside me lit up.

"Really?" I asked.

"Yeah…" As he started to tell me about his trip, he said out of the blue, "So there's a triathlon coming up, and I wanted to know if you'd be interested in training with me."

I looked at him like he had lost his mind. "Um, no." Without any hesitation, I flat-out turned him down. He looked at me dumbfounded.

"No?" he said.

"No," I straight up told him. Nothing like that had ever appealed to me.

Trying to change my mind, he said, "You're a cycle instructor, though! You're super fit, and I know you can do it." My mouth dropped.

"Yes, I know that I am, but it doesn't mean that I enjoy doing extreme activities like swimming across the ocean in my spare time!" Trying to help his case, I said, "Well, I did participate in a 5K turkey run for Thanksgiving last year." He smiled.

"Well, that sounds nice."

"It was!" I exclaimed. "I even won a free Thanksgiving dinner." I was pretty jazzed about that Thanksgiving dinner since I'm not the type of person who has any luck winning prizes.

"That's pretty cool," he told me.

After we finished talking, I started teaching my class. At the end of class, Emilia came up to me. She had observed the entire conversation and gave me her two cents.

"He likes you, Lily," she told me with a smirk on her face. I looked at her like she was crazy.

"What? No way!"

"Yes!" she said excitedly. "He was trying to ask you out." I was confused.

"Why didn't he just ask me out for coffee?"

She responded. "I have no idea."

Thinking about it, I said, "Okay, if he comes to my next class, I'll ask him out." Emilia smiled.

"You are so brave for doing this. From what I can tell based on him talking to you, he really likes you, and I'm usually pretty accurate about these things!" Trusting my friend's guidance, I made the decision to ask him out the next time I saw him.

Like clockwork, the handsome man showed up to my next cycle class. My heart was racing, knowing I was going to ask him out. The last time I asked a man out it didn't go too well for me, and so I was hesitant. But I had to do it. I couldn't let my fear hold me back because if I did, fear would win, and I wasn't about to let that happen. So, after class, with my heart wildly beating, I approached Anthony. We made small talk about stretching as he was sharing where in his body he was tight from working out and asked for my advice.

All the while, I was thinking, *I'm about to ask this guy out, and this is what we are talking about?* I looked over at Emilia, who was two bikes away from us, and she was giggling. She pointed at my shirt, and I looked down. I was wearing a tank top that had "*love*" repeated on it three times. Once again, I was a walking billboard for love.

Embarrassed by this thought, I did my best not to look in her direction and laughed at myself. When a short break came in our conversation, I cleared my throat and said, "I have a question for you."

"Sure. What's your question?" *Here it goes*, I thought to myself.

"I was wondering if maybe you'd like to have coffee sometime." Anthony's mouth dropped as his eyes widened with excitement.

"Yes, absolutely!" he said without hesitating. My mind went blank. He followed me to my bike, and I grabbed my phone. I felt so rusty since I hadn't exchanged phone numbers with a man in almost fifteen years. Closing my eyes and taking a deep breath, the muscles in my hand twitched as I typed his phone number into my phone. I felt myself slowly open back up to the possibility of love like a plantain lily lying dormant in the wintertime and getting ready to blossom again.

39

———

A date. *I'm actually going on a date.* I couldn't believe it. If someone had told me five or even ten years ago that my life was going to resemble a hair-raising rollercoaster ride and end with me going out on a date with a handsome man, I wouldn't believe them. But here I was. Anthony and I made plans to meet up for coffee the weekend after my vacation with Emilia. The night before our first date, I sat at my kitchen table rather hesitant about going out with this shy and good-looking man from my cycle class.

Praying to God, I expressed my concerns. *Oh, I don't know God if this is who you want for me.* Suddenly, a voice inside me said, *"You wanted a man who was a Christian, and that's what I'm giving you. Give him a chance."* It felt like I was being lectured by my dad.

"Okay." I finally said. "I'll give him a chance, but he better not hurt me!"

The next day, I was looking out the window of my favorite coffee shop in town, wearing my pink and beige floral romper with my tan high heels accented with a cute bow. I waited patiently for Anthony to show up for our first coffee date. I finally saw him walk across the parking lot wearing jeans and a nice button-up shirt. Unexpectedly, a fluttery feeling formed in the pit of my stomach. *Wow, he's really handsome*, I thought to myself. He looked different from the typical gym attire that I was used to seeing him in. He walked in and looked rather surprised to see me in something other than gym clothes as well.

"Wow, you look beautiful," he told me sincerely. I was beyond flattered.

"Thank you," I told him with a coy smile on my face. As we were talking, I learned he was an engineer for the military. *Oh my gosh, of all things he could be*, I thought to myself. *He really is my type.*

As we were talking, Anthony received a text message from his pastor. They were supposed to meet up to go mountain biking together, but his pastor canceled. I was pleasantly surprised to hear this. On top of everything, he was friends with his pastor, and they hung out outside of church. I was beginning to believe this man may be a good fit for me after all. We talked for more than two hours. The conversation seemed to be endless and just flowed naturally. We talked about our jobs and our family, including my two dogs, Max and Charlie. He didn't have any pets so a lot of the concepts that I talked about he had never heard of, but I didn't mind educating him. My dogs are the one topic that I could talk forever about. As we talked and took in the moment, I could tell he was trying his best not to stare at me too much, changing up my gym attire for my floral romper.

It seemed like time flew by while we sat in that coffee shop. Anthony asked me if I wanted to go for a walk outside, and I said sure. After we walked for about ten minutes, he looked down at my dainty high heels.

"Your shoes are really nice," he commented. I smiled, thinking about how he noticed my shoes.

"Thank you! I own a lot of shoes," I admitted to him. He laughed. In thinking about my shoes, I realized that my feet were feeling sore from walking around in heels. "I should probably get going," I said to him. I had plans to attend a friend's birthday party right after my date with Anthony.

"Of course, let me walk you to your car." As we stood in front of my car, I thanked him for the nice time. We made plans to meet up the following weekend. I wrapped my arms around him, gave him a hug, and realized he was much taller than me. I looked up at him as his face lit up with a smile.

I got in my car and realized that this was the coffee shop where I had planned for Jack and me to meet. We could have finally talked about what had happened in the past year between us. But instead of Jack, it was my handsome cycle guy. The universe sure did throw me a curveball. This was not at all how I planned for my life to turn out, but I also knew that everything was working out for my highest and best good. I had to learn to let go and trust.

40

We should go to the zoo for our next date! The idea popped into my head like someone dropped it into my mind. I also thought of making him my famous chocolate chip cookies since he mentioned during our coffee date that he liked cookies. I had a feeling he would appreciate the thoughtful gesture. The cookies were also a favorite with my family, who gobbled them up every time I made them. I stumbled upon the recipe one day as I was thumbing through a recipe book I received as a Christmas gift a few years prior. Even though the recipe called for chocolate chips, I loved giving it my personal spin by mixing white chocolate chips into the dough, along with brown sugar, flour, and melted butter. My stepdad was even convinced that if I were to quit my job, I could make a good living selling my cookies, which made me laugh.

After baking the cookies that weekend, I went to the mall. I handpicked the cutest box with polka dots and a bow to put them in. I brought the box home and gently placed the freshly baked cookies in the wrapped box.

"It's perfect!" I told myself.

As he pulled up to the house to pick me up, I carried the perfect little box with my delicious cookies inside. We walked to his car. He opened the passenger side door for me which I took note of and got inside. With the box of freshly baked cookies in my hand, I told him,

"I made something for you." He smiled.

"Oh, wow. You didn't have to do this for me! I'm nobody special." I looked at him, completely bewildered.

"Yes, you are!" I told him. He smiled and gently opened the box to discover the freshly baked chocolate chip cookies.

"You made these for me?" He asked, surprised.

"Yes, I did," I proudly replied. He took a bite of a cookie. A look of excitement flashed across his face.

"Wow, these are delicious." I smiled, excited that he loved my cookies.

"I'm glad you like them," I told him. He ate one cookie and a second.

"I can't stop eating them!"

I laughed. "Yeah, they have a tendency to do that to people," I said jokingly.

"Yeah, no kidding!" he said.

As we drove down the freeway, making our way to the zoo, I was excited because this particular zoo held a special place in my heart. It was a place I had imagined going to for a date before. Zoos normally make me sad because I hate seeing animals in captivity, but this is one zoo that didn't leave me feeling depressed after visiting because the animals seemed happy living in something close to their natural habitat. I also loved the train that people could ride, giving a behind-the-scenes tour of the zoo. I was excited to see my two favorite animals who lived at this zoo: The flamingo and the giraffe.

As we walked into the wildlife refuge, making small talk, Anthony spotted the herd of bright pink flamingos and remembered that I mentioned they were my favorite animals.

"Hey, let's snap a photo in front of them."

I smiled. "That's a good idea!" And there, in the middle of the zoo, I took my first photo with the handsome cycle guy. As we walked around the park, I noticed that he took the time to read about all the animals. I loved how we were strolling casually, with no rush to end the day, as kids happily ran around with their families also excited about seeing the animals. Time seemed to stand still. I felt like I could be there all day with him. Walking next to him, I had the urge to hold his hand, but I held back. As we walked about admiring all the animals and watching them play, we stumbled upon the train and knew we had to ride it.

"This is my favorite part of the zoo," I told him excitedly. "We have to go on it!" Flashbacks of riding the train with my brother, sister-in-law, and my niece came flooding back into my mind. Seeing the smile on their faces as the train made its way through the zoo made me smile. I was excited to be sharing this special moment with this soon-to-be special man who was now in my life.

We bought our tickets, and it was our turn to board the train. The caboose on the train was rather small since it was made mostly for kids, but we managed to squeeze in the bright red seat. Anthony carefully placed his arm around my shoulders so he wouldn't hang off the side of the train. We snapped our second photo together. As kids were eagerly boarding the train, the conductor got on and introduced himself.

"Hi everyone! My name is Jack, and I'll be driving you around the zoo today." I sat there feeling like I was being haunted by the ghost of Jack as I was trying to move on with my life. I did my best to push the thoughts out of my mind and be in the present moment, enjoying the day with Anthony next to me.

As we listened to the conductor talk about the history of the park, including where the animals all came from, we approached the giraffe enclosure, and I got excited.

"There's the giraffe," I said like an excited little girl. Anthony looked over at me and smiled at seeing how happy I was to see this giant animal. The giraffe was walking around with her little baby giraffe. They walked up to the trough holding their food that looked as tall as the Empire State Building, and they started to eat. We learned the mama giraffe was pregnant, which was very exciting for the zoo. "We have to come back after the baby's born!" I told Anthony excitedly.

"That's a good idea...I think we should come back," he said with a pleasant smile on his face.

After walking around all the paths, we got into his car. Since it was still early, Anthony had the idea of stopping at a brewery he had enjoyed in the past to grab a bite to eat and something to drink. We walked into the brewery, and I saw two wooden swings hanging inside the restaurant on a rope. The little girl in me loves a good swing and couldn't resist wanting to get on one and swing. As I walked over to it, I noticed there was part of a quote printed on the swing. I looked down and couldn't believe what I was reading. *You are braver than you believe, stronger than you seem, and smarter than you think.*

Thinking back, I remembered seeing this quote last

Christmas when I was walking around downtown, leaving an Apple store after getting my phone repaired. A Christmas pop-up shop caught my eye. I walked into the glittery shop filled with beautiful Christmas ornaments and antique furniture hoping it could lift my spirits with the current drama happening in my life with Jack and being let go from my job. There, in a framed poster, was this exact quote. It brought tears to my eyes because it summed up exactly how I felt about Jack. Now here I was, looking at this swing on my date with another man, reading the same exact quote I saw four months prior. First, Jack the conductor, and now this.

What does this all mean? I asked God.

I got on the swing and started to move back and forth as thoughts were also swinging back and forth in my mind. Anthony looked over at me and smiled. He finished ordering our food and then got on the swing next to me. We snapped another photo together, our heads in close, hanging onto the ropes of our swings. I looked at the photo on my phone and thought, *He is so cute, and his dimples are so adorable.*

We sat down at a picnic table as our meals were being prepared. He had a beer, and I had a sweet lavender cocktail with whiskey and honey. I was not much of a beer drinker, so I was happy to learn this brewery also had cocktails. He started to tell me more about his family and where he went to school. Anthony was from a small town in Arizona, where he was the youngest of two siblings. He graduated from the University of Arizona with a degree in electrical engineering. He loved the idea of working for the Army while giving back to his country and decided to make a career out of it. I told him about my little brother, how he was a wildland firefighter, and some of the adventures he had been on fighting fires.

"Wow, I have so much respect for what they do. Their jobs are incredibly hard," he said.

I responded, "Oh, they sure are. I don't know how he does it, but he does it very well." I loved how he respected my brother's profession and made a note of that in the back of my mind.

Sitting at the picnic table with the sun shining above us and a few clouds sprinkled in the sky, our conversation flowed and seemed endless. No awkward moments of silence. We seemed to fit together perfectly. I looked up and saw our waiter approach our table with our food. Anthony had ordered a hamburger and fries, and I decided on a Caesar salad with shrimp. The delicious smell of his hamburger and fries filled the air. "Wow, these fries look great! Did you want to try one?" Anthony asked.

"Sure, I'll try one." I excitedly told him. Fries are my weakness and, in my mind, should be its own food group. Anthony grabbed a few fries and set them on my salad plate as I reached over and took a bite. "These are great fries! I love the garlic seasoning."

Anthony casually popped a French fry into his mouth. "You're right! They did a great job making these."

I smiled at Anthony as I cut my shrimp into tiny pieces and sprinkled it throughout my salad. I looked up and saw kids playing in their own section of the restaurant as families were laughing and enjoying the day. My heart felt full as a comfortable warmth filled my face. *Wow, this day is perfect. I couldn't have asked for a more perfect date,* I blissfully thought to myself.

After our meal, we made our drive back to my house. He carefully pulled up to the curb, making sure not to park next to the big tree in my front yard so I could get out. After we stopped, Anthony walked over to my side of the car and opened my door like a total gentleman. *Wow, I've never had a guy hold the door open for me, and this guy has done it twice already*, I thought to myself, impressed. He walked me to my front door, and I turned around to face him.

"I had a great time. Thank you so much for today and for our trip to the zoo." He smiled.

"It was my pleasure; I had a great time as well." I leaned in to give him a hug, and I could feel his heart racing. *He must be nervous*, I thought. I hugged him once more, and I could tell that he wanted to kiss me, but he was too shy. So there, standing on my front porch with my arms wrapped around his neck, I leaned in, and we shared our first kiss. Thinking that I shouldn't get too carried away, I started to giggle afterward.

I opened my eyes and said, "I better get going." We told each other goodbye, and I went inside the house.

I ran upstairs to my bedroom and flopped down on my bed. I grabbed my pillow, giving it a huge hug with a beaming smile on my face. I was floating on a cloud. This guy was everything that I hoped for and so much more. But in the back of my mind, Jack was still lingering. Part of me still wondered how things would turn out and if he called. To everyone on the outside, it seemed crazy to hold onto that tiny drop of hope, but I couldn't help it. I told myself that I couldn't fall in love with Anthony. I just couldn't.

41

———

A few days after my zoo date with Anthony, I got a call from Alice, my cousin Sophia's daughter. She was moving out of her dorm on campus and needed help relocating to her new apartment with the graduate students from her program. Knowing Anthony had a bigger car, I thought maybe he could help us out and meet Alice for the first time. "Let me talk to Anthony and see if he can help out with your move."

After hanging up the phone, I called Anthony and told him about Alice and her situation. "I would love to help her out," he said excitedly.

"That is nice of you Anthony, and she will be so thankful for your help, but I need to warn you that she is a little spitfire and will keep you on your toes!"

He started to laugh and said jokingly. "I'm sure she is, but that's okay. I still want to meet her, and besides, you're a little spitfire when you're teaching cycle, so I think I can manage." I laughed at his comment. I also knew what a big deal this was. He wasn't only helping Alice move but meeting a family member of mine for the first time, and Alice meant a great deal to me.

Anthony and I pulled up to the beautiful college campus. Gazing outside, the campus was lined with iconic red brick buildings. Large palm trees provided shade over vibrant green manicured lawns and a beautiful waterfall in the middle of the quad. We saw Alice waiting outside with a large platform moving cart, wearing purple corduroy overalls with white Converse sneakers and a gray t-shirt. We got out of the car, and Alice ran up to give me a big hug. "Hi, Lily! Thank you so much for helping me out."

"Of course—we're happy to help!" Anthony then smiled at Alice.

"Hey, Alice, I'm Anthony. It's nice to meet you. I've heard so much about you from Lily."

She smiled at him. "It's nice to meet you too, but honestly, I haven't heard *anything* about you. I didn't even know Lily was seeing someone…" I started to laugh and looked over at Anthony, who took her comment in stride.

"Oh yeah? Well, from the stories Lily told me about you, I can totally tell that you guys are related," he said with a smirk on his face.

We dutifully made our way up to Alice's dorm with the rolling cart in tow. *Well, if he can survive Alice and get her seal of approval, then he's a keeper,"* I thought to myself.

The three of us made the trek down to Alice's dorm. Walking down the hall, I caught sight of flyers hanging on the walls about various campus events, including a movie night at their recreation hall and a meet-and-greet for students living in the dorms. It reminded me of my college days when I lived on campus. Alice had her own private dorm whereas I wasn't so lucky.

She unlocked her door and walked into her dorm. I was shocked. It looked like a bomb had gone off. She had her belongings littered all over her room. I saw Cheetos bags and Gatorade bottles on the side next to her mini refrigerator, her clothes piled up, and her shoes everywhere. I looked back at Anthony as his eyes widened and his mouth slowly dropped open.

I turned to Alice and commented. "Alice, did you not do any packing?"

"No, I tried to make it back sooner but got caught up doing something for class, so I couldn't make it over in time," she replied.

Looking around her room I asked her, "How in the world did you pile so much stuff in your broom closet of a dorm?"

Anthony started laughing. He decided it was best not to step foot in her dorm like it was an active war zone.

"I know I'm a hoarder, but I just never know when I'm going to need something!" she remarked, not caring about her messy room.

I bent down and looked under her bed to find Alice's orange tabby cat, Odin, hiding in the midst of the carnage that was her dorm room. His large eyes were wide and darting back and forth.

Feeling lost and not knowing where to start, Anthony read my mind and spoke up. "I will go back down to my car and get the cardboard boxes that I brought and bring them back up for us to start packing."

I looked over and smiled at him. "Thank you so much." I was so thankful to have his help.

Formulating a plan of attack in my mind, I turned to Alice. "Okay! Let's start with your food first. We will pile it up in one spot, and then we can move on to your clothes and handbags."

"Sounds good!" she said excitedly.

As we sat on the floor organizing her food, Alice remarked. "That was nice of Anthony to come help me move. I was surprised when my mom told me you were dating someone, but we will see if he can pass my tests."

I laughed at her sassy comment. "I think he's doing pretty good so far. He even brought an entire tool kit, including Allen wrenches and screwdrivers, to help you move. I think that's pretty impressive."

"I'll be the judge of that," Alice joked.

Anthony came back with the cardboard boxes. "I will stay out here in the hallway and tape up the boxes while you guys pack. Besides, I don't think there's much room for me anyways."

I looked around at her packrat dorm room. "Sounds good," I told him.

We started organizing her food and putting it into cardboard boxes as we chatted about her school year. She was double majoring, with one major being neuropsychology, so she had a lot of responsibility on her plate, on top of working part-time. I was always so proud of how hard she worked and how far she had come so early in her college journey.

After packing all her snacks and meals, I moved to her clothes and spotted a cute, jean-colored Coach purse. "Alice, this is a nice purse!" I held it up, examining it.

Anthony started laughing. "Alice, you better keep an eye on your purses, or Lily may steal one from you." I began to laugh. He was already getting to know me all too well. He knew I loved fashion. Alice was the exact same way. She and I were cut from the same cloth.

Piling up the boxes, I started to hand them to Anthony one by one as he loaded them onto the cart. I then reached over to a chest decorated with various stickers in the back of her room to give to Anthony when Alice stopped me. "Oh, be careful with that one! I have some special goodies in there." She told me with a mischievous grin. It was then I caught a whiff of pot. *Oh Lord, please help me*, I thought to myself. I flashed Alice my most convincing parent look. Trying not to lecture her, I said, "I know you're an adult, but don't let Anthony know you have pot in your chest, please." A big smile came across her face.

"Got it!"

She grabbed the chest from my hands and walked over to Anthony as he tried to take it from Alice to place onto the cart. "Don't worry, I'll put this one away." Unexpectedly, she tripped over the cart. The lid popped open, and her "goodies" flew everywhere. I froze. Anthony looked down at the ground at the gummies and looked back at me with a smirk on his face.

"I am so sorry." I mouthed to him. He gave me an understanding smile and then looked down at Alice.

"Well, what do we have here?"

She quickly picked up the candy. "I'm sorry about that! I just eat them occasionally when I need to relax from studying."

Well, so much for that, I thought to myself.

Once the cart was packed up, we made our walk back to our vehicles to load up her boxes. As we were marching down the hall, I gave Alice a big hug. "I sure did miss you! I feel like we never get to see each other enough, even though we live so close."

She hugged me back, hanging tight onto me. "I know, and I'm so glad you guys came to help me move. I was crying earlier to my mom because I was so stressed and didn't think this was going to work out."

"Oh, don't worry. We've all been there with moving out of college dorms, and you will always have me to help you anytime. I'm only a phone call away." I told her soothingly.

We squeezed into the tiny elevator with Alice's cart filled to the top with her entire college life in cardboard boxes when Anthony's butt accidentally pushed the emergency call button. An operator came on the loudspeaker asking if we needed assistance. "Oh no! I'm so sorry! I accidentally pushed the button." The woman hung up the phone.

The three of us busted up laughing. "You must have a lot of junk in the trunk!" Alice remarked jokingly to Anthony, referring to the size of his butt.

He quickly responded, "I guess so!"

We wound up making two more trips to our cars, loading up more clothes, food, and college dorm furniture than I'd ever seen in my entire life. With Odin secure in his backpack, we made the drive over to the new college dorm, following Alice in our packed cars.

On our drive, I asked Anthony his thoughts on Alice. "So, what do you think about Alice? I wasn't kidding when I told you she was a little spitfire."

Anthony laughed. "No, you weren't kidding, but I really like her. She is sweet and smart. I can tell she has a bright future ahead of her."

His insight into Alice brought a smile to my face as we drove through the campus passing students walking to classes with their friends. "She really is smart, and she works so hard. She gets that strong work ethic from my cousin Sophia," I told Anthony. I then added, "She means a lot to me, and you meeting her is a big deal."

Anthony replied, "I can tell that you love her very much so I can understand that."

Pulling up to Alice's new dorm, we loaded her cart once again with all her boxes. I walked behind Alice and Anthony as they pushed the cart. I carried her large collection of squishmallow pillows to her new dorm. I smiled to myself as I overheard them talking about Alice's classes and campus life. We walked inside the college apartment and let Odin out of his backpack so he could explore his new home. He had developed a reputation among the college students as the resident dorm cat. They all pitched to care for him, even though he was Alice's cat.

Setting Odin down, he made a run for Alice's new room, hiding under her bed. *Oh, poor Odin. He certainly does roll with the punches as a college cat,* I thought to myself.

After we finished unpacking her boxes and organizing her kitchen, it was time to say our goodbyes. Alice had the bright idea of giving Anthony a small parting gift as a token of her appreciation.

"Anthony, I want to give you something as a thank you for helping me move." She ran into her room and emerged with the gummies from her chest. "Here. You can have some!"

Anthony looked over at me, and I could tell he was trying not to laugh.

I respond. "Alice, that is so thoughtful of you, but he can't eat those gummies."

Alice was confused. "What do you mean?"

I continued. "Alice, he's a government employee, so he can't have any pot, but that is nice of you to offer."

Not satisfied with my answer, she said, "Why the heck not? Is he James Bond or something?"

Anthony and I both laughed. "No, he's not James Bond, but he can't eat those, but thank you anyway."

Alice shrugged her shoulders. "Okay. Suit yourself, but these are the good gummies!"

Laughing, Anthony and I looked at each other. "Oh Alice, you are too funny! Please let us know if you need anything else as you're getting settled in your new place," I told Alice with a loving smile on my face.

I reached over and gave her a big hug. "I know. Thank you again for everything," Alice happily replied.

She then walked over to Anthony and gave him a hug. "I'm sure this isn't what you imagined when Lily asked you to come help me move, but I appreciate everything you did for me today. I hope it wasn't too much."

He smiled at her. "Of course not—it was fun, and I'm glad I was able to help."

On our way back home, I thought it would be a good idea to call Sophia and give her a rundown on Alice's move. "Hey, Sophia, Alice is all moved into her new dorm," I told her.

"That is such a relief. Thank you both for making the trip down to help her out. I was so bummed that I couldn't make it, but I felt better knowing you two could help her move out of her dorm," Sophia replied.

"Of course! But we do have to tell you something…Alice

did try to offer Anthony some drugs as a parting thank-you gift for our efforts," I hesitantly told her.

"She did what? Oh my gosh, I am so sorry, Anthony! What did she offer you?" Sophia replied, horrified.

Anthony started laughing. "It's okay! Really, it's fine. She tried offering me gummies."

"Oh, my goodness, I'll have a talk with her. I'm sorry again, Anthony," Sophia said apologetically.

Anthony quickly responded. "Really! It's okay. That was a first for me."

We both started laughing. *I knew the day would be memorable, but I had no idea it would turn out this way,* I thought to myself.

After we hung up with Sophia, Anthony and I continued chatting about our adventure when he said unexpectedly. "I have to let the cat out of the bag about something."

Confused, I quickly replied, "What is it?"

He slowly responded. "I'm allergic to cats, and that's why I didn't want to go into Alice's dorm."

I started to laugh. "What? Why didn't you say anything sooner? I saw you sneezing, but I thought it was allergies!"

"No, I'm allergic to cats. I just didn't want to say anything," he said slowly.

"Ahh, that's okay! I guess we won't be getting any cats in the future…" I told him jokingly.

He responded. "Yes—all animals are fine except cats."

I smiled at the thought of us having a farm filled with rescue animals, minus cats. "Noted, I'm good with that." I lovingly grabbed his hand as we continued driving back home.

———

DINNER NIGHTS, movie dates, and trips hiking with Anthony and my dogs filled my calendar as I spent more time with Anthony. We were together just about every weekend for a month straight, and before I knew it, I was wholeheartedly falling in love with him. We fit together perfectly like two puzzle pieces that had been searching for each other. All the while, the memory of Jack began to fade little by little, and I thought maybe I was starting to get over him.

One night, I confided in Anthony about the prayer I had prayed at the church concert the month before we started dating. I told him that I was letting go and letting God take over control of my love life and who *He* wanted me to be with.

We cuddled on the couch in my living room as my roommate, Aiden, worked the overnight shift at the hospital. Anthony quietly took in every word when he finally said, "I also prayed that same prayer—asking God to bring me a woman who loved God and put *Him* first. I also let go and told God no matter how long it takes, I will wait for her."

I couldn't believe it. We had prayed almost the exact same prayer at the same time. We were each other's answered prayer. God was leading us to each other all along, but we just didn't know it.

Things were also going wonderfully at my job. I was a few months into my new role. I was thankful to finally be working in a healthy work environment where I was supported by my new boss and team, who expressed their thankfulness for the work I did. I took on a large project, completing a communications plan for a division within the new agency I was working with. I knocked it out of the park. That was my first time leading a huge project, and thanks to my amazing co-workers, my boss, and the client were very impressed.

During my weekly check-ins with my new boss, Samantha, she gave me feedback on my performance so far. She was a soft-spoken woman in her early forties who had a strong public affairs background working for the government and the military.

"You have a great background, Lily, and you're doing a great job. If you ever want to work in Washington, D.C., there are a ton of great opportunities here, just so you know." My clients also echoed the same sentiment and gave me similar feedback. I never thought about living and working in the nation's capital, but I was open to the idea and thankful to Samantha for seeing something great in me. I also knew that moving away would impact my new relationship with Anthony. I decided to sit down and tell him what my boss told me. So, one night after work, as we sat around a firepit at his apartment complex, I broke the news to him.

"Wow, that's great," he said. "That's awesome that they see something in you and are recognizing all the hard work you're doing." Anthony lovingly smiled at me as he reached over and poured us a glass of red wine. It was a crisp, chilly night with the stars shimmering above us as we sat close to the fire, trying to stay warm.

I responded, "I agree, but I can't help but feel a little sad because if I moved, what does that mean for us?" He looked at me with love in his eyes.

"It'll be okay. We will make it work, but if you have this opportunity, go for it. I took an opportunity like this when I graduated from college and look where I am now. I don't want to hold you back." I was so thankful for his support, but in my mind, this made my decision even more difficult.

"I appreciate what you're saying, but I can't help but feel sad because I don't want to leave you." A sympathetic look came across his face.

"What? Don't feel sad! This is amazing news. I want you to be happy. We will make our relationship work, don't worry. It's going to be okay." I reached over and tightly hugged his arm as he kissed the top of my head.

My heart still felt heavy, but I was also excited for the opportunity.

I made plans to visit Washington, D.C., the following month—to meet all my co-workers in person, including my boss—and visit my stepbrother Isaac, who lived in New York City. He was excited about the trip and the opportunity to play tourist and sightsee in the city. I also saw this as an opportunity to see if Washington, D.C., was a good fit for me if I decided to make it my permanent home.

Spring 2022

42

———

Oh no, what if I see Jack? As I sat on the plane enroute to Washington, D.C., I couldn't help but think about him. I knew he was living in the city since he had just accepted military orders there. I wondered what might happen if I ran into him on the street, possibly stopping to say hello or ignoring me like I was another stranger walking by. My mind began spiraling as I started to second-guess myself for even taking this trip to begin with. I held my warm green tea in my hands as I did my best to get lost in the jazz music playing in my headphones. My hands began to sweat as I started to feel faint.

No, that won't happen, Lily. What are the chances of you running into him? You have nothing to worry about. I quickly thought. With so many people living in D.C., I figured my chances of seeing Jack were pretty slim. I decided to push him out of my mind and focus on making this trip the very best it could be. I was very excited to be visiting the city again after leaving fifteen years ago when my ex-husband and I were stationed on the East Coast. I was now visiting as a newly single woman with potential career opportunities, and I couldn't be happier.

Unfortunately, the universe had other plans for my trip. The trip got off to a rocky start the moment I stepped off the plane. Walking up to the counter to pick up my rental car for the week, the woman with the car rental company pulled up my itinerary and said, "Did you reserve an electric car?" I looked around, confused.

"No, why?"

She continued, "Well, it says here you reserved an electric car."

I shot back. "No, I didn't. Why in the world would I reserve an electric car?" In the back of my mind, I reviewed the receipt and didn't remember anything about an electric car.

She continued, "Well, that's what it says here, but if you want a regular gas car, then it's an extra hundred dollars."

Feeling completely blindsided, I practically yelled, "What!" At this point, I had no choice. I had to eat the extra cost of the car, so I didn't have to worry about being stranded in a city that I didn't know very well, trying to find an electric car charging station. "Okay, just give me a gas car, and I'll pay the extra cost." I couldn't believe this was how my trip was starting, with me paying extra money that I honestly didn't have, saving up just enough money to cover my expenses.

I went into the parking garage and picked out a cute silver Toyota Corolla. I shoved my luggage in the back seat and put in the address for the Airbnb I was staying at in Alexandria, Virginia, just outside of the city, into the GPS on my phone. As I drove out of the airport trying to leave, I discovered a little too late that the signs weren't very clear. I wound up driving around the airport for about twenty minutes, trying to figure out how to leave. Everyone was flying past me, and my anxiety level was through the roof. This was my first solo trip without my now ex-husband and without any friends, and I was pretty terrified.

After I figured out the correct exit to take, I finally left the airport after feeling like a trapped hamster running on a wheel, going absolutely nowhere. Driving on the freeway, I tried to calm myself and take in the luscious green trees all around me. I had forgotten how green and pretty it was on the East Coast since it had been more than a decade since I visited the area.

Driving down the freeway, I took the wrong exit to connect to the next freeway and wound up downtown. As my mind raced to try to figure out which direction to go, I accidentally drove down a one-way street and almost hit a guy wearing a crisp business suit carrying a brief case crossing the street.

"Hey! Watch where you're going!" He yelled at me as I swerved around him.

"I can't believe this is happening!" I said aloud.

I pulled into the parking lot of a drug store, trying to calm myself down. I pulled the directions back up to my Airbnb. After studying the map, I got back on the road. Somehow, I managed to leave the city and get back on the correct freeway.

As I approached Alexandria, a strong feeling of déjà vu hit me. This looked just like Maryland when I was stationed there with my ex-husband. I felt like I had stepped back in time. The town was very small, but everything still looked the same. The signs for the streets were the same sad brown color and while the buildings looked outdated and old, I had a feeling the historic architecture in the town had some amazing stories to tell. Regardless, I now remembered why I wanted to move back home all those years ago and why my ex-husband volunteered to go to Afghanistan just to get us out of the East Coast. I just knew it wasn't a good fit for me. Nonetheless, I was still optimistic and open to this opportunity.

Maybe this time it will be different, I thought to myself. I had a feeling that I was wrong.

I finally found the Airbnb that I was staying at and as I pulled up to the driveway, the home looked picturesque. The cute little blue and white cottage had white shutters on the windows and was surrounded by beautiful green trees with pink flowers. A wood swing hung from a big oak tree in the front yard. I got lost in the moment, and I realized this wasn't where I was staying. I was staying in the home in the back. I drove past the adorable, quaint home to find a small brick building that looked abandoned. There were cobwebs on the cloudy windows. It looked as if nobody had lived there in about twenty years. *This can't be it!* I thought to myself.

I read all the reviews, and this didn't fit what was written about the home. The photos online looked vastly different from the outdated mother-in-law cottage sitting in front of me now. But nope, I was wrong. The Airbnb was my home for the next week. I sat in my car staring at the house that looked like it was built in the early 1900s. I was completely horrified and didn't want to step inside, but I knew I had to go. I had nowhere else to stay, so I decided to suck it up, hoping the inside wasn't as bad as the outside.

. . .

As I APPROACHED the house and opened the front door, a strong odor hit me. It was a cross between wet clothes and mothballs. I was horrified. *This place needs some Febreze,* I thought critically. I walked around the tiniest kitchen I had ever seen in my life. It was obvious this place was in dire need of a major update. The bedroom, which sat in the back of the house, had a low ceiling that I was sure I could actually touch. The room had a queen-sized bed with a cute photo of an elephant hanging above it.

I peeked outside the bedroom window and saw the sun starting to set. I was terrified to stay in this old, outdated house alone. It honestly looked haunted. I did my best to push the thought out of my mind. After unpacking, I called Anthony and gave him the lowdown.

"Babe, I'm sure it's not that bad," he said.

"Oh no, it is that bad!" I told him. He asked to FaceTime with me to see the place for himself, so we chatted over video. I gave him a little tour of the house and showed him what it looked like outside.

"Well, the area outside is really pretty and green," he said hopefully, but admitted after seeing the rest of the house, "Yeah, I see what you mean about the house. It is old." I remembered from my time living on the East Coast that many of the homes here were old. I also remembered my friends who lived here, and almost all of them lived in a house that was haunted. It was the norm for them, and they didn't think much of it. But as an outsider, I found this utterly alarming.

"I'm so scared to go to sleep in this house!" I told Anthony. "How in the world am I going to get any sleep in a place like this?"

"Just make the best of it, babe. You will be okay. Before

you know it, you will be home. Besides, no ghost in their right mind would want to mess with you." I let out a small laugh.

"Okay, but I'm sleeping with the lights on tonight." And I did. I didn't turn off a single light all night. I put on my ocean waves on my phone and did my best to fall asleep at my haunted Airbnb.

43

———

A pounding headache greeted me the next morning as I woke up not feeling as refreshed as I'd hoped—especially since I was meeting my co-workers and my boss for the first time in person. Gathering my things, I decided to take a cycling class in the city. It was pretty early for me, considering I was now three hours ahead, but I made it work. I needed a little something to lift my spirits, and cycling did the trick.

I drove into Georgetown, thankful I was able to locate the cycle studio in one piece. I got out of my car and walked into the pristine, beautiful cycle studio. I took a deep breath.

"Now, *this* is my home," I said to myself. I put my bags in the locker, walked into the cycle room, and clipped into the bike. I looked around and saw other people starting to file into the room and clip into their bikes. As the lights dimmed, the instructor got on his bike, and loud dance music started to fill the room. I realized that no matter the city that I was in, being in a cycle room felt like my home away from home. I let my mind get lost in the music and tried my best to sweat out my frustrations from my trip.

After the class ended, I got ready for my first big day in the city. Since it was still hot and humid, I did my best to look professional and cute while trying to stay cool. I wore black dress slacks with closed-toed high heels and a light pink dress tank top. I was trying not to sweat from the humidity and realized that keeping makeup on in this weather was going to be a challenge. I stepped outside and saw people dressed in business suits and blazers, which blew my mind.

"It's ninety degrees and hot! How in the world are they wearing jackets?" I said to myself, bewildered.

Thinking I had some time to kill before seeing my boss, Samantha, my phone rang, and it was Samantha. She had an event that ended early and wanted to meet up earlier for lunch, so I said sure. I was ready to go, so I didn't mind meeting up early. Then, I got a text message from my co-worker Angela. She was a bright and ambitious woman in her mid-twenties with shoulder-length dark blonde hair and chocolate-brown eyes. She had been working for my company for more than a year. I always saw her as the glue that held the team together. No matter the problem, she always had a solution. She was in the office and overheard my conversation with Samantha. She offered to move up our coffee plans before my big lunch, and I agreed.

As I drove through Georgetown and crossed over the Arlington Memorial Bridge, I took in all the breathtaking monuments on my way to the restaurant. I saw two bronze statues in different poses on one side of the bridge. One of the statues was of a bearded muscular man on a horse with a woman and a child. This wasn't something I was normally used to where I was from. At that moment, I felt so proud of myself for how far I had come. Despite everything that had happened, I tried my best to just make this trip the very best possible.

I parked my car in the parking garage and walked outside. I quickly realized high heels weren't the best thing to wear as pain started shooting up my legs. As I tried to navigate this new city on foot and find the coffee shop where I was meeting Angela, I couldn't get over how big the city was. After about ten minutes of not finding the coffee shop, I called Angela.

"Hey," she said in a chipper voice. "I'm so excited about finally meeting you in person. Where are you at?"

I replied, "Well, that's why I'm calling. I can't find the coffee shop, and I think I'm lost."

She quickly replied, "No worries. I'll guide you. Just tell me the street you're on." After some navigating, we finally found each other. I reached over and gave her a big hug. I felt like I had known her forever, and we clicked right away.

As we walked to the coffee shop, she started to talk about the warm weather. "It's normally not this hot this time of the year—this is very unusual weather for us."

I commented, "Yeah, I noticed it's pretty hot and forgot how humid it can be here." I realized that maybe moving here wasn't a good idea after all, but nonetheless, I kept trekking on. A cold gust of wind hit me as we opened the front door to the coffee shop that sat in the lobby of a modern office building. We found a seat at the coffee bar and started to talk about our work and my trip over coffee. She asked me what I thought about my role now. "Oh, I love it," I told her. "This is that mission-driven work that I enjoyed doing for the military, and I'm glad I'm able to tap into that again."

She looked at me and smiled. "That's so great! I'm so glad

that you're enjoying your new role with us." I really was, and I felt so blessed to be working where I was.

We continued talking and I kept an eye on the time to make sure I was not late meeting my boss. Especially being in a new city, I knew I had to give myself time to find it. Luckily, Angela knew the city well and was happy to help. "The restaurant is only ten minutes from here, so you'll be fine to walk," she said.

"Great! Thank you for your help." We exited the coffee shop and walked outside as she gave me directions to my next destination. We hugged and said our goodbyes and promised to see each other again soon.

After ten minutes of walking to the restaurant, I was again reminded that high heels were the *wrong* choice for footwear as I was doing a lot more walking around the city than expected. My feet were killing me, and they were very unhappy. Regardless, I did my best to make it quickly to the restaurant, giving my feet a well-deserved break from walking. I stepped into the seafood restaurant where I was meeting Samantha, and the smell of fresh fish hit me. It looked similar to a restaurant back home. It made me smile as that feeling of home came over me once again.

Sitting at the table, my boss Samantha showed up. She was a petite woman with amber eyes and dark brunette hair. She was wearing a crisp black suit with her hair pulled up into a bun. A warm smile flashed across her face as I gave her a hug and thanked her for coming out and meeting me.

"No, thank *you* for coming out here all the way from Arizona!" Samantha said. I smiled at her. It was so nice to finally meet her in person. As we laughed and talked about work, Samantha said, "I am so thankful for all the work that you've done so far. You've really grown since you first started with us, and it really shows." I was blown away by the compliment.

"Wow, thank you so much for saying that—that means so much to me."

I glanced over the lunch menu and decided to order a lobster roll with French fries. "Everything looks so good! I could order one of everything but I'm thinking of getting the lobster roll."

Samantha looked up from her menu and smiled. "Everything here is good, and the lobster roll is a great choice! I think I'll get the same thing."

After the waiter came and took our order, I looked around the restaurant and just took in the moment sitting with Samantha. I couldn't get over how much things had changed in my life. I felt so blessed to have an amazing job and boyfriend that I loved so much. My life had received a much-needed makeover.

Almost as if Samantha read my mind, she looked at me and smiled. "The environment here is much different than what you're used to, I'm sure!"

I smiled back at her. "Yes, it is but different in a good way! It was the exact change that I needed."

Samantha replied, "It is certainly different than Arizona that's for sure! Have you done anything outside of work since you got here?"

My eyes lit up with excitement. "Oh yes! I went to a cycling class this morning in Georgetown, and I had a blast! It was nice to get a good workout in after sitting for so many hours on a plane."

Samantha quickly replied, "That's amazing! I forgot that you taught cycle back in Arizona!"

I could feel the glow in my eyes grow as I squealed, "I love it! I could easily do it for free but it's nice that they pay me." We both laughed.

"Yes, that's great that you have something you're so passionate about! Side hustles are never a bad thing to have, especially one that keeps you healthy."

After we were done eating our lunch, we said our good-byes She thanked me once again for coming out. Walking back to my car, I realized that I needed to stop and sit. I found a nearby place to take a break from walking and give my feet some breathing room. I finally made it to my car and headed to downtown Washington, D.C., to meet up with my co-workers for my highly anticipated happy hour meet and greet. I planned this happy hour a month in advance to meet all my co-workers in person and couldn't wait. After researching several restaurants in the area, I picked a restaurant off Dupont Circle that was close to everyone. I pulled up to the restaurant about an hour early and decided to wait inside.

I walked in and the first thing I noticed was the loud music. Something told me this probably wasn't a good place for me to pick but I was already there. I decided to make the best of it. As I sat at the table looking over the menu, I saw a group of younger guys in their twenties wearing suits sitting at the table across from me. I overheard them saying a co-worker of theirs got busted for wiretapping. I couldn't believe what I was hearing and how, to them, it seemed normal. I realized the culture in this city is much different from what I remembered the last time I lived on this side of the country. Not knowing what to order, I decided to order my usual lemon drop martini.

Looking at the clock and slowly sipping my drink, I realized that it was getting close to the hour that people should be coming, but nobody had arrived yet. I looked down at my phone and received a text message from one of my co-workers saying he was sorry, but something came up, and he couldn't make it. Before I knew it, other text messages started coming in. They were dropping like flies. My heart dropped. I soon realized that nobody was coming out to my happy hour meet and greet. I couldn't believe it. I was getting stood up by my own co-workers. I stepped outside the restaurant as I could no longer hold back my tears. I called Anthony, upset about how things were turning out.

"This entire trip has been a disaster! Nobody is showing up for my happy hour…I went through all the trouble to plan this trip, and nobody is coming!" I heard his heart breaking in his voice.

"Babe, I am so sorry! If I were there, I would wrap my arms around you and give you a big hug. We would be exploring the city and having fun."

I shouldn't have been surprised this trip was going south. From the moment I got off the plane, it was a total train wreck. Even as I was sitting at the light in my car, I saw people honking at each other and arguing in the street. I felt like Dorothy, and it was apparent that I wasn't in Kansas anymore. I was out of my comfort zone with no support whatsoever.

Standing outside of the restaurant feeling defeated, I continued to vent to my sympathetic boyfriend. "I just want to come home," I cried to Anthony. "I'm homesick, and this place isn't what I'd imagined."

Trying to encourage me, he said, "Babe, Isaac will be there in the morning. Just try to hang on a little longer. I promise it will get better."

I sighed. "I know you're right babe. Thank you for the pep talk."

Anthony replied, "Call me anytime. You know I am here for you. I am just a phone call away." I smiled as I hung up the phone with him and waited another ten minutes. I finally decided to call it a night and drove back to my haunted Airbnb in Alexandria.

44

———

The next morning, I woke up early and made the short drive back to Washington, D.C., to pick up my stepbrother Isaac from the Washington Union Station. Driving up to the monumental train station reminded me of the Smithsonian. It was by far the most beautiful train station I'd ever seen, with three American flags proudly flying in front. I sat in my car, waiting for Isaac to come out of the station. He had to leave New York at four a.m. just to come see me. Knowing him, a recent college graduate, that was very early, but I was thankful that he was coming.

As I watched people quickly filing in and out of the station, I saw Isaac walk up with his luggage. He had a big welcoming smile on his face. He was wearing a fun multicolored tye-dyed shirt with jean shorts, his black Doc Martins, and brown eyeglasses. His beautiful, long black hair was pulled back into a low ponytail. Even though it had been two years since I last saw him, it was almost as if no time had passed. I reflected on the last time we saw each other. We were standing in the middle of a football field at his high school graduation in my small hometown as he was looking over a photo collage book I had made of all his plays since he was a young boy. Now, here he was two years later, taking his luminous inner light and living in the Big Apple, pursuing Broadway acting. I was so proud of him for making such a scary jump, but he was thriving in New York. He was paving his own way.

He ran up to me and gave me a big hug. "Lily! Oh, my goodness, I've missed you!"

Trying to hold back the tears, I told him, "I missed you too little brother! You have no clue what's been happening on this trip!"

After he put his luggage in the back seat, he got into the passenger seat and said, "Okay. Tell me about it! What's been going on?" I gave him a rundown of the trip so far. He was shocked.

"Wow! Your trip has gotten off to a rocky start for sure! I am so sorry!" Trying to lift my spirits, he said, "Well, I am here now, and we are going to turn this trip around." I smiled, hoping that he was right.

The first thing Isaac asked for was coffee. He was exhausted and needed a caffeine boost. We found a cute mom-and-pop coffee shop in a quaint neighborhood on the corner tucked away in between the beautiful federal-style homes. As we sat down over coffee, I realized that he had no clue what had been going on in my love life the last year and he didn't know that I started seeing someone. I decided to tell him about Jack and Anthony. After I was done telling him the story of my life, Isaac's eyes grew large. He was leaning into the table across from me, hanging onto every word.

"I had no idea this was happening in your life...this is by

far the craziest story I've ever heard, and honestly, it sounds like a movie. I want to know how it ends!"

I smiled at him. "It really is a crazy story, and I'm not sure how it's going to end. Honestly, that's okay. I'm just trusting that everything will work out for my highest and best good."

"Yes," Isaac said as he reached from across the table and lightly grabbed my hand. "I agree with you, and it will all work out. You'll see."

In the back of my mind, a small part of me was still hesitant about fully jumping in with Anthony and giving him my heart. At the same time, I felt like part of my heart was with Jack. I confessed to Issac about my uncertainty regarding my relationship.

"Even though I know it will all be okay eventually, a small part of me is still hoping for Jack to come for me. I can't help but wonder if the day will finally come when I will stop pining for him and wanting him to consider a future with me."

Isaac looked at me with a sympathetic smile. "Anthony sounds like a great guy who really loves you and appreciates you. You can't live your life for Jack with the hope that he *may* see the light of day and come for you. You need to think about what will make you happy. From what I can see, Anthony makes you happy, and honestly, you're glowing, girl. I've never seen you this happy."

I paused and took a deep breath. Issac was right. Anthony did make me happy. Even in all my years of being married, I didn't know happiness like this existed. "You're right, Isaac. I do have a great guy. He is everything I've ever wanted in a partner, and it seems like he was sent straight from Heaven just for me."

Issac smiled and exclaimed. "I know—that's what I've been

saying! You two seem to complement each other so well. I can't wait to meet him one day."

After leaving the coffee shop, we made plans to visit our first Washington, D.C., museum, the Museum of Natural History. As we parked in front of the National Mall, I got out of the car and looked around at all the monuments. I couldn't help but think about Jack. I wondered if he ever made the time to visit these life-size monuments and amazing museums or if he was too busy with his new job working in the city.

We walked into the museum and caught sight of a large African Bush Elephant with its tusk in the air on display in the rotunda. "Isaac! He is huge!" I exclaimed. Isaac ran over and stood next to me reading all about the model elephant.

"It says that he weighs eleven tons and is thirteen feet tall!" I glanced across the rotunda and saw a mega-tooth shark hanging from the atrium.

"Issac, we have to take our photo in front of that shark. Let's go!" Issac snapped his head up and stared at the shark.

"Oh yes! We have to do that!" We walked over and snapped our first museum photo in front of the fifty-two-foot-long model female shark.

After spending more than two hours walking around the museum and reading about the exhibits, Isaac and I decided to grab lunch at this adorable, locally-owned Italian restaurant downtown. The restaurant donned framed family photos from the owners of the restaurant, along with famous people and former presidents who had also dined there on the walls. This was my first time at an authentic Italian restaurant on the East Coast, and we shared a delicious seafood pasta plate. We sat next to a large window looking out onto the street as people casually strolled down the sidewalk. In between enjoying our lunch, Isaac couldn't wait to tell me all about life in the big city since graduating from college, including going on auditions for different roles. He was doing so well, and I couldn't have been happier for him.

"What you're doing is so brave. I admire how you've really hit the ground running in a city that is so new to you. It's not the small town that we lived in before," I said. He laughed at me.

"I know, but I love it! I can't imagine myself living anywhere else." I agreed with him.

"The city fits you well and you've grown so much personally and professionally since you've moved there. I have no doubt it will be no time before you land your first big role—just keep at it, and God will open a door," I told him encouragingly.

After spending the day in D.C., I drove Isaac back to my less-than-luxurious accommodations in Alexandria. I prepared him for what he was about to experience.

"Okay, bring it on! I'm excited to see this place," he said unphased. As we drove up, his tone changed as he caught sight of the rundown house. "Wow. You weren't kidding. It really does look haunted…"

I laughed. "See? I wasn't lying." We walked into the small brick mother-in-law house with his luggage trailing behind us. He looked around and was appalled but tried to hide it.

"Well, it is quaint looking, and it could use a nice candle," I laughed at him as he was referring to the old musty smell.

"It needs a lot more than a candle, Isaac!" I told him jokingly.

We sat down on the couch and settled in for the night. As we relaxed, the idea of Isaac and Anthony finally meeting popped into my mind, so we called him over FaceTime. I've told Anthony all about Isaac over one of our dates, and I knew he was excited to meet him. As we talked over video, I saw the look of relief on Anthony's face when he saw me laughing and smiling with Isaac.

"There's that smile and laugh! Isaac, you have no idea how much it means to me that you made the trip from New York to see Lilian," he said. "Just to see her happy brings so much peace to my heart. Seeing her cry last night just broke my heart that I couldn't be there with her, but it's obvious you two have a close bond, and you both love each other very much. Thank you for making her feel better."

My stepbrother had a big smile on his face and gave me a tight hug. "There's nowhere else I'd rather be than here with her. We will have a great time and turn this trip around." Isaac started to talk about his life in the big city with Anthony as he listened attentively. Anthony asked Issac about his new job working at Trader Joe's, which he proudly said was the busiest Trader Joe's in America. I sat back as they talked. A wave of peace came over my entire body. I felt so much happiness in my heart for how they were getting along so well.

After we hung up the phone with Anthony, Isaac turned to me and said, "I really like him a lot, Lily. It's obvious that he loves you and cares a lot about you." I smiled.

"He really does. He was a Godsend, that's for sure."

45

———

I woke up the next morning excited and refreshed, almost as if the string of unfortunate events I first encountered after landing in D.C. were in the review mirror. Issac and I were ready to take on the day. The first activity on our agenda was seeing George Washington's estate in Mount Vernon. I loved presidential libraries since college, and I visited three so far in my life. I was so excited to see the home where George Washington himself lived and add that one to my list. I also remembered how my Aunt Victoria told me a while back that we were related to his wife, so I had a personal tie-in. It made me even more excited to see his estate. It breathed new life into the visit.

We drove through the countryside leading up to his estate. I couldn't get over the picturesque foliage from the leaves turning beautiful tones of red and gold. Every home looked like a beautiful mansion straight out of a Hollywood movie. Huge yards and gorgeous, luscious trees surrounded the neighborhoods. Looking around in awe, I told Isaac, "I absolutely can see myself living here…"

He exclaimed, "Oh yeah! It sure is beautiful. I don't remember the last time I've seen homes this large." I agreed with him.

As Isaac played DJ in the car, singing some of his favorite Barbra Streisand songs, we finally made our way to the highly anticipated estate. We got there early in the morning, which meant we beat the crowd. Since I bought our tickets ahead of time, we walked right into the museum. We grabbed a map of the grounds and excitedly made our way through the museum and out the back doors toward the estate.

As we followed along the dirt path lined with wood fencing, the first thing I noticed was how far-reaching the property was. A large green field lay in front of the house. It looked like it went on forever as the mansion sat on top of a hill overlooking the Potomac River. As we waited in line to get into the estate, we were standing with a large group of junior high-aged kids also waiting to take a tour of the home. Isaac and I started to giggle as we listened to the kids talk back and forth about the school trip and teenager gossip about someone they knew having a crush on their friend. Finally, the line started to move, and we made our way into the home.

We walked into the main foyer of the house and listened attentively as the tour guide told us about the history of the house. In the living room were huge oil paintings hanging on the wall that I was pretty sure I had seen in my high school history books. Vibrant turquoise green wallpaper covered every inch of the walls. We learned that wallpaper was a symbol of wealth back in that time. If you had wallpaper in your home, that meant you had money. It was so interesting to hear what was valued back in that time, whereas nowadays, we take something like wallpaper for granted. As the tour guide went into detail about George Washington's family history, he also commented about George Washington's characteristics, giving us a glimpse into who he was as a person.

"George Washington was a man of exemplary character and conviction. While he had a tall, commanding presence about himself, he also placed the welfare of others above his own and possessed a true servant-leadership spirit." I listened to the tour guide talking about the admirable characteristics that made George Washington a great president. A small grin came across my face. These same traits also reminded me of Jack. I realized my old brigade had their very own George Washington, and they didn't even know it.

I looked across the foyer and spotted the family's parlor and music room that housed George Washington's harpsichord that he had commissioned for his step-granddaughter. I started taking piano lessons back in January, and I developed an appreciation for the instrument and the harpsichord was a closely related instrument. Studying the parts of the harpsichord made in the late 1700s, it was probably older than the house itself. The instrument was dainty and yet had a large and beautiful presence all at the same time. It possessed two sets of keyboards and an opened music book. I imagined the music that was played on that very harpsichord and the famous people who sat in that chair, not thinking much about what they were doing but enjoying the beautiful music it played.

We moved on to George Washington's study, which was lined with historic books on the wall. Two antique desks and a telescope sat on one of his desks. They complemented his study with his portrait hanging on the wall above it. The tour guide, an older man in his late 60s with gray hair and light brown eyes, was particularly animated. He was acting out some of the scenes to drive the point home of the important work George Washington did in that study. I looked around at everyone in the room and back at the tour guide. All of a sudden, I started to giggle under my breath. Then I was giggling some more. Before I knew it, I was in the midst of a giggling attack. I had to step out of the room so nobody saw. Meanwhile, Isaac did his best not to look at me, but he was obviously laughing as well.

As we moved into the next room, Isaac ran up to me, laughing. "Oh, my goodness, that was so funny! I was trying so hard not to laugh and look at you!" I was busting up laughing. I couldn't remember the last time I had a laugh this good. I knew my soul needed it. I gave Isaac a big hug. He was right, he did turn this trip around. I was having the best time and it was all because of him.

We made our way out of the house and stepped onto the back patio facing the Potomac River. As I stood in awe, looking at the beautiful river and the beautiful green mountains all around, I also caught a glimpse of the highway across the way with cars driving by. Suddenly, time stood still. While the world continued to develop and change with the times, this house stayed exactly the same. Not a single thing was out of place. No painting on the wall changed with everything looking exactly the way it did when George Washington lived there with his family. With a light breeze blowing all around us, I closed my eyes. I allowed myself to be transported back in time to a period when things were easier and life wasn't as complicated as it was today. Wishing for a simpler and easygoing life, I opened my eyes and saw Isaac standing next to me, listening to the tour guide talk about the river. A small grin formed across my face. I knew I was exactly where I was meant to be.

46

———

The tour ended just in time as I felt my stomach start to rumble from hunger. We decided to take a break and grab some lunch at a restaurant in downtown Alexandria. Driving through the town, I couldn't help but notice how old the colonial buildings and homes were, with so much history behind their walls. Each home had a lantern hanging in front of it with a hand-painted sign reflecting the home number on it. They were so beautiful. *Maybe I could live here*, I thought to myself. I also realized going from living in Arizona to Virginia may be a culture shock.

Isaac and I found a small pub facing the Potomac River to eat lunch. We sat outside enjoying the sunshine, waiting for our food to come, and reflecting on our day. Without warning, dark clouds rolled in. It started to sprinkle. To everyone else, this was completely normal. They didn't move a muscle. For Isaac and me, we started to freak out like a downpour was going to happen at any moment.

"Oh no…we haven't even gotten our food yet!" he said

worryingly. The sprinkling lasted maybe a minute, and it was over. We were safe. I started to laugh.

"I love how us being the out-of-town people are freaking out, and the locals are cool as cucumbers," I told him. He also laughed.

"All I kept thinking was, wait! We haven't gotten our food yet!" I knew I was out of my comfort zone on this trip, but I was so thankful to have Isaac with me.

Before we knew it, the day was over. It was time to go back to our Airbnb and get ready to take Isaac back to the train station in the morning and for me to make my way back to the airport to fly home. On the drive back home, I told Isaac, "Thank you so much for coming. You will never know how much it meant to me that you came here to literally save me. If it wasn't for you, this trip had disaster written all over it, but you turned it around." He looked at me and smiled. He reached over and gave me a big hug.

"I'm so happy I was able to make you smile, and I'm happy that we spent this time together." Something also told me this was a trip I'd never forget.

That night, a big thunder and lightning storm blew in and brought rain in a way that I'd never seen before. As I was getting ready for bed, I looked out the bedroom window and saw flashes of light tear across the night sky. I ran to the window and called out to Isaac.

"Isaac! Get in here! You have to see this!" Isaac came running into my room.

"What is it?" he asked curiously.

A flash of light streaked across the night sky, lighting up huge storm clouds in the distance, turning nighttime into daytime with such ease, accompanied by rolling thunder.

"Look at the lightning!" I yelled. He ran to the bedroom window next to me as we watched in amazement the most beautiful lightning show we'd ever seen. "I've never seen anything like this before in my life!" I told Isaac. He agreed with me.

"We can't see anything like this in the city because of the huge buildings."

In between us *oohing* from our bedroom window, we couldn't take our eyes off the clouds as the rain came pouring down. Lightning danced across the beautiful night sky in a new way that night. The last time I watched the rain come down was the day after I was let go from my job. During that time, it felt like the rain was also coming down on my life, literally and figuratively. This time, it was different. The same rain that came down on my life that day was coming down once again. This time, it looked like a beautiful work of art in the making.

As Isaac and I watched the rain come pouring down, breathtaking lightning danced freely across the sky. I realized that I was making my life something beautiful again after all the trials I'd gone through. I was dancing once again, just like the stunning lightning in the sky that night.

47

———

Before we knew it, morning came, and I drove Isaac to the train station to make his way back home to New York. I got out of the car as Issac ran over to me and gave me a big hug. "I am going to miss you! I'm so happy that I decided to meet up with you in D.C.!"

I held back the tears, and I gave him another hug. "Oh my gosh, you coming out here meant more to me than you'll ever know. You really did turn this trip around, and something tells me we will never forget this trip." We promised to stay in touch and text to let me know when he made it back safely. I promised to do the same. I drove away and made my way back to the airport, where I was more than ready to come home.

Sitting in the terminal waiting for my flight to board, I looked out the large window in front of me with planes flying in and out…cars driving about on the freeway…and my mind wandered to Jack. Part of me wondered where he was at that moment—if he was happy living in Washington, D.C., and with the choices he made with his life. With my heart overcome with emotion, I started to cry. Sentiments that laid dormant for the past nine months came to the surface.

Feeling like I had to get these emotions out, I got up from my chair and found a little kiosk selling journals. I handpicked a beautiful silver journal lined with hearts that came with a pink glittery pin. It had *me* written all over it. I bought the journal and took it back to my seat. Sitting in the middle of this busy airport in Washington, D.C., with tears running down my face, I decided to write him one last letter. But I didn't plan on sending him this letter. Instead, I let the words from this letter be sent directly from my heart without knowing if he received the words. Regardless, I had to get them out, almost as if I was sending out an SOS to the universe. I was finally letting him go once and for all. Almost as if my pen had a mind of its own, I started to write:

I'M SITTING in an airport in Washington, D.C., knowing that you're here somewhere in this huge city. My heart is faced with the realization that this is probably the closest to you that I will ever get. I was chasing a ghost while you hid behind your military heart of steel. It's easy for you to do and it's the only thing you know how to do—shove your feelings deep down in your soul, lock them away so you don't have to see them, let alone feel them. I wish I could do that, but I just can't. I'm not built that way.

I saw you my entire time here. I saw you in the freeway exit for your new job. I saw you walking to the National Mall, in the military monuments, in the museum visits, in the small coffee shop in a D.C. neighborhood, in the beautiful Victorian homes. I'm wondering if the time will come when you wake up one morning and realize that you let go of the one person who really loved you, all of you. Just when I think I'm over you and moving on, I decide to visit the one city in America that you happen to be in. I wonder if the real reason why I came was not to meet my co-workers or see my stepbrother but for the small chance that I may run into you on the corner of some random D.C. street. But again, I was chasing a ghost. You don't exist anymore. It's like you died, and the memory of you haunts me. So here I am, sitting in an airport in Washington, D.C., knowing you are so close and yet so far away.

Across the United States, a man is waiting for me. A man who loves me and wants me. He's not afraid of his feelings for me. He doesn't run away and hide as you do. He doesn't have a hard heart. He loves me, and he's not afraid to show it. He wants a future and a life with me. You may want that as well, but I'll never know because you're not here. You're a ghost. You served your purpose in my life, and now you've moved on, but you've left me here completely open and exposed.

I poured my heart out to you in a letter I wrote earlier this year. I hit the send button with hope and a prayer that you'd find your way back to me. Here I am, nearly a year later, still wondering if you knew that you had a beautiful woman who loved you so long ago. You're doing what you think is right. Taking the safe path with predictable turns, no surprises, no change. It's in your nature. People in the military don't like change. I should know this by now, being a former military spouse. Being married to a man who didn't like change. But he didn't love me the way you loved me with your eyes, with the soft tone of your voice when listening to you speak to me. Those moments now feel like a lifetime ago.

As I sit here in this airport with tears running down my

face, totally exposed and not caring who sees, I know that it doesn't matter that we are in the same city. You are still light years away. Even if you knew I was here, it wouldn't matter because you still wouldn't come for me. This beautiful petite five-foot-one woman with bright green eyes and beautiful long blonde hair scared the crap out of you because she made you feel. She made you feel things in your heart that you never felt before. Instead of facing those feelings and taking a leap of faith, you ran away. It's what you know, and it's what you're good at.

Stay where you are. Stay in your familiar black-and-white world with your wife whom you don't love anymore and maybe never really loved. You know what you felt for me; you never felt for her, but she's safe and stable, which is what you think you wanted, but what you needed was me, and you know it. You loved me, and you carried me around in your heart, but you were choosing not to let me out into the light. It was easier to keep me in the dark so nobody could see me. They wouldn't think less of you if they didn't know about me. They wouldn't know on that fateful day more than a year ago, you fell in love with that beautiful woman who walked into your auditorium and stole your heart with just one look. She's the one you should be with, and you know it, but it's easier to run away and hide.

So here I am, locked away in your cold heart because it's the easy way out. You love her, and you know it but letting her go is easier than having to fight for her and face your feelings to keep her. Thoughts of doubt plague your heart and mind because she is not the safe path, the seen path. She is the unseen path. In the end, fate played its role in bringing us together, so now I will honor your free will and let you go because I know deep down in my heart I deserve love. I deserve to be happy. I'm with someone who loves me and makes me happy. Just know that in the end, I only wanted what was best for you and your happiness.

WITH THAT LAST THOUGHT, I closed my journal just as I heard my flight number called by the flight stewardess. I took a deep breath and exhaled out loud, almost as if I was letting something go from deep inside my heart. I got up from my seat and dried my tears. I made my way to board my flight back to Arizona. It was time to go home.

I sat on the plane in a daze as I was absorbing my trip to D.C. I watched the map on the seat in front of me, tracking the distance as I flew back home. Emptiness filled my chest as I started to feel the sting of being away from Anthony. Feeling homesick, I wanted more than anything to call him. I took a deep breath and closed my eyes, allowing the jazz music to play in my headphones. I fell into a dreamless sleep.

As I walked through the airport after landing in Arizona, I couldn't be happier to be home. I made my way down the escalator with my luggage trailing behind me, feeling emotionally and physically exhausted from my trip to D.C. I looked down and saw Anthony standing at the bottom of the escalator. He was holding a beautiful bouquet of red and pink roses with that gorgeous dimple smile that I loved so much. I dropped my luggage and ran up to him, wrapping my arms around his neck. I allowed myself to take in the warmth and love of his long-overdue embrace. He gazed at me, and with love in his eyes, he said longingly, "This was the longest week of my life. I really missed you, babe. I was afraid that I was going to lose you and never see you again. I love you so much…I can't picture my life without you."

We stood in the busy airport, hugging for what felt like minutes. The type of hug that held the world together. I realized Aaron had been wrong all those months ago. I did get my happily ever after. Even though it wasn't what I pictured, it turned out even better. The journey was messy. It wasn't perfect, but it was the path that God wanted me to take. It ultimately led to where He wanted me in my life. I also finally saw what Jack saw in me that first day working for the military: A beautiful, genuine woman who had the entire world at her fingertips. She loved with her whole heart. Her light radiated from the inside out. That's what he saw in me that day, and now I finally saw it for myself. The light was there all along. It's shining bright for the entire world to see and will continue to shine bright for many years to come. Jack taught me how to love on a deeper level than I didn't even think was possible. He opened my eyes to new possibilities. I went from seeing the world in black and white to seeing the beautiful rainbow colors of the technicolor world.

I looked up at Anthony and smiled as he cupped my face in his hands and kissed me ever so gently. We walked out of the airport hand in hand leaving the ghost of Jack behind in the city where he belonged. With a heart filled with love and gratitude for the gifts he gave me, I finally let him go.

"For what it's worth, it's never too late or, in my case, too early to be whoever you want to be. There's no time limit; stop whenever you want. You can change or stay the same; there are no rules to this thing: We can make the best or the worst of it. I hope you make the best of it. And I hope you see things that startle you. I hope you feel things you never felt before. I hope you meet people with a different point of view. I hope you live a life you're proud of. If you find that you're not, I hope you have the courage to start all over again."

-F. Scott Fitzgerald

ACKNOWLEDGMENTS

First and foremost, I want to thank God for always guiding me even when I felt most alone in the trials that I faced. I know that I am truly never alone. He's always been my bright lighthouse through everything in my life, and for that, I am eternally thankful. He's given me strength when I felt weak, wisdom when I felt lost, and love and grace when I needed it the most. I am incredibly grateful for this platform He's given me to spread His message of light and love to those who read this book.

My readers: I hope this book shows you that you are worthy of love and that you are perfect and beautiful just the way you are. I hope that by sharing Lily's story of trials in search of love and light that you, in return, find your light in the journey that God has you on and that you are never alone.

Teri: Thank you for being by my side as I navigated through the ups and downs of working for the military. I love how we came full circle, with you being the first one to edit my novel after editing my articles for the military. So many great things came out of me working for the military and you are at the top of that list. Thank you for your constant support and advice and for always being there for me.

Natalie: Thank you for your endless reviews and edits of this novel, for making this story shine bright by providing your experience and insight, looking at this story in a new light. This book wouldn't be where it is at this moment if it wasn't for you. Thank you for your patience with me as I asked you many writing questions. This entire experience has made me a better writer, and it's because of you. Thank you.

Charlotte: Thank you for being my final set of eyes in reviewing my novel. I appreciated our conversation in talking about my book and your suggestions for books to read for my next novel. Thank you for your flexibility and quick responses to my text messages and questions. Thank you again for everything.

Kim: All I can say is I love my cover! You are talented in so many ways. Thank you for your wisdom and patience as we navigated the design of my cover when I didn't know what I really wanted. Thank you for guiding me through the publishing process and being able to lean on your years of experience as a successful author. I am so lucky to have you in my corner. Thank you.

Mom: Thank you for your insight as I shared parts of my journey that I went on and heard my story with grace and love. Thank you for always encouraging me to go after my dreams, for always believing in me, and for letting me know that you're always there for me, even when I feel most alone. Thank you, Mom, for your daily calls, emails, and endless packages of vitamins you send me and for just always finding ways to show me that you love me and that you're thinking of me (a lot). All those years I spent growing up plastered in front of my computer screen, writing endlessly, paid off. SE loves you.

Mike: Thank you for always being there for me and for praying for me throughout the years. I appreciate your Godly insight when I shared my issues with my marriage. I am so thankful that God led my mom to you. Thank you for being her rock and for being there for me. I love you.

Dad: You have been there for me in my darkest times with my divorce and the other ups and downs in my life. Thank you for always encouraging me throughout my journey, and even when I needed something, I always knew I could count on you. Thank you for your constant encouragement and love. I know I got my strong work ethic and drive from you. I hope I make you proud to call me your daughter. I love you.

Stacey: I am so thankful for all the times you've been there for me, and I've been able to call you when I've needed advice: From life advice to finance/tax advice. I always know that if I need anything, I can call you. Thank you for your support. I love you.

Ben: Thank you for being there for me when I confided in you about my marriage issues and the advice and love that you showed me at my most vulnerable. I'm so excited to see the journey God has you on and how you've grown over the years. You've overcome adversity in so many ways and I have always admired that about you. Thank you for always praying for me and being there for me. I love you.

Katie: All the times I've called you crying because of something going on in my drama-filled life between my divorce and my job and all the times you've made me laugh and cheering me on in my life victories. Thank you so much for always being a listening ear, for giving me advice, and for praying for me. Thank you for supporting me to write and pursue my dreams. I feel so very blessed to call you my sister-in-law. Thank you for reading my book and for giving your feedback. I love you.

Aunt Valerie K: I love you so very much. Your support,

love, and advice as I've navigated through my life, college years, and even my adult life have been an integral staple of my life. Thank you for giving me a place to live when my parents were navigating through their divorce, for teaching me how to boil chicken and eggs (a must for any college student), and for all the advice you've given me over the years that I still hold dear to my heart to this very day. Thank you.

Aunt Valerie T: Thank you for always supporting me throughout my life. All the letters you wrote me in college encouraged me to keep striving for my dreams. I loved all our visits throughout the years. Your advice, support, and love mean more to me than you will ever know. I know if I need someone to talk to, you are always there. Thank you, and I love you always.

Mike C.: It goes without saying that you are an answered prayer in more ways than one. Thank you for showing me the very best in what a supportive and loving relationship can offer. For being my biggest cheerleader and encouraging me to go for my dreams, including writing this book. Thank you for your grace, love, and patience as I told you my crazy story. Thank you for reading my book and for being my extra eyes and brainstorming ideas with me. I know I can do anything in life with you by my side, and I'm so excited for what our future holds. Know that I will always be your little spitfire. I love you.

June, Annabeth, Kaylynn, Leanna, and Brendyn: I am so proud of you, more than you will ever know. Continue to go for your dreams, whatever they may be or how crazy they may seem. God placed those dreams in your heart for a reason. Always stay true to your voice and know that you are never alone. God is always with you. Keep reaching for the stars and beyond. I love you so much and will always be there cheering you on!

Isaiah: I know I always say how proud of you I am, and I really mean it. You took a chance leaving our small town behind to live in The Big Apple and stuck with the talents God has given you and look at how much you've grown! Don't ever let your light go dim, and know that all your hard work is paying off and will continue to pay off. I will always be here in the front row, supporting you and cheering you on. I love you!

Gilda: You have always been my sounding board since the moment you came into my life, being my emergency line if I need someone with our personal SOS emergency alert system. Your constant advice and words of wisdom have always been exactly what I needed at the right moment. Thank you for everything you've done for me and continue to do for me and for being the older sister that I never had. I love you!

Grandma Green: You've always taught me to be proud of my Native American heritage and to always give back. I hope that sharing our heritage through this novel makes you proud and shines a light on our Native American tribe. Thank you for taking the time to share your story with me, for giving me an excuse to shop for shoes (since you always liked to steal mine), and for passing down our Native American traditions, including showing me how to make Indian Tacos and how to dance in pow-wows. I am so happy that I had the opportunity to share my book with you before you gained your angel wings in Heaven. I will always love you.

Grandma Ball and GrrAlex: I wouldn't even be half the writer if it wasn't for you, Grandma, instilling the art of good resume writing at a very young age and critiquing my resumes. The jobs and internships I now have under my belt are because of you. Even though we don't live close and don't talk often, your love and support mean so much to me. I'm so glad that I got to share a little bit of my book with you before you passed away. I know you're in Heaven cheering me on. I love you. Consider yourself hugged.

Michelle: You've had such a big impact on my life since the moment I met you when I first moved into town. You've shown me my passion for fitness, and I got a lifelong friend out of it. Thank you for being there for me through happy times and sad times, always giving me "free therapy" when I needed it the most. Your drive and passion for life have always been an inspiration to me. Thank you for being my beta reader and for your invaluable notes and feedback after reading my novel.

Marissa: Look how far we've come from our years working in the fashion industry! We've both grown so much personally and professionally with you being a successful wedding planner in Mexico and just thriving. I cherish our dinner dates when you come into town and our girl chats. You've always been my cheerleader and supported me in all that I want to do. I feel so blessed to have you in my life and I'm excited for you to plan my wedding one day.

Alexa: Oh, how happy I am that you decided to take my cycle class and "collect" me as part of your group of girlfriends after hearing about my divorce. You and Becca both keep me laughing, and I will always be thankful that you both accepted me into your girl posse with open arms. Thank you for always telling me that I look like I'm in my thirties, which always makes me laugh, and for our endless chats filled with love, support, and laughter. I know that we will all be friends for life.

Rick: I will always be thankful that you took a chance on me, letting me live in your home. You and your family welcomed me with open arms as I was fresh from my divorce and hadn't lived on my own for a very long time. You guided me through my divorce, the drama with my job, seeing me get a new job, and starting a new relationship. Thank you for always being there and for guiding me on this new journey I was on. Thank you for giving me grace when I did things that irritated you—like using all the spoons in the kitchen, my obsession with lemon water, and letting a stranger into our house who wanted to talk about fitness.

Claire: I still can't believe that we've been friends for twenty years! Even though times have changed, you are still the same crazy Chica that I met when I first started working in the TV news business some twenty years ago. I love how we always fit together so well, like two peas in a pod, and we balance each other out. I will always cherish our crazy times in college, your great relationship and life advice, your love for 80s music, and where I credit my vast knowledge and appreciation of music I now have. You've always shown me how to live outside of my comfort zone and live life to the fullest. Thank you for being my partner in crime and my best friend.

Cycle Tribe: You have no idea how much it means to me that you come to my cycle class every week! Your faith and support in me have given me the courage to let my light shine bright on this new platform. I always pinch myself every class that I am your cycle instructor, and you all respond with such genuine love and encouragement. Thank you.

Shannon: I couldn't have asked for a better roommate and friend. Thank you for supporting me as I write this book and for being my first beta reader. Your insight was extremely invaluable, and I am so thankful that you took the time to read it and provide your feedback. Thank you for welcoming me and my boys into your family. Your family and Lucy will always hold a special place in my heart, no matter where life takes me.

Sarah: I will always be grateful for the wise insight you've always given me throughout my professional career. We've both come so far on our journey and I'm excited to see the direction God is leading you in your life. Even though we don't live close, you will always hold a special place in my heart. I will always cherish your wisdom and how we've been each other's cheerleaders in life. I know God has great things in store for you. Thank you for everything.

Last but not least, to "Jack": I never guessed on that day when I stepped foot on that military base as a contractor that God would have allowed the amazing man that you are to be the catalyst in changing my life forever. Even though I have no idea where you are now in your life, my prayer is that you are happy with the life you are living. I hope when you retire from the military and reflect on your career and all your accomplishments, you remember with fondness that blonde-haired, green-eyed girl whose life you impacted by just being you. Thank you.

ABOUT THE AUTHOR

Latasha Ball has a B.A. in Journalism from California State University, Northridge, and an MBA from the University of La Verne. She grew up in Mariposa, California, and currently lives in Southern California with her boyfriend and their three adorable rescue dogs: Scotty, Elvis, and Daphne.

f